Praise for Anita Whiting's
A Killer Among Them

Rating: 5 Stars and a Recommended Read "...a fast paced and fascinating murder mystery that will keep you guessing right up until the end. ... Anita Whitings style of writing really draws you into the story making it almost impossible to put down. ... So if you enjoy a good murder mystery along with some romance and a little of the paranormal thrown in then you're going to love The Killer Among Them..."

~ *Kasey's Reviews*

"Anita Whiting weaves a compelling and tangled web of suspense in THE KILLER AMONG THEM. With its many options of capable suspects—including some obvious and not-so-obvious ones—this suspense delivered on all levels, including some that I hadn't expected. ... If you like well written suspense edged with mystery and an added touch of the paranormal, then THE KILLER AMONG THEM might just be one for you."

~ *Romance Reader at Heart*

Rating: 5 Blue Ribbons and a Recommended Read "...a suspenseful thrill ride that had me guessing until the very end. ... Ms. Whiting drew me in from the beginning scenes to the very last word, never letting go as she revealed the shocking truth. ... THE KILLER AMONG THEM is a fast paced, well-written novel that will continue to cement Ms. Whiting's place in the romantic suspense genre. A real must have and a recommended read for certain."

~ *Romance Junkies*

The Killer Among Them

Anita Whiting

A SAMHAIN PUBLISHING, LTD. publication.

Samhain Publishing, Ltd.
577 Mulberry Street, Suite 1520
Macon, GA 31201
www.samhainpublishing.com

The Killer Among Them
Print ISBN: 978-1-60504-006-6
Digital ISBN: 1-59998-855-0

Editing by Sarah Palmero
Cover by Dawn Seewer

First Samhain Publishing, Ltd. electronic publication: January 2008
First Samhain Publishing, Ltd. print publication: November 2008

Dedication

Home. It's always where the heart is.

Chapter One

"I'm frightened, Kat. I'm locking doors I've never locked before. Please come home."

Katarina sank into the couch, switching the phone to her other ear as she unhooked an earring. "Aunt Evelyn, I'm sure the police are doing everything they can."

"It's not enough," her aunt responded. "Marie and Paul Sulin lived in this town all their lives. To have them murdered in their own home not two streets away gives me the shivers." Her aunt's Southern drawl grew thicker as it always did when she was upset. "Brings back memories I thought I'd finally forgotten."

Kat took a deep breath. "None of us will ever forget. You know that. But that was almost fifteen years ago."

"Doesn't matter," her aunt retorted. "It's the same thing all over again. All that hoopla and they still never found your parents' killer. They're not making much of a dent in *these* murders either. Honey, you've got that big city experience. You might see what others don't."

Kat felt herself weakening. "It's not that easy, Aunt Evelyn. I've got cases on the calendar, depositions I can't put off. Besides I doubt Chief Powell would be thrilled if I horned in on his investigation."

"Charlie retired not two months after your last visit, Kat. Moved to Florida. He brought some man in from Birmingham to run for the position. Endorsed him as well. Of course, that didn't sit well with Jerry Landers."

Kat heard the amusement in her aunt's voice, her own lips twitching at the memory of the portly deputy. "I imagine it didn't. He's been with the force for a long time. Why pull someone from the outside?"

"Because Charlie knew how most people in town feel about Jerry. Good old boy who moves as slow as molasses on a cold day."

Kat laughed, curling her long legs underneath her. "Then you've got some big city experience already. You don't need me."

"I don't like looking over my shoulder all the time, young lady. I do need you. This town needs you."

"Aunt Evelyn, I'm a lawyer not a detective," she argued, already sensing she was losing the battle before it had begun.

"But you work with the police all the time. You told me so yourself."

"I do but *they* are the ones doing the investigating. I just take what they give me to defend my clients."

"Then it shouldn't be too hard for you to do the same here," her aunt said firmly. It was a tone Kat recognized. "This is your home. These people know and love you. If there's anything to be found they would be more apt to tell you than a new sheriff."

Kat sighed, rubbing a hand across her forehead. "Okay, okay. It'll probably take a few weeks for me to get things organized and then I'll take some vacation." She smiled ruefully into the phone. "Why is it I get the feeling I've been very successfully manipulated?"

"Because you have been," her aunt said impishly. "See you soon and say hello to that partner of yours."

"I will. Give Andy my love."

"I'll do that if I see him. I swear that brother of yours spends more time working than breathing. He's garnered quite a name for himself around these parts in the real estate market."

"What's his opinion of these murders?"

"Thinks I'm making too much of what he believes was a simple robbery gone bad. My instincts are telling me there's a lot more to it than that."

Katarina was silent for a moment. "Define instincts."

"You know exactly what I'm talking about, young lady. Just because you don't want to admit you were born with the family gifts doesn't mean they aren't there."

Kat sighed loudly. "Let's not discuss that again."

"I'm not discussing, I'm simply stating a fact."

Kat knew better than to argue with her. It wouldn't do any good. "I'll arrange things as soon as I can." Suddenly, unexpectedly, she felt incredibly homesick. "I miss you, Aunt Evelyn."

"And I miss you. Let me know the day you're coming and I'll pick you up at the airport."

"I will."

Shaking her head, Kat hung up the phone and stretched. Rising, she shed her suit coat, tossing it on a chair as she headed for the kitchen. As she busied herself preparing dinner, her thoughts strayed back to her conversation with her aunt. Evelyn Hadar might look like everyone's idea of a typical Southern belle. However, underneath that soft exterior beat the heart of a very strong woman. Strong enough to handle being widowed at a very young age and then within the year having to raise two orphaned teenagers. She wouldn't have called unless she was really worried. Worried just like back when...

Kat thrust those thoughts away, not ready to deal with the memories. It had been over a year since she'd visited Brookdale although she made a concerted effort to talk with her aunt once or twice a month. They had discussed the murders in previous conversations so it was rather strange that it was only today that she had mentioned her fears.

Filling a pot of water, she put it on the stove. Her thoughts were still on the conversation as she turned the burner on. She wouldn't put it past her aunt to have an ulterior motive buried somewhere beneath that worry even if it was truly genuine.

She glanced at her full briefcase, conceding that the idea of getting away from all the deadlines and pressure was beginning to sound very attractive. A few weeks' vacation might not be such a bad idea after all.

Wandering to the window, she suddenly found the sights and sounds of New York less appealing. Usually she loved the pulse of the city, loved the fact that there was always something to do every minute of every day. In spite of its layer of sophistication, there was toughness, a blue-collar kind of atmosphere about the people that appealed to her. Her gaze slid to the site where the Twin Towers once stood. Each of them had needed every bit of that endurance and stamina during the terrible days after 9/11. Instead of pulling the city apart, the tragedy had served to unite its diverse population. There had been a feeling of us against the world that hadn't entirely disappeared in the years afterward.

Leaning against the window, she continued to watch life go by below. She had learned so much here. Her first apartment had been literally one room and the rent had taken almost everything she had made. Yet somehow, someway, in one of the most competitive markets in the world, she had managed to find a job with a well-known firm. Granted, it was a lowly position, but it had been a start. She had worked long, hard hours and within five years she had been offered a partnership. Although flattered, she had been young enough and maybe foolish enough to say thanks but no thanks and put out her own shingle. Many of her clients followed. Among them had been several well-known television personalities, including a rock singer by the name of Joel Skinner. It was his rape trial and acquittal that had truly cemented her reputation.

She turned at the sound of boiling water. Lowering the flame, she bent down to take out the colander. Running a hand along the granite countertop, a smile tugged at her lips. The smooth surface was a far cry from the cracked one in her first place. She took stock of her spacious kitchen and living area with its panoramic view of the park and for the first time almost missed the old neighborhood.

There had been the permeating smell of garlic from the Italian restaurant next door. She had been roused from sleep almost every morning by the sound of the volatile couple who owned it arguing in their own brand of broken English. Every day had been a challenge, a chance to push her way up a ladder that, at times, seemed insurmountable. She still loved what she did but there was something to be said about living on the edge, not quite at where you wanted to be. Thinking each case might be just the one that would make all the difference.

She shook her head. She was being introspective and that wasn't like her. She had a lovely apartment in the best part of the city along with a partner and a host of people who worked for her now. She should be satisfied, she told herself, testing the noodles with a fork, instead of being ridiculously nostalgic.

The phone rang, startling her. Debating on whether to answer it or not, she shrugged and reached across the table to grab the portable.

"Kat, it's Dan. Got a few moments?"

"Sure, what's up?" She glanced at her watch. "Are you still at the office? It's after seven, Dan."

"I know, but I'm stumped on this Keenan case. I'm beginning to wonder if our client's high profile is getting in the way of my being objective. I've gathered a whole lot of evidence with no one to point it at."

"The DA would say it points directly at our client."

"Yeah, I know, and unless I can disprove that theory, I don't like our chance of an acquittal."

Okay, she thought, *here goes*. "Speaking of that, I'm not so sure you're going to like what I have to say either."

He groaned. "Please don't tell me you've accepted another case. Kat, we're overloaded as is."

"Nope. I'm taking a vacation."

The groan was louder this time. "Come on, Kat, we're up to our necks in litigation right now. This isn't exactly the best time to leave."

She turned off the stove and drained the pasta, tilting her head to keep the phone at her ear. "I know, but I just got off the phone with Aunt Evelyn."

"Problems at home?"

"Maybe. I'm sure your father wrote you about the Sulin murder a couple of months ago."

"He did. But what has that got to do with you, Kat? I'm sure Charlie is investigating the case."

"Charlie's retired and I got the impression my aunt isn't overly impressed with the new chief."

"Jerry's okay. A bit dim but okay. He'll go by the book."

"It's not Jerry but some man he brought in from Birmingham. Anyway, you know how small towns are, Dan. Unfortunately, Brookdale is growing and you know as well as I that a growing town means growing crime. Of course, Aunt

Evelyn wouldn't buy that so I didn't even waste my breath. She's worried and I couldn't tell her I wouldn't come home. I did say it would take me a few weeks to get everything together so there is that."

She shifted the phone to her other ear as she poured sauce over the noodles, waiting for the reaction she knew was to come.

"Kat, I'm not sure I can handle everything without you."

"Come on, Dan. I covered for you when you went home. Turnabout is fair play. To be honest, I've felt incredibly guilty that I haven't been able to offer my condolences to Sam and Ellen in person after their parents' death. This will be my chance. Besides, didn't you interview another attorney yesterday?"

"I did, and it went very well, as a matter of fact. Man's name is Jack Steinman. Smart with a pretty complete resume in the five or so years he's been out of school."

"Then set up an appointment and I'll meet him in the next few days. If I'm as impressed, we'll hire him and he can take some of the load off your shoulders until I get back. Deal?"

"You got it." There was a slight pause. "Honey, just be careful. I wouldn't want anything to happen to my fiancée."

It was her turn to groan silently. The push toward a commitment was getting less and less subtle lately. "Nothing's decided yet, Dan. You know how I feel about you, how I've always felt, but..."

"I know, I know. You want to make sure our roots and partnership aren't coloring your decision. Okay, take your vacation but think about us while you're relaxing."

"I will," she promised, relieved that he had let the subject drop so easily.

"Kat, I want you to co-chair when the Keenan case goes to trial next week. This is a tough one and I've got a feeling I'm going to need all the help I can get."

Kat rubbed a hand across her forehead, frowning. "That's going to be a problem, Dan. Opening arguments for Senator Tabor's tax evasion case are scheduled to start on the same day. I can't be in two places at once."

"You can if we switch cases."

She could feel the familiar irritation working its way through her. "You're perfectly capable of working that case."

"Yes, but to be fair to our client, I think you're the better choice."

Kat's fingers tightened on the receiver. This was the very reason why she found it so hard to commit to a more serious relationship with the man. She liked Dan Rogers. She really did. He was suave, good-looking and from her hometown. What she didn't like were his subtle manipulations. It was becoming more and more apparent that when the cases got tougher or the client famous, he found a way to back off, leaving her to handle things. Didn't stop him from taking the credit afterwards, she thought cynically and then was immediately ashamed. "Okay, why don't you fill me in on what we haven't already discussed and we'll work out the particulars."

Dan spent a few minutes bringing her up-to-date on the most recent evidence.

"I talked to John Freeman the other day. Why don't you give him some of this and see what he can come up with."

"The PI?"

"I've used him on several cases. Give him a call. Do some poking around. Have him put a tail on several of our suspects and see what shakes out. Tell him to make sure they know he's following them. It's amazing what a little pressure will do to a person's tongue."

There was silence for a moment and then laughter. "You're good, lady, you know that?"

"I do. Night, Dan."

"Sleep well, Kat. See you in the morning."

She curled up in front of the television with her dinner, refusing to dive into her work for at least an hour. Impulsively, she set her plate aside and stood searching through the videos sitting by the television. At the very bottom of the pile she found what she was looking for. Slipping it in, she settled back on the couch. As the images began to flicker across the screen, she slid into another time and place, the familiar tears stinging her eyelids. Slowly, the screen blurred as her mind took over, taking her back to that day.

The sun shone hot and bright as she ran out the door, a tall lanky ten years old. She launched herself into her father's arms.

"Daddy, what are you doing home?" she asked, wrapping her arms around his neck.

"You don't think I'd forget my best girl's birthday now, do you?" He grinned, his big arms pulling her close, smiling at her mother as she took the video from the front porch.

"Mom, you knew about this?"

Her mother laughed. "You bet. Run inside and get your swimming suit on. I have a picnic lunch packed."

"We're going to the beach?"

"It's your favorite place, isn't it?"

She flew up the porch steps, long blonde hair flying in the wind. "Yes!"

Her own memories took over, the film playing in the background fading as she relived the next few moments. That day, every hour of it, had remained permanently ingrained in her mind.

Tearing up the stairs to her room, she could hear her father and brother throwing the football to each other through the open window.

"Mom," Andy shouted, "take a picture of me going for a pass."

"All right, ready, set...go!"

She peeked out the window as she slid into her swimming suit, grinning as her father chased after her brother, tackling him in the soft grass, their laughter drifting upward. Everything had been so perfect that day, so wonderful.

Impatiently, she brushed the tears from her cheeks as she tapped the remote and the picture disappeared. It had been a long time since she had watched that tape and now she knew why. That aching pain had dimmed, but all it took was the sound of those voices to bring it back with startling clarity.

Resolutely, she switched the news on and finished her dinner and then forced herself to make some headway with the paperwork she had brought home. By the time she climbed into bed, she was exhausted.

Yet, as she felt herself drifting to sleep, new images appeared inside her head, slowly emerging into focus. She found herself standing in her father's office, knowing she was about to see a scene unfold in front of her. A scene that was horribly familiar.

She watched Cathy, her father's nurse, leaving with a backward wave. The sun was low in the sky, throwing shadows inside as she drove away. The scene shifted back to her father as he ran a hand through his still-blond hair and stretched, sliding the last chart back into the filing cabinet. The sound of a key turning in the front door caught his attention. He turned, smiling when her mother walked in.

"You look tired, John," she said, massaging his shoulders as he pulled her into his arms. "It's late."

"Better now that you're here," he smiled. "Speaking of that, why are you here?"

"It's Friday. I thought we'd go out to dinner. Kat is staying at a friend's house and Andy's out with a group of his buddies."

He absently stroked her dark hair, smiling. "They're growing up, Emily."

Her mother nodded. "Makes me feel old."

"Not in my eyes, my love," her father said, bending down to sneak a kiss. "Let me finish just a few things and then dinner it is."

"I'll close up while I'm waiting then."

"Good idea. Cathy already locked the doors before she left. Just do me a favor and make sure all the exam room lights are off."

Even in her sleep she could feel herself tense. She knew what was to come and wished with all her heart she could stop it from happening. Desperately, she attempted to fight through the layers of sleep. It was too late. The visions were too intense, too real and too horribly familiar.

She could hear her mother's receding footsteps just as the back door opened slowly. She watched as the knob turned. The late evening shadows masked the figure that entered quietly.

Cool evening air filtered in through the door he hadn't bothered to close behind him. He edged swiftly behind the front desk, apparently knowing exactly where he was headed. She heard the click as the narcotic cupboard swung open. Gloved hands rapidly filled a backpack with the contents inside. She saw him jerk around as her mother's heels clicked on the tiled floor. Pushing the cupboard door closed, he crouched behind the desk, out of sight.

"I've checked everything," she heard her mother say over her shoulder as she walked toward the waiting room. "Reservations are for eight o'clock, so finish up as quickly as you can."

"Almost done. Give me five more minutes."

She could see her mother shaking her head in amusement, glancing at her watch. The smile turned to a frown as she felt the chill of the evening air coming from the open doorway.

"John, did you know the back door was open?"

"It wasn't a few moments ago. I'll be right out," her father called, concern in his voice.

Kat felt herself sobbing in her sleep but she couldn't stop the images, had never been able to.

Her mother peered out into the dusk and, shaking her head, closed the door and turned the lock. Sensing a presence, her gaze strayed to the desk and her blue eyes widened, not with fear, but with recognition.

"Now what on earth are you doing here? I thought..."

The gunshot was loud as it echoed in the empty room. Her mother's beautiful face froze in surprise and then she slowly crumpled to the ground.

Her father's chair scraped loudly as he shoved it back and tore down the hall. Freezing for just a second at the scene that greeted him, his gaze shot toward the figure standing against the wall, gun pointed at his wife's crumpled body. His expression mirrored his shock.

"My God! What have you done?"

The figure slid toward the door, the pistol shaking in his hand. "I'm sorry. Really sorry." The voice was trembling as much as the gun in his hand as he aimed it again and pulled the trigger.

Her father grabbed his chest and stumbled, falling to his knees. Managing to crawl to his wife before he lost consciousness, he cradled her against him as their blood mingled.

The door slammed loudly as the killer fled, dropping vials of narcotics from the still-open backpack as he ran into the night.

Kat's eyes shot open, the sheet gripped in her hands soaked with her tears. Shaking, she shoved it back and rose, walking to the bathroom. Rinsing her face with cold water, she reached numbly for a towel. The face that stared back at her was pale, the blue eyes, so much like her mother's, bruised and swimming with tears.

It had been a long time since she'd had the nightmare. It had haunted her dreams for days, years after her parents' death. The psychologist had diagnosed it as post-traumatic syndrome. They had prescribed pills and she had taken them, hoping for some measure of relief. But even through the drug-induced sleep, the dream came. Almost as if her parents were trying to tell her something, warn her of something... If only she could see his face, the man who had destroyed her life. She had tried so hard for so long, but his features had always remained in the shadows, mocking her.

Taking a couple of aspirin, she climbed back into bed, rubbing her temples to ease the headache that was beginning to make them throb. She should never have watched that tape. It had awakened painful memories that she thought she had finally dealt with.

The illuminated dial of the clock said three a.m. Yawning, she nestled back under the covers, knowing the dream wouldn't return. Yet, as she drifted back to sleep, just for a moment she could see her father's horrified face staring at...

"I'm sorry. Really sorry."

That voice! She knew that voice!

As her mind fought to identify who it was that spoke those chilling words, her body gave in to the exhaustion. Moments later she slid into a deep and dreamless sleep.

Chapter Two

"Mr. Frank, what time of day was it when you saw my client leave the victim's house?"

"Around eight o'clock."

"In the evening?"

"Yes, in the evening," he answered irritably, shifting in his seat.

Kat stood for a moment, arms crossed, eying the witness steadily. In the past five years, she had perfected that look, had perfected the timing. She also knew how to dress the part. The red suit she was wearing, accompanied by the discreet makeup and sleek hair, downplayed her femininity. It also made a statement about her skill and control of the situation. At least it seemed to appear that way from the reaction of the prosecutor's star witness. The man was tanned, good-looking and, from the subtle signs she had learned to recognize, nervous. "And how many times had you met Miss Keenan?"

He shrugged. "Once or twice?" he answered, avoiding eye contact.

A smile tugged at the corner of her lips. It was so very hard to lie and look someone directly in the face, especially on the witness stand.

"Interesting," she said slowly, exaggerating the hint of the South in her voice. "My client agrees with you in that. She says she met you exactly twice."

A gleam of triumph lit the man's eyes. "That's right."

Katarina walked toward him, sensing the eyes of the jury focusing on her. Good, she had them listening.

"Then how is it you have such a keen recollection of not only my client's face, but what she was wearing at a time that you yourself admit was almost dark?"

"Your client is well known, Miss Ramon," he said disdainfully. "Besides, I have both very sharp eyesight and a very good memory."

"Apparently." She paused again for effect and glanced at the table where her client sat looking chic and frightened at the same time. "Miss Keenan also has a rather good memory. She remembers you making unwanted sexual advances on both those occasions."

"That's a damn lie!" Adam Frank shouted, glaring at the petite brunette, his jaw working visibly. "She wanted it. I could see it in her eyes."

"Objection!" the prosecuting lawyer demanded, jumping to his feet. "Assumes facts not in evidence. Besides, I see no relevance to the case at hand. Is there a question here?"

"Miss Ramon?" the judge asked, lifting a brow.

"There is, your Honor," Kat said smoothly, sliding a look at the desk where their new partner, Jack Steinman, sat, trying to hide a grin. She leaned forward, placing some papers in front of the witness. "Did these women want it as well, Mr. Frank?" She read from a paper she still held in her hand. Walking toward the jury, she lifted her gaze to them, her voice clear and strong. "Did you see the same thing in the eyes of a Bonnie Powell in Cleveland, Ohio? Or a Donna Freeman in Chicago?" She spun back toward him. "Or was it just in the eyes of the two women right here in New York that petitioned for restraining orders against you?"

"Objection! Relevance."

"Objection sustained," the judge said. "Miss Ramon, where are you going with this?"

"To the heart of the case, your Honor." She strode forward to stand directly in front of the witness stand. "You knew absolutely everything about my client, didn't you, Mr. Frank? You knew when she awoke, when she went to sleep. What room she slept in and her every movement every minute of every day, didn't you? Because you were stalking her just like you were those other women."

"No!" he denied emphatically, his expression tightening, an angry flush coloring his cheeks.

"Then why were you observed outside of Miss Keenan's home on at least ten occasions and outside of her workplace on at least five other occasions?"

The eyes became just a little wider, a little wilder. "That's ridiculous!"

Kat walked back to the table, smiling at her client reassuringly while she appeared to search for another paper, knowing the seconds would seem like hours to the man sitting in the witness stand behind her. She had learned long ago to use the ebb and flow of a criminal trial to her advantage.

"Do you drive a two-door dark blue BMW, Mr. Frank? One with a license number of GS4527?"

"Yes," he answered reluctantly.

"Then it was your car that was seen at those locations at least fifteen times, Mr. Frank. Are you saying that it was simply a coincidence? Fifteen times a coincidence?"

"Objection!"

"Overruled," the judge said, turning toward the witness. "I'd be interested in hearing your response to Miss Ramon's accusation, Mr. Frank."

The man cleared his throat. "We have similar business locations. Similar interests."

"You're a computer specialist, aren't you, Mr. Frank?" Kat asked, raising a brow cynically. "Could you explain to me what mutual interests you and the star of *Good Morning New York* have in common?"

Adam Frank swallowed convulsively, clearing his throat once again.

Okay, Kat thought, *it's time for the kill.* She leaned against the mahogany witness box and smiled. "What's the matter, Mr. Frank? The question is simple enough." She waited again, crossing her arms casually.

"Well...we, uh, jog at the same time of day. Frequent the same gym."

Katarina nodded, although inside her mind was working at top speed. She almost had him. "Is that the gym on 22nd

Street?"

"Yeah."

Kat straightened, the smile and relaxed façade disappearing. "The same gym that is only half a block from the victim's apartment, isn't that right?" She made eye contact and felt rather than saw the fear in his expression. "You followed her to Grady Jackson's place that evening, didn't you? Just like you had followed her before."

"No and you can't prove it," he growled defiantly.

"Are you sure?" She walked away from him and toward the jury, carefully making eye contact while she continued her questioning. "You knew they were involved and you hated that, didn't you? Hated the thought of that man's arms around your woman? But she wasn't really your woman, now was she, Adam? All those mornings, all those nights parked in your car imagining what was going on behind those closed doors, behind those curtains. You had to make her pay for taunting you, isn't that right? If she wouldn't come to you, then you would eliminate the competition." She spun back, the silken curtain of her golden hair flying. "That's what you did, isn't it, Adam? You waited until Alicia Keenan left that apartment, and then you killed Grady Jackson. Killed him and set up the woman who had rebuffed your advances. Isn't that right, Mr. Frank?"

"Objection! Miss Ramon is badgering the witness."

Adam Frank flew to his feet, his face a mask of uncontrolled fury. "The bitch wouldn't even answer my phone calls." He pointed a finger at her. "I wasn't good enough for you, was I?"

"Mr. Johnson, control your witness or I'll have him removed from the courtroom," the judge said sternly, pounding his gavel as the conversation from the spectators grew louder. "Let's have order here."

At that instant, amid the gavel pounding and the buzz of excited conversation, an image flashed in Kat's brain. As the prosecutor attempted to calm the irate man, she allowed her lashes to flutter closed for just a moment, focusing, familiar with the aura that meant something was about to be revealed to her. Normally she fought the lack of control, denied what she still didn't completely understand. Not today. She cleared her mind, letting the courtroom and its occupants fade, allowing the images in. Almost instantly the scene sharpened, became clear.

Adam Frank waiting in his car, watching. She recognized the victim's luxurious apartment complex, the high decorative iron fence with the buzzer. Saw him opening the car door as the pizza delivery van with Mamma Santos painted on its side pulled to a stop at the curb. Saw him glance at his watch and then casually walk up the sidewalk behind the boy. She could see a quick gleam of satisfaction as he watched him try to balance four pizzas with difficulty while attempting to reach the buzzer. She could hear Adam offering to buzz the apartment for him, smiling as he held the door open. The boy turning, thanking him...

She focused harder as she saw something on the boy's shirt...something...

There it was: a nametag. Daryl! His name was Daryl.

Her eyes flashed open just as Adam Frank was shoved back into his seat by the bailiff. His expression was ugly as he stared at her, breathing heavily in his agitation.

"Just one more question, your Honor," she said quietly, walking slowly back to the witness stand. "Mr. Frank, how did you get inside the victim's residence that day?"

"I told you I was never in that apartment," he said through clenched teeth.

"Strange. That's not what Daryl from Mamma Santos told me. He said you followed him inside at exactly eight-thirty the evening of the murder. Who were you visiting in that apartment building, Mr. Frank? Just give me a name so I can confirm your whereabouts. That should be simple enough."

"I wasn't there!" The voice was just a shade higher, a shade more desperate.

"I'm sure the judge would allow a short recess in order for me to locate Daryl and bring him in to identify you."

He shook his head, his gaze swiveling again toward Alicia Keenan then back to Kat. The blatant hatred in his expression almost caused her to take an involuntary step backward

"We were perfect for each other, you know. I had to kill

him." He flipped back to Kat, his glare glazed and dark. "All you women are alike, greedy and selfish, begging for attention. Asking for it and then acting so hard to get. No one plays that game with me." His gaze slid back to the woman sitting still as a statue at the table, her eyes wide with horror. "Did you enjoy teasing me? Shaking that ass at me? Taunting me?" He leaned back in the chair, his expression frighteningly calm, almost as if he were unaware of the judge and jury. "At least now you won't shake it at him. I took care of that."

The courtroom erupted. Doors flew open as reporters headed for the cameras outside in an attempt to be the first to report the breaking news. The judge began pounding his gavel loudly with little effect as cameras flashed through the open doorway. Alicia Keenan broke into quiet sobs while the prosecutor, looking slightly bemused, tried to stop his witness from incriminating himself further.

"No further questions, your Honor," Kat said just loud enough to be heard. She turned her back on Adam Frank deliberately, unwilling to admit she was just a little unnerved by the almost maniacal expression on his face. That didn't stop his eyes from boring into her back. She could feel and sense it.

"You tricked me!" he roared, flying to his feet again, jumping from the witness stand. "I'll make you pay for this."

Kat spun just in time to avoid being punched, dodging at the last minute. With a quick twist of his arm, she expertly flipped him to the ground. He landed hard, fighting to breathe.

The flashbulbs went off again, capturing the sight of the slim blonde standing over the prone victim, the surprised deputies in the background.

"Clear the courtroom," the judge ordered loudly.

The deputies sprang into action, hauling Adam Frank to his feet and handcuffing his arms behind him. Several more began escorting the excited spectators out, having difficulty with the reporters who were still snapping pictures at a furious rate.

The judge wasn't happy with the turmoil, shifting his gaze to the man being held in front of him. "Mr. Frank, you are under arrest for the murder of Grady Jackson. Read him his rights, gentlemen, and get him the hell out of here."

Katarina leaned against the defense table, crossing her arms slowly, indicating a calm she was far from feeling. Her client continued to cry quietly behind her and the sound was enough to push the fear back and replace it with anger.

"I believe, Mr. Frank, you'll be the one paying. For twenty five years to life."

"Bitch!" he spat.

"I've been known to be," she responded coldly.

The deputies escorted him out of the room before he could say anything else.

The big courtroom had been vacated, the noise outside barely muted by the thick wooden doors. Kat moved to stand next to Jack Steinman, who had a hand on Alicia Keenan's shoulder in an attempt to comfort her. He caught her eye.

"Nice work, counselor," he murmured. "Are the judo lessons included in the orientation?"

Her lips twitched but before she could answer the judge spoke. "Miss Keenan, although this is redundant at this point, for the record you have been found innocent of all charges and are free to go."

"Thank you," their client said huskily, tears still damp on her cheeks.

They stood until the judge as well as the jury had left the room and then Alicia hugged Kat long and hard. "Thank you seems so inadequate," she said fervently, the horror still reflected in her expression. Those famous green eyes strayed to the back of the courtroom. "I had no idea he was following me but now it all makes sense. I always seemed to catch a glimpse of him wherever I went." She shivered, wrapping slim arms around herself. "I sensed he was unbalanced, but I never thought he was capable of something like this!"

"I know," Kat said, sliding an arm around her client and squeezing reassuringly. Alicia Keenan was a well-known personality and a truly nice person. "It's over now, Alicia. Why don't you let Jack show you the back way out of here. Unfortunately there's a good chance you won't be able to avoid all the reporters."

Alicia straightened, the composure she had lost returning along with a hint of color in her pale cheeks. "No. I have no intention of hiding from those reporters." She slid into a peacock blue jacket that matched her skirt, the color automatically highlighting her creamy complexion and ebony hair. "You know, Kat, stalking was something I reported on the morning news, something that happened to other people." She closed her eyes briefly. "Poor Grady."

"Take some time off," Kat advised. "It's going to take awhile for life to return to normal."

Alicia shook her head, moving toward the doors. "I don't think life will ever be normal again," she sighed. "Maybe that's a good thing." She managed a smile and slipped an arm through Jack's. "You don't mind if I lean on you just a little when we go out there, do you?"

Jack grinned. "You've got to be kidding."

For the first time, Alicia laughed, turning the attractive face of their client into a truly beautiful one. Kat had to hide a smile at the look on her new associate's face. Jack Steinman wasn't handsome in a classical way. He had a steady, calming manner and quick intelligence that she could see reflected in his dark eyes as he gazed down at the woman leaning against him.

His last minute help in this case had proved to be invaluable and she counted herself lucky to have grabbed him before another firm did.

"Looks like you've got a willing escort, Alicia. Jack, why don't you brave the crowd out there and then take Alicia somewhere quiet and expensive for dinner at the firm's expense. I've got a feeling you both could use a break." She glanced at the ornate wooden doors. "Just make sure you're not followed or you'll never have any peace."

"Sounds heavenly," Alicia said gratefully, glancing up at Jack. "As long as you're okay with that?" She shivered. "The thought of going back to my apartment and being alone right now just doesn't appeal."

"I'm more than okay with that," Jack assured her. "Why don't you join us, Kat?"

She shook her head. "Unlike Alicia, I want nothing more than to soak in a hot tub for a very long time. Have a couple of drinks on me."

"You got it."

Kat watched them leave and then turned back to the table. She began gathering papers, the adrenaline disappearing, leaving her feeling drained emotionally as well as physically.

"How do you do it?"

She turned, the exhaustion easing somewhat as she smiled at the prosecutor. "Do what, Ron?"

"You know damn well what. Manage to run rings around me. Must be getting old."

She laughed, eying his fit body and dark hair tinged with just a hint of gray at the temples. "You'll never be old."

"I knew Frank was a risk but he was my best witness. We were informed about his past but the man had never been violent. I figured he was just a nutcase who had witnessed a murder."

Kat stuffed the last of the papers in her briefcase. "Stalkers sooner or later become physical. You know that."

He waved to his assistant as he left the courtroom and then turned his attention back to her. "You really have a Daryl hidden away somewhere or was that just a bluff?"

Kat smiled. "Guess you'll never know, will you."

He shook a finger at her. "You're just sassy because you won, young lady." He walked with her toward the exit. "Just remember, any time you want to join forces, you let me know. I'd be glad to have you."

"I'll keep that in mind, counselor," she tossed back.

The minute they opened the doors, they were bombarded by reporters and cameras. Kat had to fight her way to the car and finally was able to escape, relaxing for the first time all day. She moved her neck from side to side trying to work out the tension kinks. It wasn't often she drove, but today she was glad for the diversion, the traffic. It gave her time to wind down.

What would have taken a brisk fifteen-minute walk took almost forty minutes by the time she reached her apartment. She unlocked her door and immediately eased out of her heels, groaning with pleasure as she stretched. Tomorrow she'd leave for home and right now the time couldn't go by fast enough.

She automatically glanced at the answering machine and pushed the button while she poured herself a cold drink. Her aunt had called along with several of her friends. She listened, sinking down on the couch and leaning back against the cool cream leather. The machine announced a fourth message and, at the sound of the voice, Kat's eyes flew open.

"It seems I am allowed to make one phone call and I chose to call you. Strange how things work out, isn't it? I know where you live and I know your number, Katarina. It's only a matter of time. Someday, someway, I'll find you and..."

She could hear the sound of muffled voices and then there was nothing but a dial tone. Setting her glass down with a trembling hand, she stood and rewound the tape. She grabbed the phone and began dialing with short, quick stabs. It only took a moment to connect with whom it was she wanted to speak to.

"Who the hell allowed Adam Frank to call my apartment?"

"Sorry, Miss Ramon. We had no idea he had your number when we let him make his one phone call. Don't worry, he's locked up safe and sound and will be for a very long time. Guy's a nutcase."

"That's an understatement," she said dryly. "I'm going out of town tomorrow so tell Chief McCreary I'll drop the tape off in the morning. I'd like him to file it away for when Frank comes up for parole. Maybe it will help keep him in prison for a long, long time."

"I'll do that."

She hung up the phone, replaying the message again. She opened the machine and dropped the cassette in her purse. Not feeling particularly hungry, she ran a hot bath and slid under the fragrant suds, allowing the heat to ease some of the tension in her muscles. Unable to prevent it, she relived the trial. It wasn't the first time she had experienced the wrath of the guilty and it wouldn't be the last. Yet, there was something about Adam Frank that went beyond that. Something sinister. Usually she was able to shrug these kinds of things away but not today. She reached for the soap, trying to erase the image of those eyes staring at her.

"I know where you live. Someday, someway, I'll find you..."

She stilled, a thought pushing its way inside. In all the

drama, she had forgotten one thing: her number was unlisted. He couldn't possibly have known it and yet he had.

Shrugging, she reached for the towel and stepped from the bath. Rubbing herself briskly, she caught sight of her reflection in the mirror. That confident persona she had exhibited in the courtroom had disappeared and had been replaced by a woman with a pale face who couldn't stop the chills from prickling her skin.

Stop it, she told herself. *The man is sitting in a jail cell awaiting trial. Even if he does know where you live, he can't hurt you.* Just as she reached for the light switch, her eyes met those of her reflection.

Or could he?

Chapter Three

Cole waved at Ben Stolarski as he eased the squad car into a parking place downtown. He unbuckled the seat belt, stretching. He ran a hand across his eyes to relieve some of the tension just as a group of teenage girls walked by.

"Hi, Chief Collins," Amy Singer said, leaning against the open window. The tight tank top she was poured into accented her blossoming curves, her big brown eyes eating him alive. The girl would be a beauty in a few years, he thought. Or pregnant.

"Morning, Amy," he said, stepping from the car. "Girls." He nodded toward her companions. Locking the door, he headed for Mandy's, the only full service restaurant in the small town.

Amy kept pace with him. "Are you going in for breakfast? That's great because Donna, Stephanie and I are too. Maybe we could share a table."

Cole groaned silently. Damn it, the last thing he needed was to sit with a trio of oversexed teens right now. The door squeaked open and instantly every diners' eyes were on him and then greetings came from all sides. He smiled and waved, knowing most of them by name. Brookdale might be growing but it was still a very small town. In the eight months he had been here, it hadn't taken him long to get to know almost every resident. He knew the people in power and he knew the troublemakers and those somewhere in between. His job was to see that one group didn't clash with the other.

While he waited for a table, he leaned against the counter, deliberately avoiding eye contact with Amy in an effort to discourage her. She was chattering with her friends but standing near enough so that her rather strong perfume competed with the aroma of the food being served.

His gaze roamed around the restaurant. The tables were covered with plastic and the walls had an eclectic mix of framed pictures and various photographs of the football and baseball teams that Mandy's had sponsored over the years. The atmosphere was homey and welcoming. The place was small by big city standards. However, what it lacked in size, it made up for in food. As far as he was concerned, Mandy's made the best bacon, eggs and grits anywhere around.

It was just a little after nine and the warm spring Saturday had people out and about. The three waitresses were kept busy filling coffee cups and serving meals but that didn't mean that the Southern hospitality didn't shine through. Each patron was greeted personally and ribbed unmercifully if there was something to tease them about. It was an atmosphere that had appealed to him the moment he accepted the job here. He liked these people and, for the most part, they had accepted him. He felt honored because this was a tight-knit town. Close and protective of each other, tied not only by proximity but by heredity as well.

"Hey, Cole!" A plump gray-haired woman called to him from behind the counter. "How's the handsomest man this side of the Mississippi?" Not waiting for an answer, her blue eyes twinkling, she surveyed the room while managing to fill a customer's coffee cup and put a plate of food in front of another. "Give us a few and we'll have a table for you." She motioned to a group of women at the back of the room. "Those ladies are just jawing. I'll give them a few more minutes and then kick 'em out."

Cole nodded, grinning. Mandy Stanislaus and her husband had owned the restaurant for years. After his death, she took over as sole owner and it hadn't taken him long to find out that no one, absolutely no one, challenged her. When she said git, they got.

Because he was a stickler for detail, he had made it a point to research the history of the place he was to call home. Even if he hadn't, it wouldn't be difficult if you took the time to really look at the patrons to know that most of them came from the same ethnicity. The high cheekbones and occasional lapse into Slovak or Russian spoke of their ancestry. Brookdale had originated as a mining town and, when that industry had slowly disappeared, it had evolved into a dozen small mom-and-pop type of businesses. It was a far cry from Birmingham and the past he was trying hard to forget.

"Chief Collins, they have a table ready," Amy said, interrupting his thoughts, sidling up to him and placing a pink-tipped hand on his arm, lashes fluttering.

Hell! He could tackle barbed wire, prisoners and God knows what else, but for the life of him he wasn't sure how to get out of one aggressive fifteen-year-old girl's clutches.

"Amy Singer, aren't you supposed to be at cheerleading practice?" a voice said from behind him. He turned and sighed with relief. Evelyn Hadar stood in back of him, hands on her hips, brown eyes flashing.

The change in the girl was almost comical. In an instant, the femme fatale disappeared and in its place was a teenager with an attitude.

"I decided to skip practice this morning, Mrs. Hadar," she said, her expression mutinous. "They shouldn't have it on a Saturday anyway."

"Really. Then perhaps you should let Sherry Mitrovich take over as head cheerleader. I just left the school a few moments ago and I have to admit she certainly has the squad looking good in your absence." She motioned to the vacant table. "On second thought, why don't y'all have a nice meal and just forget I mentioned anything." She turned her back on them and smiled up at Cole, eyes dancing. "Beautiful day isn't it, Chief Collins?"

"It sure is, ma'am," Cole replied, finding it hard not to grin.

"That little witch!" Amy muttered, spinning back toward the door, blonde hair flying. "*I'm* the only one that's going to lead those cheers. Come on," she ordered her friends, "let's go."

Cole waited until the door slammed and then turned back to the woman standing in front of him, rolling his eyes. "Evelyn Hadar, I owe you lunch, big time. Anything on the menu as a matter of fact."

Evelyn laughed, following him to the table, greeting people as she passed them. "You looked just a tad overmatched so I thought I'd lend a neighborly hand."

"Overmatched is one way of putting it. Scared stiff might be more accurate."

"Fifteen-year-old girls will do that to you. Believe me, I know."

Cole slid into the booth, motioning for her to join him. "You actually enjoy teaching that age?" He shook his head. "You have my undying admiration."

She laughed gracefully, tucking herself across from him. "Just some of that heavenly smelling coffee and a cinnamon roll for me, Julie," she said, smiling at the cute redhead that came over to take their order.

"Okay. And the usual for you, Chief?" she asked, pouring both of them a cup of the fragrant brew.

"That'd be great, thanks, Julie."

"No problem."

Evelyn took a moment to study the man sitting across from her. No wonder the girls were after him, she thought. He stood out like a sore thumb, especially in this town. His dark hair and sea green eyes spoke of his Irish heritage, not to mention the breadth of shoulder and cleft in his chin that deepened when he smiled. She had a strong feeling that the female population of Brookdale had come out in record numbers to vote because of those eyes. He was friendly, efficient and had secrets. She was aware of some of them but her intuition was telling her there was a lot more to Brookdale's new police chief than he allowed people to see.

"You do realize that someday that sweet little girl of yours is going to become a teenager? Believe me, parenting a girl that age is never easy."

He groaned, taking a sip of his coffee. "Lord, I don't want to even think about that. I'm having enough trouble dealing with an eight-year-old."

"That's because she's precocious. I've already been told she's the brightest kid in her class."

A flash of pride lit his eyes. "Maybe so, but that only makes reasoning with her that much more of a challenge."

Julie brought their food and both were silent for a moment as they dug in.

Cole took another sip of his coffee, enjoying the company. Although he had it on good authority Evelyn Hadar was in her mid-fifties, he would never guess that was the case. She was petite, had sparkling chestnut eyes, dark hair that didn't show a hint of gray and an accent that flowed as smooth as silk. And he had learned within weeks of arriving that beneath that soft Southern charm was an intelligent and level-headed woman with an uncanny ability to be at the right place at the right time when someone in the town needed her. *Just like today*, he thought, an image of Amy Singer's expression as she stormed out flashing in front of him.

Evelyn leaned back a few minutes later and unashamedly licked her fingers, sighing. "I swear there's no one in these parts that makes cinnamon rolls like Mandy's. Best I've ever had." She waited until he was finished; the hands curling around the coffee cup tightening slightly. "I hate to ruin a beautiful morning, Cole, but how's the investigation going?"

He shook his head, easing back in his chair, meeting her gaze with a steady one of his own. "Slowly. Very, very slowly. It would help if I could find a motive but as far as I can see there simply isn't one. Even though the house was torn up, my instincts are telling me robbery wasn't the reason those people were killed. There were several rings left in the jewelry box that could have brought some big bucks as well as some nice pieces of silver in the dining room hutch. No fingerprints, no hair, nothing evidence-wise. In fact, nothing was taken according to the couple's kids."

"I know. I've talked to both Sam and Ellen." Her brown eyes darkened, grew angry. "It's bad enough that two good people are gone but what's worse is these murders bring back memories the people in this town would rather forget."

He eyed her silently for a moment. Another thing he had learned about Evelyn was that she knew how to get a point across without appearing to do so. "I know about your brother and his wife's murders, if that's what you're hinting at. And, if you're asking if the two cases are related, I've found no evidence of that so far."

She met his gaze candidly. "I know. Charlie assured me before he left that he had briefed you on everything he had regarding the investigation." She shook her head. "It's not enough. I lost two people I loved dearly all at once. I want whoever it is that is responsible for their murders to be punished."

He fingered his cup of coffee, weighing his words carefully. "Fifteen years is a long time, Evelyn. The case is cold, witnesses either dead or their memories are tainted with the passage of time."

"Are you saying you can't find their killer?" she challenged him.

"I'm saying that all I can do is my best," he said quietly. "I know what it's like to lose someone close to you. Sometimes, it's better just to let it go after awhile."

Evelyn's brown eyes warmed, grew sympathetic. "Did you?"

He wanted to lie but instead found himself shaking his head. "No."

"Then you know how I feel."

Julie came back to refill their cups. Cole shook his head. "Thanks, Julie, but I've got an appointment in about an hour." He waited until she left. "What I can't seem to get past, Evelyn, is that these murders happened just after Charlie announced his retirement and before I was elected chief."

Her eyes widened. "What are you thinking?"

He hesitated. He trusted Evelyn and he wasn't one to trust easily. "Let's just say when a motive for murder doesn't just sit up and slap me, I look for other reasons, other explanations."

"As in past history?" she asked shrewdly, taking another sip of her coffee.

"Or the present with a link to the past."

"What frightens me, what has always frightened me, is that the person who murdered my brother and his wife as well as the Sulins could be any one of the people sitting here. People I have known my entire life."

"I know. Crime is a lot easier to deal with in a big city where anonymity is a factor and people don't leave their doors open at night."

She laid a hand on his arm. "That's why I'm glad Charlie chose you, Cole," she said sincerely. "And that the people in this town had enough sense to elect you instead of Jerry

Landers." She frowned, sliding her gaze to several men sitting at the bar. "You've been here long enough to know Brookdale takes care of its own and some of its own aren't exactly model citizens."

He nodded, rising and slapping some money on the table. "Learned that a long time ago, Evelyn." He moved to the side as Julie passed with another loaded tray. "Nice having breakfast with you, ma'am." He grinned.

She returned the smile. "Give that little girl of yours a kiss for me."

"I'll do that."

She watched him walk out, eyes narrowing thoughtfully. She knew from her own investigation that Cole Collins was good. Navy Seal kind of good. That meant his instincts were sharp. She had a feeling when he set his mind to something, he wouldn't let go until he had answers. All the answers.

Standing, she took a last sip of coffee, smiling to herself. The man had the same type of determination as her niece, the same quick intelligence. It was a good bet that sparks would fly when the two of them met. In fact, she was sure of it. And, shame on her, she was looking forward to the confrontation.

She tossed a look at the restaurant clock and, waving to several people, headed for her car. Kat was due in at noon and it was about an hour's drive to the airport. She had just put the key in the ignition when Jerry Landers pulled up in front of her. He opened the door and heaved himself out of the car, spying her as he turned to close it. He began lumbering toward her, the buttons on his uniform straining against his round belly. She started her car, not wanting to encourage conversation. Once Jerry starting talking in that slow deliberate drawl of his, it was hard to get away. Besides, since his wife divorced him a few years before, she knew there was an attraction he felt toward her that she didn't reciprocate.

"Morning, Evelyn," he said, out of breath from the simple exertion.

"Jerry." She nodded, smiling simply because it wasn't in her nature not to be polite. Besides, the deputy was a good man. Not her type, but a good man nonetheless.

"You're looking mighty pretty this morning."

"Thank you."

It was then she noticed Brian Landers, his son, stepping out of the other side of the patrol car. He was better looking than his father in a rakish sort of way, tall and rangy like his mother. Where Jerry was simply a small town deputy, there was something about his son that she didn't like. The boy had always had a giant chip on his shoulder and that hadn't changed over the years.

She eased the car forward, smiling. "Sorry to leave so quickly, Jerry, but I've got to pick Katarina up at the airport."

"Kat's coming home?" Brian asked, leaning inside the passenger window, his dark eyes flickering with interest.

"For a couple of weeks," Evelyn said. "Really, I've got to go, gentlemen. Have a good day."

She watched them in her rear view mirror as she pulled out. Damn but something about that boy irritated her. She waved at Cole as he pulled away in the opposite direction.

Cole saluted her, his lips twitching at the wink she leveled at him as she passed. Evelyn Hadar was something else, he thought in amusement. The smile slid away however as he slowed next to Jerry and his son.

The deputy was one of those who hadn't accepted him for a number of reasons, not the least of which was his being elected chief. That hadn't stopped him from accepting Cole's offer of staying on as deputy however, he thought somewhat cynically. In reality, he knew that Jerry might not be the quickest man but he was methodical and thorough. Just, according to Charlie Powell's opinion as well as the voting public, better at being a deputy than being in charge. In spite of their uneasy relationship, however, Cole trusted him.

Not so his son. Brian Landers out and out disliked him and Cole had a hard time not feeling the same way. Not endorsing Jerry Landers for chief had been a slap in the face to the whole family, Brian included, even though Charlie Powell hadn't meant it to be.

His thoughts abruptly returned to the present as Brian Landers deliberately walked in front of his car just as Cole began to brake, forcing him to tap the brakes harder than he normally would have.

"Looks like you need to watch where you're going, Chief Collins," Brian said, his smile unpleasant as he rapped the hood sharply.

"Guess I do at that," Cole said easily, switching his gaze to his father. "Morning, Jerry. I've got some business to attend to. If you need me, I'll have my cell on. I should be back midafternoon."

Jerry's face was already glinting with sweat as he nodded, lifting his hat to rub a hand through his crew cut. "You think I'm capable of running things while you're gone?" he asked sarcastically.

Cole caught his gaze and held it. "I wouldn't be leaving if I didn't think you were."

The older man challenged him silently for a moment and then nodded.

"Just not capable enough to be boss, is that it, Collins?" Brian said, animosity playing across his features as he stepped to the other side of the car.

Cole didn't even acknowledge him, instead rolling up the window on that side. "See you this afternoon, Jerry," he said evenly, putting the car in gear and moving forward. Looking back, he could see his snub had hit home from the look on Brian's face. The man was itching for a fight.

He drove slowly through downtown, admiring as he always did the cleanliness of the sidewalks and the attractive shops. Brilliantly colored flowers bloomed in pots attached to the old fashioned streetlights while people strolled along window-shopping. An image of Mayberry from the old Andy Griffith series came to mind as he passed the only barbershop in town.

He stopped for a red light just as Deanna Ross pulled next to him in her minivan piled high with boxes of food. The delicious smell of fresh baked bread wafted through his open window and he sniffed appreciatively.

"Morning, Cole," she said, lowering the radio. She motioned to the back of the vehicle. "Church social tomorrow. You coming?"

He pulled off his sunglasses and grinned at the petite redhead. "Any of your lasagna in that pile?"

"Four boxes worth."

"Then you can count me in."

"Great," she said, smiling. "Stella was just saying how she hasn't seen you in awhile. She'll be there tomorrow so wear your glad rags."

He sighed loudly enough for her to hear. "On second thought..."

Her laughter was loud and infectious. "Come on, Chief. You can handle one very determined divorcee now, can't you?"

"I'm not so sure about that."

The light turned green and she spun the volume dial on the radio back up. "Bring that adorable daughter of yours as well," she shouted above the country music, grinning. "That might just put her off a bit."

He laughed, turning right as she turned left. Damn if he didn't like this town!

Although there was only one elementary and high school, there were several churches clustered on Main Street. People here took their backgrounds and their religion seriously. The women still got together to prepare meals for the elderly and infirmed. He had attended more than one wedding where all the food had been homemade by dozens of women who cooked for weeks ahead of time. It was a little bit of the old country in a contemporary time and just the kind of atmosphere he wanted for his daughter.

Olivia was his life now, although he was still trying to convince her of that fact. He silently cursed his ex-wife for what she had done to their child. Poisoning her against him was one thing, but exposing her to drugs and alcohol was something entirely different. The guilt he still felt at not recognizing the signs of chronic drug use came rushing back. The constant activity, the inability to sleep, the disappearance of valuables around the house little by little. Christ, he was trained to recognize that stuff!

Yet he had found himself making excuse after excuse when she hadn't been there for their daughter's recitals or school plays or conferences. Never realizing how much he was enabling her. Their marriage had been in shambles almost from the very beginning, but after she became pregnant, he had clung to the hope that motherhood might change her. It had, for the worse.

Allie Sandoval was spoiled, rich, an only child and had no intention of letting pregnancy ruin her body or mess with her good times. It was a miracle she hadn't terminated it. She had preened at the baby showers, enjoying the attention, but once the baby came, she lost interest quickly. It was only later that he had discovered just how often their daughter was left alone or with babysitters for long stretches of time.

He drove around a sweeping curve and saw the sign that announced he was entering Roaming Hills. While Brookdale's roots were blue collar, everything about this town spoke of just the opposite. The houses were large and elegant and the residents were lawyers and doctors and politicians who worked in Birmingham and the surrounding county. It was an old and established community that screamed wealth. It was also where he had met Allison Michelle Sandoval, daughter and only child of the wealthy Sandovals. She came from a family prominent in politics not only all over the South but in Washington, D.C. as well. Dallas Sandoval was mayor as well as major stockholder and owner of Sandoval Construction, while his wife, Sonya, spent her days at the country club or jetting around the country. It was a lifestyle Allie expected when she married him. A lifestyle he had no intention of living, although he hadn't known that at first. That realization had come later.

He barely glanced at the mansion as he passed it, the bitterness he felt toward the entire family threatening to consume him. If he had self-recriminations, Allie's parents should have a boat load. They had turned a blind eye to their daughter's addictions just as they had ignored their grandchild's mental abuse. In the eight months since he had finally been awarded custody of his daughter, they had never asked to see her or even talk to her on the phone.

He turned into the parking lot of a very attractive stone building and parked, taking a moment to gather himself. He should have seen this coming but he hadn't. He opened the car door, slamming it shut with unnecessary force. Moments later, he was being ushered into a plush office. The blond-haired athletic-looking man sitting behind the desk stood and extended a hand, his gray eyes crinkling as he shook Cole's firmly.

"Damn! It's good to see you, buddy," he said, motioning for him to take a seat on one of the two cream-colored leather chairs.

"How's Gina?" Cole asked, leaning his big frame back in the comfortable cushions.

"She's great. Keeping busy with the boys. She sends her love and an invitation to dinner tonight if you're free."

Cole shook his head regretfully. "Olivia and I are going to the zoo later. Tell her I'll take a rain check though." He took a deep breath, mentally preparing himself for what he suspected was to come. "Okay, why don't you just lay it on me right away, Barry. No use trying to avoid the inevitable."

"It's not that simple, Cole. First, let me say that the fact that you were awarded custody of Olivia will weigh things heavily in your favor."

"But..." Cole said dryly.

"But you know what money can buy and the Sandovals are loaded with it."

Cole's hands fisted. "Why the hell are they seeking custody now? After eight months of not having a thing to do with their granddaughter, they suddenly discover they want to be doting grandparents? That's bullshit!"

"I agree," Barry said calmly. "I firmly believe this is all Allie's doing. I've done some investigating and I've got some eyewitnesses who claim they overheard her asking her parents to sue for custody on her behalf."

Cole stood, pacing. "Why would she do that? She doesn't give a damn about Liv. She hasn't since she was born so why the act? What is she hoping to gain?"

Barry leaned back, his gaze following Cole's angry movements. "My guess is more money."

Cole swung back, pounding his fist on the desk. "I'm not giving that woman one more cent! Hell, she took me to the cleaners with the divorce as it was even though I wasn't the one having the affairs."

"You could have fought her."

Cole shook his head. "It wasn't worth it. I thought Liv's happiness was the most important thing at the time." He sat back down heavily. "If I had only admitted back then what I knew subconsciously..."

"Cut it out, Cole. Gina and I were fooled as easily as you were. What counts is you did what you had to do to get your daughter back."

"Yeah but for how long?"

"Forever, if I have anything to do with it." Barry grabbed a folder and opened it. "Okay, here's the story. We both know Allie must have an ulterior motive for this move. She's manipulative enough to fool her parents. She's been doing it for years. So that begs the question of why."

The anger in Cole's eyes changed, interest taking its place. "You've got an idea?"

"She's hurting for cash. It's that simple. Her parents are relatively young so, barring a catastrophic accident, she isn't going to inherit anytime soon. In addition, rumor has it her father has put a clamp on her credit cards in the past few months. Seems she's maxed to the limit on almost every one of them. Combine that with the loss of child support and she might be getting desperate. The woman lives high and chances are good that she has no intention of giving up that kind of lifestyle. She knows how you feel about Olivia and she knows you'll do anything in your power to keep her, even if it means paying big bucks."

Cole grimaced. "Allie's idea of big bucks differs markedly from mine."

Barry's lips twisted briefly. "Cole, don't kid yourself. She knows what you're worth, what your father is worth."

"Damn it, that's blackmail!"

"That's one word for it." Barry leaned back in his chair contemplatively. "Did you ever tell her about the trust fund?"

Cole's expression grew darker, obviously following his friend's train of thought. "The one my mother left me?"

Barry nodded.

"No way."

"Someone did. I'll stake my reputation on it. Dangle several million dollars in front of a drug addict and you've got yourself a hell of a motive to fight for custody one way or another."

"So what do I do about this?"

Shuffling through some papers in the folder he held, Barry

pushed several toward him. "I've already provided these same papers to the private investigator I use but I figure you'd want a peek at them as well."

Cole picked them up and began reading. "I recognize some of these names."

"You should. That's a list of some of the people we used as corroborating witnesses at the custody trial. The second page is a list of people who knew Allie before the two of you met. It's my intention to prove that her parents were aware of her alcohol and drug addictions and did nothing to remedy the problem. According to what I've discovered so far, your ex was a good-time girl way back in the eighth and ninth grades. We prove that, then we can make a case that her parents aren't suitable candidates for raising an eight-year-old girl. Combine that with the fact that you're her biological father and I'd say we have a good chance of nipping this whole thing in the bud."

A flash of relief crossed Cole's face as he put the paper down. "You think you can make that stick?"

"I'm sure as hell going to do my best, pal."

For the first time, Cole laughed freely. "I'll take that." He stood, offering his hand. "Thanks, Barry."

Barry stood as well. "How are things going with Olivia?"

Cole shook his head. "Damn slow. She doesn't trust me and I think she misses Allie, rotten mother that she was."

"Be patient, Cole. She's dealt with a whole lot in a very short period of time. The kid is smart. Sooner or later she'll figure out that you really love her."

"God, I hope so." He opened the door, turning back. "Let me know if you come up with anything."

"I will," Barry said, moving to stand in front of him. "Does Jared know what's going on?"

"Dad's got enough of his own worries," Cole responded firmly. "Although he's running for reelection, I don't think his heart is in it."

"Missing your mother?" Barry said sympathetically.

"We all miss her," Cole said quietly. "You know what's most ironic? Liv looks just like her. She has the same dark hair and green eyes, same delicate build and dimples." He shook his head. "I can't tell you how many times I've thought if only…"

Barry slapped his friend on the shoulder. "And I can tell you, pal, that I knew your mother and she would never want you to worry about what you can't change." He wagged his finger dramatically, imitating Cole's mother. "I can just hear her saying, 'Bartholomew, if you would just put a little more effort into your studies and a little less into your parties, those grades would go up'."

Cole laughed, the tense furrows in his brow easing. "Thanks."

Barry shrugged. "I'm only telling the truth. I don't think I'd have finished college without her urging."

"Nagging, you mean?"

"You said it, not me, buddy."

"Call me as soon as you've got something, will you?"

"I'll do that. And don't forget we've got that rain check."

"I won't and thanks, Barry."

"No thanks are necessary," he said. "Now take that little girl to the zoo and let her gorge on food and pop like we used to. Best part."

"Yeah and then we paid for it later with stomachaches."

"Hey, that's part of being the parent. Gotta take the good with the bad, right?"

"At least I've got the opportunity to enjoy the good again," Cole replied "If Liv will let me in."

"Nothing like watching a couple of monkeys to ease things," Barry joked. "Just imagine they're your ex and her parents."

Cole laughed. "How'd a guy with a sense of humor like yours get to be one of these lawyer types?"

Barry raised a brow. "How do you think I keep sane?"

Cole was still smiling as he walked back to the cruiser. He slid his sunglasses into place and stopped as the glare from the sun disappeared, throwing the white words spray-painted on the black side of the car into focus.

CHIEF COLE COLLINS
RIP

Underneath was a crude drawing of a cemetery stone.

Cole walked closer, furious, his eyes scanning the parking lot and the hilly road running in front. There were only a few cars scattered around, none of them occupied, and traffic was light.

He was reaching for the door handle when he heard the sound of a car accelerating. Instantly his training took over as he felt the familiar warning tingle up and down his spine. He threw himself down on the pavement just as a car came barreling around the wide turn. A barrage of pellets hit the cruiser, shooting bits and pieces of gravel around him. Tires squealed as it took the next turn heading downhill into town.

He was on his feet in one fluid motion. Squinting through the sunshine, he was able to focus on part of the license plate. He didn't recognize the car but he would if he saw it again. They could count on it.

He reached down and picked up one of the pellets. BB gun type, he thought. Not enough to kill but enough to damn well hurt if they had hit their intended target. Thoughtfully, he palmed a few of them and slid into the car.

Frowning, he flicked the ignition and then simply sat there. Someone either resented his presence in the town or wanted to make sure he was kept busy investigating malicious mischief instead of more important things. Like murder.

He started the car and backed out, his brow narrowed in thought. The obvious answer would be Brian Landers or one of his cohorts.

Then again, he was never one to go for the obvious.

Chapter Four

Cole saw her the minute he walked into the church hall. Even if she hadn't been the only person he didn't recognize, it would have made no difference. She had the kind of body and face that drew attention. Model tall and slender with shoulder length gold-spun hair, classically high cheekbones and brilliant blue eyes. Even in the casual clothes she was wearing, she screamed high society and wealth. His jaw tightened, fighting an antagonism he knew he shouldn't be feeling.

At that moment, she looked up and their eyes connected across the room. Instead of turning away, however, she continued to hold his gaze for a long moment and then transferred it to the girl standing at his side. Even at that distance, he could see her expression soften before she turned her attention back to the people with her.

"Afternoon, Chief." Deanna Ross smiled as she breezed passed him with a basket of bread, her short red hair curling about her head, her cheeks flushed with exertion. She stopped for just a moment to smile at his daughter.

"Well, young lady, you certainly look pretty in that lovely blue dress."

"Thank you," Olivia said politely, her voice solemn and expressionless.

Deanna shot a glance at Cole and then leaned down. "You know, honey, I could use some help in the kitchen. Do you think your father could spare you for a little while?"

Cole could see the indecision flicker across her face and so did Deanna.

"Would it help if I told you Tiffany is back there driving me crazy? She must have asked me fifty times if I knew when you and your dad were coming."

Olivia's green eyes widened. "Tiffany's here? I thought she was grounded."

Deanna nodded. "She was and is. I just thought a suitable punishment would be for her to do the dishes. Now I'm not so sure." She motioned toward the kitchen. "Go on, she's dying to see you."

"Is that okay?" Olivia asked, glancing up at Cole.

"Sure, Liv. I'll be waiting for you out here. Just behave yourself."

She eyed him with that flat expression that tore at his heart. "I always behave myself," she said quietly, walking toward the kitchen.

Deanna put a reassuring hand on his arm. "Don't worry. I'll keep an eye on her if you want to mingle a little. Food's over that way and there's juice, pop and coffee on the other table. Help yourself."

"Thanks. Let me know if there's any problem."

"There won't be."

Cole grabbed a plate of food, including a large chunk of Deanna's famous lasagna, and started for one of the tables that were set up in rows in the large room.

"Over here, Cole," a familiar voice said to his right. He turned, inwardly groaning at the sight of the plump brunette. Damn. He'd forgotten about Stella. The woman had pursued him with a vengeance in spite of his attempts to discourage her. The words *not interested* simply weren't in her vocabulary.

She smiled seductively, patting the chair next to her. "I saved you a seat. Come on, sit down and tell me what you've been up to," she drawled.

He took stock of the crowded table and the amused glances and shook his head. "I'd love to, Stella, but Liv's with me. No room."

"Oh, someone will be leaving soon. Right?" she challenged the two men nearest her.

Before they could move, Evelyn waved to him from two

tables down, her brown eyes dancing. "Cole, there's room down here," she called.

Stella's head swiveled, her expression changing to one of annoyance as she caught sight of Kat sitting next to her aunt.

"When did *she* get here?" she muttered almost to herself.

Cole didn't answer but weaved his way toward Evelyn, sliding into one of the several empty chairs across from her.

He heaved a sigh of relief, his gaze encompassing both women in front of him as he set his tray down. "I've decided you're my personal guardian angel, Evelyn."

She laughed. "I've been called a lot of things but never that. Cole, I'd like you to meet my niece, Katarina Ramon. Kat, this is our new chief of police, Cole Collins."

The blue eyes were even more spectacular up close, he thought. The impeccable makeup, red silk shirt and designer jeans confirmed his initial impression. Rich city girl home for the obligatory visit. His jaw tightened as he extended a hand, almost recoiling when she put her slender one in his. He couldn't have felt that tingle, that shock that wasn't physical but mental, but he had. From the brief widening of her eyes, he could tell she had felt it as well.

"Nice to meet you, Chief Collins," she said casually, removing her hand.

The voice was crisp and precise but the image was softened somewhat by the hint of the South in the words.

"Cole will do just fine," he responded easily. He turned to greet someone down at the other end of the table.

Kat took stock of the man up close. Dark, curly hair, green eyes, chiseled jaw and tall enough to tower over her five-foot-nine inches. She only knew what her aunt had told her about the man, but before she went back to New York, she was going to know a whole lot more. If for no other reason than the vibes she had just felt when they touched.

She sipped her iced tea as he ate, simply observing. Evelyn and several of the women on the other side of the table pulled him into their conversation. She liked the way he listened, giving them his full attention. There was an aura of strength about him she found appealing. What was even more intriguing was the flash of dislike in his eyes she noted before he was able to mask it. Dislike that made no sense considering they had never met.

Her thoughts were interrupted as a pigtailed girl came barreling across the room, the food on her tray sliding precariously as she bounced to a stop next to Cole.

"Mom said we could sit by you if that's okay, Chief Collins." She turned impatiently. "Come on, Liv!"

Kat followed her gaze and watched as the girl she had seen with Cole Collins walked slowly toward them, carefully balancing her tray and drink.

"May we sit here?" she asked politely.

"Of course," Cole said patiently. "Liv, this is Katarina Ramon. Miss Ramon, this is my daughter, Olivia."

Kat extended a hand and, after a brief hesitation, Olivia put her tray down and took it, blushing slightly. "It's very nice to meet you, Olivia. Please sit down."

She slid gracefully into the seat next to Kat, folding her napkin primly on her lap. While Tiffany Ross chattered incessantly, Olivia ate quietly. She finished her lunch and then folded her napkin across the empty plate.

Kat felt herself drawn to the girl. There was something sad and lost about her, even though she was truly adorable with dark curly hair framing her elfin face and beautiful green eyes that were lowered at the moment. She was aware of some of the personal history regarding Brookdale's new chief and his daughter, thanks to her aunt. She waited until Cole was engaged in conversation with one of the men sitting across from him and bent toward the child.

"It's hard living somewhere new, isn't it?" she said, lowering her voice. "Hard to make new friends, get used to new teachers?" She had the girl's attention, although she didn't respond but just gazed at her with those big eyes. "You know, Olivia, I grew up in Brookdale before I moved to New York City. There were days I was so homesick I could hardly stand it."

"Did it get better?"

Kat smiled, nodding. "It did. I made new friends and now it's home just like Brookdale was."

The child eyed her with an almost adult concentration. "Did you miss your mother?"

Oh brother, she thought. *How do I answer that one?*

Fortunately, she was saved from replying by Tiffany Ross.

"Let's go see if they have any peanut butter cookies, Liv," she said enthusiastically, pushing her chair back so hard it almost fell over. Kat grabbed it, swatting the girl playfully.

"Gentle and graceful as ever I see, Tif," she teased.

Tiffany stuck her tongue out and then ruined it by throwing her arms around Kat's neck. "Did you bring me anything from New York?" she asked, sending a surreptitious glance toward the kitchen door to make sure her mother wasn't anywhere in listening distance. Reassured, she chattered on enthusiastically, moving to stand next to her friend. "Liv, you've got to see the cool jeans Kat got me the last time she was home. They've got this really super gold stuff on them with sparkles and everything."

Kat could feel Olivia's eyes on hers, felt the scrutiny. Instinctively she knew something was troubling the child. Something that was a lot more complicated than simply being shy.

"Hey, Kat, are you listening?" Tiffany said, grabbing her arm. "Mom told me to ask you to come over for dinner tomorrow." She put her hands on her hips, grinning mischievously. "I bet I can still beat you at poker."

Kat shook her head, lips twitching. "Bet you can't, you little monster."

Olivia stared at the two of them. "You actually play cards together?"

Tiffany twirled a pigtail impatiently. "Sure."

Kat's heart went out at the incredulity on the girl's face. She glanced at Cole Collins and found herself looking directly into the man's eyes. It was obvious he had overheard the conversation and equally obvious he was disturbed by it.

"Tell your mother I'd love to visit tomorrow. I'll give her a call later."

"Okay. See ya," she tossed over her shoulder while pulling Olivia along with her.

Cole shook his head, following Kat's gaze. "Talk about opposites. What's amazing is that the two of them get along as well as they do."

"You know what they say about opposites attracting," she said, taking a last sip of her drink. She wanted to add that it looked like his daughter needed someone like Tiffany Ross but she didn't. Not because she was concerned about his reaction, but because she had seen the quick flash of worry in his eyes when he looked at his daughter.

"Kat," her aunt said, rising and gathering her tray. "I'm going to be tied up here for a while with clean up." She dug in her purse and pulled out a set of keys. "Why don't you go home and I'll grab a ride when I'm done."

Kat stood, shaking her head. "I'll help."

Evelyn shook her head emphatically. "No, you're not going to help. Go home, young lady."

"I'll give her a ride, Evelyn," Cole said, pushing his chair back and standing. He glanced at Kat. "I'm going right past your house anyway. Okay with you?"

"That's fine as long as you really don't need any help, Aunt Evelyn."

"I don't. Thanks, Cole."

"No thanks necessary." He turned to Katarina. "I'll go round up my daughter."

She nodded, watching him stride across the room.

"Quite a hunk, isn't he?" her aunt said casually.

Kat shook a finger at her. "Very clever."

"What?"

"Don't give me that. You're matchmaking again."

"I most certainly am not."

"Sure you're not."

Evelyn laughed. "Okay maybe I am." She nudged Kat toward the kitchen as people began to leave. "Listen, Kat, Cole Collins might be a looker but he's also sharp as a tack. Unfortunately, the same can't be said of Jerry Landers. There's still a lot of resentment there. The man needs someone who will look at the evidence objectively, someone who won't take sides between him and his deputy."

"What makes you think he's going to trust me with that

kind of information?"

Evelyn pushed open the kitchen door. "Because, my dear niece," she said smartly, "you love a challenge and that man is definitely a challenge." She waved as the door began to close behind her. "See you in about an hour or so, honey."

A few moments later, Cole returned alone.

"Where's your daughter?" Kat asked.

"Deanna has invited her to stay the night with Tiffany." He shook his head ruefully. "I don't normally allow an overnight the day before school but I couldn't hold up under the pressure."

"From Tiffany?"

He shot her a quick look. "How did you guess?"

She shouldered her purse, amused. "Because I've known that child since she was born. She turned thirty on her first birthday."

He held the door open for her, grinning. "Guess you do know her."

She followed him to his car, lifting a brow at the low-slung Corvette. "Looks like police vehicles have changed since I was here last."

He didn't reply but opened the door for her. She slid gracefully into the leather seat, admiring the sleek contours of the vehicle. When the door didn't close, she looked up and found him studying her. "What?"

"Why are you here?"

"I would think that's fairly evident. It's my home," she said coolly.

He folded his arms across his chest and leaned against the door. "No, it might have been at one time but you've got New York City written all over you."

Kat crossed her long legs and took her time answering, fighting to control her temper. "I really don't think my reason for being here is any of your business."

His eyes narrowed, his gaze focusing intently on her for a long moment. Then he straightened and closed the door. Moving to the other side, he slid in and started the car. Still silent, he pushed a button and the convertible top slid back.

Donning a pair of sunglasses that effectively hid his expression, he merged into traffic.

She leaned back against the seat, taking a deep breath of the familiar scents of home. The breeze felt pleasantly cool against the heat of the afternoon and she could smell the honeysuckle and aroma of dinner cooking through the open windows of the century homes that lined the street.

She stole a glance under her lashes at the man sitting next to her. He had already managed to get under her skin. It wasn't often someone could catch her off guard but Collins had been able to do just that. It was obvious from the blunt question he had just asked that he suspected she was here for more than a visit. He wasn't happy about it either.

Well, that was just too damn bad. In spite of her reticence at becoming involved in the Sulin case, she felt a perverse desire to ruffle this man's feathers. She told herself she was well past the stage to be impressed by sunglasses and a sports car but she had to admit the chief intrigued her.

Her aunt had told her he was divorced and that, just until recently, his ex-wife had custody of their daughter. Kat knew better than to ask her where she had obtained such private information but she was sure it was reliable. Courts didn't order custody changes unless something warranted it. Against her better judgment, she was going to find out what that something was.

"Damn!" he swore, swerving to miss a bicycle left on the curb.

In the small confines of the car, she found herself jostling shoulders with him. The electricity, the connection, was there before she could prevent it. She did her best to pull away without being too obvious, leaning against the door. Damn her intuition.

She had begrudgingly adjusted to the sixth sense she had been born with. From the time she had been a little girl, she knew things, sensed things that no one else seemed to. It had scared her then. Now it simply annoyed her.

Settling against the seat more comfortably, she began to relax. Cole turned the corner and slowed, frowning. She glanced at him and then followed his gaze, immediately recognizing the Sulin house. The faded pieces of yellow police tape along with the abandoned look of the property made it clear this had been the scene of a crime. A dart of pain rushed through her as she gazed at the familiar surroundings. This house was part of so many of her memories.

He pulled to the curb and stopped, easing himself out of the car. "Thought I saw something. Stay here," he said curtly.

She held onto her temper with difficulty as he strode away. She wasn't a stranger to police procedure but Cole certainly could use some instruction on common courtesy. She opened the car door and slid out, slamming it behind her. Knowing better than to contaminate the scene, albeit an old one, she skirted the property, nostalgia creeping in before she could prevent it.

The Sulins' daughter, Ellen, had been her best friend growing up. She had spent many nights camping in the spacious backyard with the smell of gardenias and roses that grew near the picket fence permeating the air. That and the wonderful aroma of bacon wafting from the open kitchen window when they had managed to drag themselves out of their sleeping bags after staying up until dawn.

Because Dan had been on vacation when the Sulins were murdered, she had been unable to leave. She still regretted not being able to offer her support to Ellen and her brother.

She glanced toward the woods, surprised that in spite of the height of some of the trees, she could still see the rooftop of her aunt's house. Her parents had lived just a few doors beyond, so it had been easy for them to visit each other following a path they had made. She and her brother had spent countless summer days between the three residences.

Sighing, her gaze returned to the back of the house, saddened by the unkempt look. She moved forward to run a finger along the fragrant rose bush that hugged the fence. Paul Sulin had nurtured and cared for his lawn while his wife had grown flowers the garden club in town had envied. She reached down to pull some weeds then leaned against the fence, eying the patio, the memories bittersweet.

So many evenings, her parents and the Sulins sat on the double swing in the backyard sipping lemonade, steaks sizzling on the grill while the four children played. Her gaze moved to the tree house still standing in the big oak at the back of the property. Andy and Sam had spent long hours in that little house, gloating as they had placed a sign on the front proclaiming NO GIRLS ALLOWED.

Even after the death of their parents, the Sulins had always been there for her and her brother. When her aunt had been kept late at school, the two of them were often invited to share dinner. While Marie Sulin had been small and quiet, Ellen's father had been just the opposite. He had been a huge man with a booming laugh and strong arms that didn't hesitate to wrap her in a bear hug.

She suddenly felt the unexpected sting of tears. It had been so easy to keep her emotions in check when there had been distance between herself and her memories. So easy to forget Paul Sulin's big arms around her at her parents' funeral just holding her and letting her grieve.

Wiping a stray tear, she continued strolling along the property until she reached the stone wall that met the picket fence at the very back. She leaned against it, smiling as she recalled...

A cold chill skimmed her skin as the house in front of her began to waver, change. The sunlight disappeared and she backed against the wall, dread filling her. Something was about to be revealed to her, something that had nothing to do with the present.

It was dusk, the moon brilliant in the night sky, causing the stones to glisten. She saw him climb over the wall almost exactly where she stood, a ski mask covering his face. He glanced around the area, his gaze meeting hers almost as if he was looking at her. They were wide, the pupils dark, the expression and the gun he held in his hand sending shivers through her. His movements were quick and fluid as he moved swiftly toward the patio, taking an odd little hop as he mounted the porch stairs. He pulled something from his pocket and slid it along the back lock. Sliding the door open, he entered. Turning toward the bedroom, he moved quietly down the hallway...

She jerked, forcing the vision away, her heart pounding as she fought for control.

Cole walked around the house just at that moment and caught sight of her, furious that she had ignored his instructions. He forgot his anger as he drew closer, however. She was as still as a statue, her face almost as pale as alabaster, those striking blue eyes closed. She opened them slowly and straightened, swaying.

He strode forward and caught her, spinning her into his arms. "What's wrong?" he demanded.

She looked up at him for a moment, her eyes unfocused. The instant she gained control, he could feel her stiffen and draw back. She moved out of his arms, putting distance between them.

"Our killer knew the house."

His brow rose in surprise. *That had come out of left field.* "What?"

"I said," she repeated impatiently, "the person who killed the Sulins knew the house."

"And how did you surmise that?"

Her expression tightened at the tone of his voice.

"As it happens, Chief Collins, I was born with a sixth sense, a clairvoyance of sorts," she said briskly. "I don't particularly like knowing things I shouldn't but oftentimes I don't have the control to stop what is revealed to me. Your killer is male, about six foot one or two and moves like an athlete. He came through the woods and over this stone wall. When he entered the house, he knew exactly where the bedroom was even though it was dark."

The cynical part of him wanted to discount what she had just told him but the other part, the Irish cop part, wouldn't allow it. "We already suspect it was someone who knew the victims, Miss Ramon."

She shook her head. "He didn't just know them. He knew more than that." She motioned for him to follow her toward the patio. She stopped just before the door and pointed downward, nudging the loose board on the first step with her toe. "I saw him skip this step. Mr. Sulin was always going to fix it but never did. It squeaks when you step on it. It got to be a family joke. He used to tell us his kids could never sneak in the back without him hearing." She brushed a stray lock of hair back from her eyes, her gaze finding his, clear and direct. "Your killer instinctively avoided that step."

He kept her gaze for a long moment, considering. He lifted his foot, putting his weight on the step. The squeak was loud and definitely noticeable.

She pointed to the third window to their right. "That was their bedroom."

Cole turned, scanning the back of the house and then moved forward to check that the patio doors were locked. "Someone was in the house when we pulled up. I found the side door unlocked."

"Did you see anyone?"

He shook his head. "No, but it's obvious whoever it is, he is after something inside. This is the third time I've found evidence of a break-in. It's a good bet they're looking for something they weren't able to find after they killed the victims." He looked at her. "You have any idea what that was?"

The tone of his voice had her glancing at him sharply. "If that question is straightforward, then no, I don't. However, I'm not so sure it was. I sincerely hope you aren't hinting I had anything to do with these murders. The Sulins were good friends." Her eyes flashed a cold blue. "I've given you information that I thought you might be able to use and frankly, if you don't, I don't give a damn." She spun, walking toward the woods. "Don't bother seeing me home. There's still a path to my aunt's house from here. Thanks for the lift."

He watched her walk away, an unwilling grin tilting his lips. The woman had a temper that she obviously kept in check. The jeans hugged her shapely bottom as she bent to dodge a tree limb. A sharp tug of sexual interest was there before he could prevent it. Disgusted, he turned away. The last thing he needed right now was to get involved with another woman, especially an ex-wife look-alike.

He stood for a moment, eyes narrowed, and then walked around the stone fence, following the same path Katarina had just walked down. After five months, the chances of him finding anything were remote and yet he had this feeling.

After about fifteen minutes, he shrugged, giving up, and started back toward the car. A shaft of sunlight broke through the clouds at that moment, catching the gleam of something under a pile of twigs. Reaching in his pocket, he drew a handkerchief out and reached down, picking the object up. It was a pocketknife. From the ornate style, a relatively expensive pocketknife. The blade was dirty but the lack of rust told him it couldn't have been exposed to the elements too long. He flipped it over and found what looked like an initial crudely scratched on its handle. Could be any number of letters, he thought. Maybe even an R as in Ramon. He dismissed the idea. The woman might rub him the wrong way but there was a lack of motive for her, or her brother, for that matter. Besides, she had been truly upset when he found her.

He wrapped the knife carefully and carried it to the car. What was more likely was that one of the local kids dropped it while walking along the several paths that crisscrossed through the woods.

He turned the ignition and headed for home, his thoughts returning to Katarina Ramon. There was no doubt she had believed what she had told him, and if he was honest with himself, she had been right. It was the best lead he'd had thus far. If the killer had been in that house enough to know about a noisy step, then his list of suspects would narrow significantly. He wasn't unfamiliar with psychics and, although he had never personally worked with one, he knew their help could be invaluable. She sure as hell didn't look the part, he thought, thinking of those long legs and blue eyes.

He slowed and turned into the long driveway that curved gently up to the two-story Southern colonial with its wide porches on both levels. The house had been entirely too big for just himself when he had moved here and incredibly run-down. Yet, once he had taken a look at the old world charm inside, he was sold. It had taken every free moment he had had, along with a sizable amount of money, to bring it back to its original charm and he still wasn't finished. Yet it had been the panacea he had needed after the divorce, a way to forget how much he missed his little girl.

He parked the car and walked up the wide steps. Sliding a key into the lock of the ornate front door, he opened it. Took a moment to take stock of the changes he'd made. Changes he was proud of. The cherry floors gleamed in the late sunlight and the buttercup yellow walls met the crown molding and soaring ceilings, giving both the impression of grandeur and warmth at the same time. It still smelled of paint and freshly sawn wood, and he sure as hell could use some help decorating, but it was home. He threw his keys on the foyer table just as the phone rang. He glanced at the caller ID and his expression tightened as he answered.

"Cole, it's Allie."

"What do you want?" he asked bluntly, not bothering to hide his animosity.

"Hey, is that any way to talk to your child's mother? Why, one would think you didn't like little old me."

"Cut the crap, Allie."

"Listen, Cole, I need money and I need it now. Either you pony up, or my parents will push harder for custody. They have the money and they have the political power on their side. You give me the cash and I convince them Olivia's better off with you. You don't and..."

"Don't threaten me," he snarled, his hands fisting in fury.

He could hear her take a deep breath and knew what was coming next, what had always followed the threats.

"Come on, Cole," she whined, "you know she's better off with you. Are you willing to put her through another custody battle just so you don't have to give me a little spare change? After all, it isn't like you can't afford it, now is it?"

"Just get the hell out of my life, Allison. And while you're at it, get yourself some help." He hung up the phone before she could respond. Damn the woman! How in God's name he had ever thought he had been in love with her was beyond him.

He checked his answering machine, cursing for not thinking to record the call. It would have given Barry some ammunition. He checked in at the station before he took a shower. Afterward he tried to catch up on some bills and paperwork. An hour later, frustrated with his inability to concentrate, he slapped the file closed. Turning out the light, he glanced at the mantel clock. A little before eleven. He climbed the stairs, the house feeling empty without his daughter. He gazed out the tall window at the woods behind. The bright moonlight bathed the roses and gardenia bushes that were in full bloom. His mother would have loved this house. In fact, that was part of the reason he had bought it. Strange as it sounded, the tall ceilings and simple yet classical lines of the interior reminded him of her. God he missed her! Even after five years, the pain was still there.

He slammed the shower on, the familiar fury rocketing through him as he stepped under the hot spray.

If only she had never met Alison.

If only...

Chapter Five

"Your straight is nice but it doesn't beat my full house," Tiffany spouted, spreading her hand down on the table with a flourish.

Kat groaned, flashing Deanna a look. "So are you the one who taught this little card shark or was it her father?"

"Actually it was you, Kat," Tiffany said smartly, gathering the cards and shoving them toward Katarina. "Come on, Liv, you play a hand with Kat. She's no competition for me."

"I don't know how to play," Olivia said quietly.

"That doesn't matter," Kat reassured her, beginning to deal. "Besides, according to your friend, I'm a pushover anyway." She smiled at the child, motioning for her to sit across the table.

Deanna's eyes met Kat's over the girl's head and the message was sent and received.

"Tiffany, why don't you help me with coffee and dessert while Kat and Olivia play? Cole will be here soon."

"But I want to watch them play."

"You can after we serve dessert," her mother said firmly.

"Oh, all right," she grumbled, rising. "Why is it I'm always the one doing these things and not Doug? He never helps."

"Because your brother is not here, that's why."

"Good excuse," she muttered, following her mother with a mutinous backward glance at the two sitting at the table. She managed to slam the connecting door with a hard bang as she went through.

"Tiffany Lynn, do you want to be grounded again?" Deanna scolded from behind the closed door.

Kat glanced at Olivia, their gazes locking for a few seconds. Kat's lips twitched and, before she could help herself, Olivia returned the grin and suddenly both of them were laughing.

Kat was enchanted. Somewhere under all the adult behavior was an eight-year-old girl just crying to be set free. That smile was the first crack in the armor.

"Okay, Olivia Collins, I hear you're very bright," she said, picking up her cards and challenging her at the same time. "I'll go through the game once and we'll take it from there." She leaned forward, whispering surreptitiously, "Learn quickly because you know Tiffany will never let you forget it if you don't beat me."

The hesitation was there, the insecurity. "Don't you want to have coffee with Mrs. Ross? I'll understand if you don't want to play with me."

Kat's heart broke a little, angry at whoever had managed to beat back what should have been a natural youthful exuberance. A quick image of Olivia's father flashed in front of her. No, it was obvious he loved his daughter. It had to have been her mother then. Even worse, she thought.

She shook her head, leaning forward to touch the girl's hand. "Listen, Olivia, I'm going to tell you something my parents told me a long time ago when I was just about your age. It's advice I still use today."

She could see the curiosity fighting with the insecurity, the curiosity winning. "What did they tell you?"

"They told me to listen to the adults and be respectful but never to forget that my wishes and opinions mattered, and if they ever forgot that, I had their permission to remind them."

"Did you ever have to?"

"Once or twice. Olivia, I wish to play cards with you. If I didn't, I wouldn't have offered. Do you believe me?"

She could see the wheels turning and waited until the girl nodded, her dark curls bouncing.

"Okay, so let's start with the game Tiffany and I were playing and see how quickly you pick it up." Shuffling the cards expertly, she glanced up. "I'll make you a deal. First time you beat Tiff, I'll give you five bucks." She extended her hand. "Okay?"

A giggle escaped before the child could prevent it as she took a look over her shoulder. "Deal," she said, putting her small hand in Kat's larger one.

"All right! So let's play."

℘

Half an hour later, Cole walked up to the open screen door. Just as he prepared to knock, he stopped with his hand raised. Was that his daughter laughing? He opened the door, knowing Deanna wouldn't mind, and quietly walked into the front room and toward the dining room. He paused just before the doorway, a lump forming in his throat at the scene that greeted him.

Katarina Ramon was sitting at the head of the table with Olivia and Tiffany on either side, both girls intent on the cards in their hands. He had never seen his daughter so animated as she concentrated on her cards then laughed again at something Tiffany said. There were coins in the middle of the table and cookies to the side on a plate next to Katarina.

His gaze settled on the woman for just a moment. She had her hair pulled back in a simple ponytail, the style highlighting her flawless skin and sea blue eyes. She wore jeans and a white cotton shirt, her own face as animated as his daughter's as she dealt a new batch of cards.

"I'll bet five pennies," Tiffany said confidently, pushing the coins to the center of the table.

"Your turn, Olivia," Katarina said, winking when the child looked up at her. She immediately assumed a poker face when Tiffany glanced at her suspiciously.

"I'll call you and raise you two pennies," Olivia said.

"You're bluffing, Liv." Tiffany pouted. "Just like the last time."

"Guess you won't know that unless you give up," Kat countered.

"So, Liv, are you bluffing?"

His daughter laughed. She actually laughed! "I know better than that, Tiff. You've got to fold or raise, right?" she asked Kat.

"Exactly. What will it be, young lady?"

"Shoot! I guess I have to fold."

"I've got four lovely ladies," Olivia said proudly, spreading them in front of her triumphantly.

"Yes!" Kat said, reaching over to hug her. "Good for you, Liv."

He watched as his daughter flushed and then returned the hug. "Thanks, Kat."

"So I see you've taught my daughter how to gamble, Miss Ramon," he teased, walking into the room.

Kat saw the child's expression change instantly, the smile disappearing. "Kat... Miss Ramon was just teaching me a game, that's all."

"Evening, Cole," Kat said, touched by the hurt she saw before he masked it. "Your daughter has just done the impossible. She actually beat Tiffany Ross in four straight hands. I think that's a record."

"I just had a bad night," Tiffany sulked.

Cole grinned, putting an arm around her shoulders. "We all have nights like that, Tiffany. Don't worry; you'll get her next time."

"Not if I can help it," Olivia said, her chin jutting out.

Cole glanced at his daughter and then slid his gaze to Kat, obviously pleased with his daughter's reaction. "Good for you, love."

Deanna walked in, followed by her husband.

"Evening, Mike."

"Hey, Cole." He walked over to his daughter, ruffling her hair. "Now don't pout, Tiff. We still love you even if your friend beat the pants off of you."

Tiffany rounded on him, eyes flashing. "She did not! Only the last couple hands."

Her father laughed, lifting her right out of the chair and swinging her around until she shrieked with laughter.

Deanna shook her head. "Hey, you two cut it out before you break something." She handed Olivia her backpack and bag. "She's already done her homework, without complaint, I might add." She leaned down to kiss the top of the girl's head. "Come back anytime, my dear. We love having you here."

"Thank you, Mrs. Ross."

"Thanks from me as well, Deanna," Cole said, opening the door for his daughter. "Night, Mike and Tiffany." He turned to Kat. "Miss Ramon."

"Goodnight," they said in unison. Tiffany waved at her friend. "See you at school tomorrow, Liv."

Kat rose from the table. "I've got to be going as well, Deanna." She smiled at both of them. "Thanks for dinner. It was great."

Mike returned the smile as he put an arm around his wife. "It's good to see you, Kat. We only wish you'd visit more often. You know, like move back."

She laughed. "Goodnight." She leaned down and hugged Tiffany. "You're a good friend, Tiffany Ross," she said quietly. "I'm proud of you."

"Proud enough to bring me some more of those jeans?"

"Tiffany!" Deanna scolded, rolling her eyes.

Lips curving, Kat walked out, quickening her pace to catch up with Cole and his daughter. "Olivia, wait a moment. I believe you forgot something."

The girl turned in surprise. "What?"

Kat reached in her purse and pulled out a crisp five-dollar bill. "This."

"You don't have to give me that," she said, glancing up at her father.

"I most certainly do. I never go back on my word."

Olivia slowly reached for the money. "Never?"

"Absolutely. What's the purpose of giving your word if you don't keep it?"

"Is that something else your parents told you?"

"It is." She could feel Cole's gaze on her. "You know, Olivia, I bet your father has lots of stories just like the ones I told you about my parents. Why don't you ask him to tell you some on the ride home?"

Cole shot her a surprised but grateful look.

Kat bent to wrap her arms around Olivia, letting the embrace last longer than normal. When she straightened, she could see the warmth in the child's eyes. "I've got an idea, Olivia. Have you ever walked along the creek that runs down the south end of town by the railroad tracks?"

Olivia shook her head.

"Then you haven't heard the stories connected with that creek? My goodness, you've been here almost a year and don't know about the hobos?"

Olivia's eyes widened. "What about them?"

"Oh, I couldn't tell you now. That will have to wait until you and I take that walk." She glanced up at Cole. "Of course, if that's all right with your father?"

Olivia spun, looking up. "It's okay, isn't it?"

"As a matter of fact, it's not only okay, young lady, but Miss Ramon has piqued my curiosity as well. How about Saturday morning? I'll provide lunch."

"You've got yourself a deal, Chief," Kat said. "Only I'll provide the lunch and meet you at your house." She smiled at Olivia. "It's up to you and your father, but if you want to bring Tiffany along, that would be okay with me."

"That'd be great!" Olivia said excitedly. "Can I run in and ask her now?"

"Sure," Cole answered, watching her race up the walkway before turning to Kat. Thank you," he said quietly.

"No thanks are necessary. I always enjoy a trip down memory lane."

He shook his head. "That's not what I mean. Thank you for giving me a glimpse of the daughter I haven't seen in a very long time. The happy-go-lucky child that has all but disappeared."

Kat frowned. "Her mother?"

He nodded. "She used Liv the worst way a mother could use a child. As leverage to get what she could out of me and when that didn't work she poisoned the kid's mind." He stopped. "Sorry, I shouldn't be bothering you with this."

Kat leaned against the car, appreciating his honesty. Attraction pulled at her as she looked up at him candidly. "So you aren't the jerk I first thought you were."

He flashed a grin. "Oh, I can be when the situation arises, I guess. But I love my daughter, Miss Ramon. Make no mistake about that."

"Kat," she corrected. "Then I guess this calls for a truce," she said, putting her hand out.

He took it and gently pulled her toward him until they were pressed against each other. She knew she should move away but she didn't. She could feel his heart beating through the thin material of her shirt as she lifted her eyes to his.

"Interesting way to call a truce," she said, just a little breathlessly.

"Yeah it is, isn't it?" he said just before he bent his head.

She had been kissed before, more times than she could possibly count. But she had never been kissed like this. It lasted all of a few seconds but when they stepped back, both of them were breathing hard and fast.

"Wow," he muttered, still holding her in his arms.

"Ditto," she responded, her lips still tingling.

They both turned, startled, as Olivia skimmed down the front steps, slamming the door behind her. "Tiffany can go if she does her chores early Saturday morning."

"That's great," Kat said just a tad breathlessly, waving as she walked to her car. "See you around ten Saturday morning then."

"Bye, Kat."

"Bye, Olivia. Oh, by the way, wear old clothes and tennis shoes. There are a few caves I'd like to take you in as well."

She had to hide a smile at the girl's expression. "Real honest-to-goodness caves?"

"Yep. Goodnight, Cole."

"Night, Katarina."

She waited until they backed out of the driveway and then headed toward her aunt's house, smiling to herself. It had been an interesting evening all around.

Ten minutes later, she pulled into the driveway behind a convertible Mercedes, grinning when she saw the license plate. ARBUY. She parked her car and flew up the big old porch steps and into the front room, following the voices into the kitchen.

"Andy!" she said, meeting him halfway across the room as he lifted her off her feet and spun her around.

"Welcome home, sis," he said, smiling. He eased her back to arm's length to take stock of her. "You get prettier every time I see you."

She laughed. "You're prejudiced, but thanks anyway." Her heart ached for just a moment as she gazed up into her brother's face. He looked so much like their father. Same body build, same deep brown eyes and blond hair, same easy way of speaking.

He grabbed a cold beer from the fridge and sat at the table, waiting for her to join him. "So how's life in the big city?"

"Busy, hectic. We've taken on a new partner and that's made a big difference in our workload. That's the main reason I was able to come home."

"You actually like that kind of lifestyle?"

She shot him a quick look. "I wouldn't be doing it if I didn't, Andy."

He put his hands up in defense. "Just thought maybe you were ready for a change, that's all."

"What kind of change?"

"Oh, maybe like buying a summer house for investment purposes."

She groaned, glancing at her aunt who was busy at the sink. "You put him up to this?"

Evelyn shook her head. "No," she said firmly, turning to Andy. "What kind of summer house?"

"Remember the cabin down by the bend in the creek?"

"Clay Saunders's old place?" Kat asked, a gleam of excitement flickering in her eyes.

"That's it. Some couple from out of town bought it on the cheap a few years back and had it fixed up. Planned on using it for vacations."

"Then why are they selling it?"

"Because the husband did use it for rest and relaxation," Andy answered, grinning.

Evelyn laughed, shaking a finger at him, noting Kat's

confused expression. "That's your brother's round about way of saying the gentleman had other things in mind besides vacations with his wife. I had no idea they'd put it up for sale though."

Kat's expression cleared. "The infamous other woman?"

Andy nodded. "His plan worked very well until last weekend when his wife decided to surprise him by arriving unannounced." His lips lifted sardonically. "I listed it two days later and, suffice it to say I don't think Mr. and Mrs. Allan are still living happily ever after."

Kat laughed. "You're an evil man, you know that?"

"Nope. Just realistic, that's all."

Kat eyed him contemplatively. She had always loved that picturesque little cabin tucked back in the trees, the creek gurgling in front of it. The two of them had spent countless hours in the summer fishing and listening to the old man's stories, their feet dangling in the clear moving water, fat trout visible below.

Her brother reached in his pocket and pulled out a set of keys. "Why don't you take a look at it Saturday and see what you think? It'd be a great place to spend a quiet week or so away from that busy schedule of yours."

"And what's wrong with my house?" Evelyn asked, tapping him smartly on the shoulder.

He grabbed her hand and reached up to kiss her cheek. "Not a thing. But that doesn't mean that Kat wouldn't like the idea of having a place of her own. Might encourage her to spend more time here."

"Hmmm...maybe it's not such a bad idea after all," Evelyn mused, tongue in cheek.

"I know a conspiracy when I see one," Kat said, taking the keys. "I'm heading down to the creek on Saturday anyway so I'll take a look just to appease you both."

"Great."

"Visiting old memories?" Evelyn asked, shutting off the faucet and drying her hands.

"And making some new ones. I've invited Tiffany and Olivia Collins to join me."

"Cole going?" Andy asked, winking at his aunt.

"He is, as a matter of fact," she answered, daring him to say another word by the look in her eyes.

He put his hands up again. "Hey, don't get your back up. I just know wherever that kid goes, he isn't far behind. He's a good guy and he's trying to be a good father."

Evelyn finished wiping the counter and turned. "I'm glad you invited that little girl to join you. God knows she's had precious few times to just be a child."

Kat rose and poured herself a soda and then leaned against the counter. "Her father hinted as much earlier tonight. His ex-wife must be a real witch."

"That's one description," Andy said, lifting a brow. "I could think of a few more."

Kat glanced at him in surprise. "You know his wife?"

"You know her as well, or at least you did. Remember Allie Sandoval?"

Her eyes widened. "You've got to be kidding me! The same Allie Sandoval that stayed with her aunt here in Brookdale the summer her parents went to Europe?"

"Yep, that's the one."

Kat frowned, taking another sip of her soda. "Then I can think of a few other words as well. She was a spoiled rich girl and she made sure everyone knew she was just slumming until her parents returned. Made sure they knew she didn't like it either."

Evelyn nodded. "She hasn't changed." At Kat's quick look, she shrugged. "You know how running for office in a small town can be. I think she pushed Brian Landers to inform everyone about their divorce and loss of custody during the election."

"Then I'm surprised he was elected."

"Actually it backfired on them. People started talking and it didn't take long for them to remember Allie Sandoval. Remember how nasty she was to her aunt while she was here? Before long, it came out that the ex-Mrs. Collins also liked to dabble in booze and drugs."

"Is that how Cole gained custody of his daughter?"

"Yep," Andy said. "Needless to say, that wasn't what Brian

Landers had in mind when he started the rumors. Immediately, public sentiment was on the side of our new chief of police. Cole hadn't wanted to put his daughter in the middle of a custody fight, but when the public did the investigation for him, he went back to court."

Kat frowned. "I'm surprised he didn't see the signs that little girl had been mentally abused. I was with her for less than two minutes and it was apparent to me."

"Allie wouldn't let him see the kid," Andy said, draining the rest of his drink. "Rumor has it she isn't happy about the situation. She doesn't get all that lovely child support now."

"Can't be much on a cop's salary."

"It's not his salary she's interested in but his inheritance," Evelyn said, eyes flashing as she slid into a chair across from Kat. "His mother died a few years ago and left him a chunk of money that he'll get when he turns thirty-five, which happens to be in a few months."

Kat raised an eyebrow. "You sure seem to know a lot about our local sheriff. What's more, it appears you think he's smart and capable. Interesting, since that wasn't the impression I got when you called asking me to come home."

Evelyn gave her an innocent look. "I can't imagine where you got that. I just thought things might happen if the two of you put your heads together, that's all."

"Yeah, right." She turned back to Andy. "Why isn't she trying these matchmaking skills on you? You're older."

"Because she knows I'm a confirmed bachelor, right, Aunt Evelyn?"

"Wrong. I just haven't found the woman yet who will knock that arrogant grin off your face, young man," Evelyn returned smartly.

Kat took a moment to really look at her brother. Beneath the boyish charm was a restlessness that had been there since their parents' deaths. At the age of seventeen, she had been devastated by the tragedy but Andy had been inconsolable. Two years older than her, he immediately had blamed himself for being out with his friends instead of being home that night. It had been long months before that grin her aunt spoke of showed itself again. Long months during which he spent every available hour searching for clues as to who it was that had murdered their parents, destroyed their lives.

"Have you had a chance to ask Cole about the Sulin murders?" Evelyn asked.

Kat shifted her gaze from her brother to her aunt. "Not in so many words but something did happen the night of the church social."

When she was finished explaining, Andy leaned back in his chair thoughtfully. "I thought you didn't believe in those instincts of yours?"

Kat tossed her aunt a warning glance. "I never said I didn't believe in my sixth sense or whatever you want to call it. I just don't particularly like things coming at me when I'm not ready for them."

"Well, if you're right, sis, then maybe the motive is deeper than simply robbery."

"I can't imagine what else it could be," Evelyn replied, sighing. "They didn't have an enemy to their name that I know of. Paul would give you the shirt off his back if he thought you needed it."

"I know," Kat said quietly, "yet I'm as sure as I can be that whoever killed them knew them, or at least knew the house very well."

Andy rose, stretching. "If that's true, then that will give Cole some kind of direction to go in." He glanced at his watch. "I've got to get home. Got a closing bright and early in the morning."

"I'll walk you to the car," Kat said, rising as well and slipping an arm through her brother's.

She waited until they were at the end of the driveway before she stopped him, her gaze scanning his face. "You okay?"

He raised a brow. "Why wouldn't I be?"

"Because I know you too well. You're not happy. Why?"

He leaned against the car, frowning. "It's not so much that I'm not happy, Kat. I just keep having flashbacks about the night Mom and Dad were killed. Something is there just on the fringe of my memory. Something that I know, if I could just see it or remember it, would reveal who it was that murdered them."

Her blue eyes softened. "Andy, it's been a long time now. Don't you think you should just let it go?"

He nodded. "Yeah, I keep telling myself that, but it's as if something or someone keeps at me." His lips twisted. "I know that sounds crazy."

She shook her head. "No, it doesn't. Remember that dream I kept having right afterward?"

His gaze shot to hers as he nodded.

"I had it again about a month ago. If I didn't think it sounded nuts, I'd say our parents are trying to tell us something."

Andy eased inside the convertible. "Do me a favor and tell Cole about that dream, Kat. He's not the type to ignore evidence, even if it's the unconventional kind."

"I wouldn't be too sure about that."

The grin was back. "Rubbed you the wrong way, did he?"

She shook her head, lips twitching. "Nah, I know how to handle smart asses. Have one for a brother."

"Cute, real cute," he said capturing her hand and squeezing it. "I'm glad you're home, sis. It's not the same around here without you." He started the car. "How's Dan?"

"He's fine."

He raised a brow. "Still pushing for something more permanent?"

She smiled ruefully. "He is and I hate that I'm keeping him on the string. I just can't seem to make up my mind and that isn't like me."

"That's because he isn't the right man for you and subconsciously you know it."

Her eyes narrowed. "And when did you come to that conclusion?"

"Oh, about the time you and he became partners," he answered frankly.

"He's a good man, Andy," she said, feeling the need to defend him.

"Didn't say he wasn't. What he isn't is strong enough to

handle my very independent and willful sister."

"Go to hell."

He laughed, waving as he backed out. "Have fun at the creek and let me know what you think of the cabin."

She shook her head in amusement, admitting she'd missed him more than she had realized. She strolled up the walkway, reaching inside her car on the way to grab her cell phone. She'd left it in there on purpose but couldn't bring herself to turn it off, just in case problems arose at the office. She flipped through her messages as she continued walking and then stopped abruptly as a text message came up on the screen.

I KNOW WHERE YOU ARE, KATARINA...YOU CAN'T HIDE FROM ME...REMEMBER THAT...

Chapter Six

"How far is it?" Tiffany asked, squirming in her seat as she gazed out the car window. "Mom says she can't even remember the last time she's been to the creek."

"We're almost there," Kat reassured her. "Olivia, tell your friend to quit bouncing back there before she flies out."

"I've tried, Kat. She won't listen."

"Something new and different," Kat murmured to Cole. "Turn at the next dirt road."

"I hate to admit it but I haven't been down here either. Wasn't even aware there was a house this far away from town."

Kat glanced at the huge trees that lined both sides of the road. "Actually we're only a few miles outside. I took you the scenic route. The cabin is just around the next bend."

Cole guided the car to a stop in front of a one-story log structure enclosed on all four sides by a large covered porch. Huge trees surrounded it, keeping the sun's glare to a minimum. With the bubbling stream in front and the lack of neighbors, the scene was one of tranquility.

"Wow, Andy wasn't kidding when he said the previous owners fixed it up. It looked nothing like this when I was here last." She opened the door and slid out, her gaze moving to the newly constructed pier jutting out into the water. "That porch is new and the wood has been treated and cleaned."

"Can we go fishing?" Tiffany asked excitedly. "Dad brought worms and some poles."

"Only if you promise to stay put on the pier," Cole warned.

"We promise. Come on, Liv."

"I don't know how to fish," Olivia protested.

"That doesn't matter, I'll show you," Tiffany said, urging her friend forward.

"Well, I'll tell you right now, I'm not putting those yucky worms on the hook."

Kat shook her head, smiling up at Cole as the girls headed to the car to get their gear. "A dollar says she'll be baiting her own hook by the time we leave."

He shook his head. "Not a good bet because I know you're right."

Kat reached in her pocket and pulled out a set of keys. "While I'm here, I might as well have a look around. Andy says it's for sale and he has the listing," she explained, walking up the wide steps. She couldn't resist sitting in one of the big rockers strategically placed to view the slow moving creek.

Cole followed, noting the way the sunlight peeking through the trees turned her hair to gold and highlighted the blue of her eyes.

"I'm already in love and I haven't even been inside yet," Kat admitted as he walked up.

He had to resist the urge to run a hand through those silken strands. There was an attraction here that he wasn't at all pleased about. He had no intention of starting another relationship when he was still smarting from the last one. "Then I suggest you unlock that door and we'll take a look," he said, his voice more curt than he intended.

She gave him a long, cool stare as she rose. "You certainly don't have to accompany me, Cole. I'm a big girl, really. In fact, I don't even have to have a man's opinion. Imagine that," she finished, turning her back to him as she fit the key in the lock.

He ran a hand through his hair, irritated with himself. "Hell, Katarina, I'm sorry. I didn't mean that the way it sounded."

She turned back to look up at him. "Let's set a few ground rules here, Cole. Number one, I'm not your ex-wife. Don't use her as a measuring stick for what I do or how I do it. Number two, I'm here because my aunt thought, as ridiculous as it sounds, that I might be able to help in some way regarding these murder investigations."

Before she could turn back, he caught her arm, squeezing lightly. "I've got a few rules of my own, Kat. Number one," he mimicked, "my ex doesn't even stand on the same plain as you. Number two, as much as I hate to admit it, I sure as hell can use any help you can give me in regards to those murders."

"Damn it, you're good," she tossed over her shoulder as she opened the door. "I like to fight and you ruined it."

He laughed. "I'll remember that the next time..."

She stopped so abruptly that he almost ran her over. "My goodness, will you look at this place," she said, spinning in a circle. She pointed to the area around the fireplace. "This used to be a very small room. They've taken out the wall. What a difference."

Cole liked the openness of the floor plan. The planks on the floor were a warm pine and the ceiling soared to the open rafters. A stone fireplace dominated one wall with pretty red overstuffed couches in front of it while a small but nicely appointed kitchen occupied the opposite wall. It still smelled slightly of paint and freshly sawn wood.

"The word cabin sure doesn't seem to fit this place," he said, examining the large round oak table next to the kitchen. "It's obvious someone spent a lot of money sprucing things up. Wonder why they're selling?"

Kat opened the cupboards, amazed to find them stocked with all kinds of canned goods. "Andy told me the couple that bought the place fixed it up then had a rather nasty disagreement."

"Must have been really nasty to spend all this money and then sell."

"It was," she said, lips curving. "Apparently the problem was which couple was going to occupy the place, the husband and wife or the husband and mistress."

He raised a brow then laughed. "I see."

Kat explored the rest of the house. There was a small laundry room, a half bath and one large bedroom with its own very nice bathroom, which included a huge spa tub.

"What I wouldn't give for sinking in that tub with a bunch of candles burning and a good book," she sighed, running a hand along the fancy faucet.

"Funny," Cole said, leaning against the tile wall, "my thoughts lean more toward a glass of wine and a woman."

She could feel herself blushing at the look in his eyes. "Typical man versus woman imagination," she scoffed, straightening.

"Oh yeah?" Before she knew it, she found herself against his broad chest. Her heart began to beat faster as their gazes locked.

It was there before she knew it. A glimpse of him, face grim and set, behind bars. Jail bars. A moment later, it was gone.

"What is it?" he asked.

She shook her head. "Nothing. It's nothing."

"Kat! Kat, where are you? Wait till you see what Liv caught!"

Tiffany's excited voice had them jumping apart just as the girl dragged Olivia into the room, still holding her fishing rod with her wriggling catch on the end.

Cole knelt down and examined the fish. "Nice trout. Must be at least two or three pounds. Good job, Liv!"

His heart caught at the shy smile she gave him, her cheeks blushing. God, he'd give his right arm to see that smile more often.

"She even put the worm on and everything," Tiffany said proudly. "I had a couple of bites too but they got away."

"Want to clean and fry him?" Kat asked.

Tiffany shook her head just as vigorously yes as Olivia did no.

Cole caught Kat's glance, not sure how to handle the situation without upsetting either girl.

"I'm with Olivia on this one, Tiff," she said. "Trout isn't my favorite fish. Too many bones." She leaned down. "Besides, in case you've forgotten, I've got a whole hamper full of fried chicken and macaroni salad in the trunk. Wouldn't want that to go to waste, would you?"

"No way! Come on, Liv. Let's toss him back in the water and watch him swim away."

The two girls ran off, Olivia carefully holding the pole high enough so the wriggling fish didn't touch the floor.

Cole rose, shaking his head in exasperation. "Thanks. There's a whole lot about parenting I'm still learning. You pulled my rear end out of the fire on that one."

"Oh, I don't know. I think you're doing a pretty good job. No one's perfect at it."

He looked down at her, admiring the steady way she met his gaze and her upfront attitude. Katarina Ramon was an intriguing package. Sexy as hell, bright and yet there was something else, something beyond the obvious. He ran a finger along her cheek, noting the quick intake of breath. Good, she wasn't as unaffected by him as she appeared to be. "I feel something when I'm with you, Katarina, besides the basic attraction. There's a link and for the life of me I can't figure out what that is."

Her lips lifted. "Perhaps it's just basic lust."

He shrugged. "Could be." Stepping forward, he dipped his head just as she did the same, their lips meeting in the middle. Before he could deepen the kiss, she did, wrapping her arms around his waist and molding her curves against him. He groaned, his lips leaving hers to trail along her cheek and to the soft curve of her neck. The rapid pulse matched his. Finally, he eased back, running a finger along her full lips. "I think that pretty much rules out basic anything," he muttered. "That kiss was a hell of a lot more than simple lust."

She dimpled enchantingly. "I tend to agree with that statement, officer." Slowly, her expression changed and grew more serious. "Let's sit out on the porch and watch the girls. I'd like to talk to you."

Carefully, she relocked the door and settled in one of the rocking chairs, waiting for him to do the same.

"Does it have anything to do with what happened back there?" he asked, motioning toward the inside of the house.

She took her time answering. "To be honest, I don't know." She sighed, setting the chair in motion. "Things come to me, Cole, out of the blue sometimes. I don't much like it and I've tried hard over the years to repress these visions or whatever you want to call them. Aunt Evelyn could tell you all kinds of stories about family ancestors with the same kind of clairvoyance, or gifts, as she likes to call them." She caught his gaze ruefully. "I think maybe that's why I chose the profession I did. You know, just the facts, sir, just the facts."

"I hate to disagree with you, Kat, but the best lawyers are those who go with their instincts." He stretched his long legs in front of him, grinning as the sound of Tiffany giggling floated through the air. "So what exactly did you see?"

She hesitated for a few moments. "You're not going to like this, especially since right now it makes absolutely no sense to me. I caught just a glimpse of you behind bars, as in jail bars."

He stopped rocking abruptly. "Now why the hell would you see something like that?"

"I don't have a clue. I told you, I have no control over these visions. Or," she corrected, "at least not usually."

He rubbed a hand along his jaw, frowning. "You always right?"

"Mostly."

"Terrific."

"Listen, Cole, my brother and I were talking and he suggested I tell you about a recurring dream I've had ever since my parents were killed. I have no idea if it means anything but I'll leave that to you."

He listened quietly until she was finished. "You think your mother knew her killer?"

She frowned, looking into the distance. "It's the same every time I dream it. I see recognition in her eyes and in my father's when he rushes into the room."

"The investigation indicated the narcotic cupboard was open so it was obvious they were after drugs. Could be murder wasn't part of the plan until your mother surprised him. Probably panicked and shot her then couldn't let your father identify him." He saw the grief flicker in her eyes. "Sorry, Katarina, I didn't mean to be insensitive."

"It was a long time ago."

He nodded. "Yeah, but it still hurts. Believe me, I know."

Her gaze slid to his. "Sounds like a story is connected to that statement."

He shrugged. "Not really. It's just that I lost my mother about nine years ago and a day doesn't go by that I don't miss her."

She didn't offer her sympathy but instead reached over to squeeze his hand. "The pain dims. It'll always be there but it hurts less after awhile."

They were both silent for a time, then he turned to her again. "Interesting that you sensed the killer also knew the Sulins. A connection?"

"My aunt thinks so."

"Then there's got to be something in common between the two."

"Or someone."

The girls were heading toward them as he stood. "I'd like to compare notes before you head back to New York. Why don't we meet at my house in the next few days? Go over some things."

She lifted a brow. "I think I've heard that line before. You know the one. Come back to my house, little girl, and look at my etchings."

He laughed. "Not when you've got an eight-year-old daughter as a chaperone."

She considered. "I guess you're right, at that. How about day after tomorrow?"

"I'll pick you up around five. Even make dinner if you don't mind not having anything fancy."

She shook her head, rising gracefully. "I'll just meet you at your house. Don't be too flattered. I make it a point never to refuse an invitation when it involves food."

"I'm starved!" Tiffany said as if on cue, leaning her pole against the house.

"Me too," Olivia said, doing the same.

"Okay, lunch it is then."

About fifteen minutes later, they were all sitting by the creek on the big blanket Evelyn had provided, feasting on chicken.

"You make the chicken?" Cole asked, leaning against a tree. "Because if you did, it's the best I've had in a long time."

"I wish I could take credit but I can't. Aunt Evelyn had it ready this morning."

"You promised you would tell us about the hobos," Olivia

said. "What exactly are hobos?"

"They're like beggars, right?" Tiffany said importantly.

Kat nodded, wiping her fingers with a napkin. "You don't see them much anymore, but back when my grandmother was a little girl, they used to walk the railroad tracks from town to town, oftentimes hopping a train between. She told me many times they would knock on the door asking to do odd jobs for food and shelter, especially in the winter."

"How come the train doesn't come through here anymore?" Olivia asked shyly.

Kat smiled at her. "Because those rails were laid for mining coal. They took it from here to other locations throughout the country. The mines are all closed now."

"That's kind of sad."

Kat reached in the hamper and handed both girls some chocolate chip cookies. "Not really, Olivia. Things change over the years, people change. Sometimes when something happens that makes us sad, it just takes a little time for us to realize that maybe it happens for a reason."

"What kind of reason?"

Kat caught Cole's eye and chose her words with care. "Let's see. You know where Mary Johnson's antique store is?"

Both girls nodded.

"That used to be the old train station. When the train stopped running, she bought it for just a little money and fixed it up. She wouldn't have been able to do that if things hadn't changed."

"There's also talk of removing the rails and fashioning a bike trail from here to eventually Birmingham," Cole added, grabbing another leg of chicken.

Kat's gaze slid to his. "Now that's a great idea." She glanced back at the cabin. "Ironically, having a walking trail directly in front of this place makes it a good investment."

"Good way to talk yourself into buying, isn't it?"

She sent him a long stare. "And how would you know that?"

He took another bite of chicken before he answered. "Because if you don't, I'm going to, and I have a feeling that wouldn't go over too well."

"You guessed right," she tossed back and then couldn't help smiling at the teasing look in his green eyes.

"Tell us more about the hobos," Tiffany said impatiently.

"Well," Kat mused thoughtfully, "my grandmother also told me some of them weren't always hardworking and nice. They sometimes stole things, including liquor." She leaned forward, her voice lowering dramatically. "One night my great uncle was on his way home from work. It was almost dark and the shadows were deep. He said he was kicking stones along the track when suddenly his foot came in contact with something bigger. He leaned down to pick it up and..."

"And?" Tiffany urged her on.

"And he found he was holding a human head."

"Yuck!"

"Later on, they found that this particular hobo had gotten drunk and fallen asleep on the railroad tracks. The train came along and..."

"Cut his head off," Olivia finished. "Gross!"

Cole glanced at his watch and gathered his plate and cup. "How about let's clean up and then take a walk along those tracks?"

"Cool!" Tiffany said, jumping up. "Can we see where your uncle found that head?"

"If you really want to," Kat said dryly, stacking the hamper and tossing the garbage into a plastic bag.

They spent an enjoyable rest of the afternoon exploring. Olivia, after being somewhat shy, was soon romping ahead, keeping up with Tiffany.

"That girl has done Olivia a world of good," Cole said, lifting a branch so Kat could duck underneath.

She looked up at him, frowning. "Don't take offense, Cole, but didn't you see what your ex-wife was doing to your daughter?" A flicker of anger flashed in her eyes. "There is nothing I deplore more than a person who would stoop to using a child as a means to manipulate a marriage or a divorce."

"Oh, I saw," he said grimly. "Problem was I couldn't do anything about it. When we divorced, she threatened to make the custody battle an ugly one unless I gave in. I didn't want to put Liv through that so I agreed as long as she gave me liberal visitation rights. She lied." He kicked at a rock viciously. "What I didn't realize at the time, or maybe what I didn't want to admit, was that the sole reason for her wanting custody was for money."

Kat grimaced, glancing at the girls ahead. "Unfortunately that isn't unusual. Especially in a divorce that isn't amicable."

"It is when the money was being used to finance a drug habit that had spiraled out of control."

Kat's eyes widened, her gaze softening with sympathy. "I gather that's when you decided to file for custody?"

He nodded. "It was an ugly battle but I won." He rubbed a hand through his hair in frustration. "What I didn't know was what she had done to Liv's psyche." His fists clenched at his side. "I could have killed her for that."

She laid a hand on his tense arm. "It doesn't matter now."

"The damnable part about it is it does. Her parents counter filed for custody just last week."

Kat stopped walking, lifting a brow. "And why would they do something like that?"

"My attorney believes it's for money." He felt the familiar anger roll through him. "Allie is a manipulative bitch and since she couldn't win fighting me herself, she brought in the big guns."

"Speaking from experience, Cole, no court in its right mind would award custody to grandparents over a biological father."

"They would if they can prove I'm not a suitable father."

"It's been tried before," she said dryly. "It still doesn't hold a lot of weight with a judge unless you're doing something illegal."

"I have a bad feeling that wouldn't matter if this goes to court because the Sandovals have power and lots of it."

"Hey, Daddy, come here and look at this," Olivia called, turning back, her face lit with excitement.

Cole's expression softened. "I can't tell you the last time I've heard her call me that," he said softly.

She reached out and squeezed his hand without saying anything. When she started to release her grasp, he didn't allow it but instead tugged her forward as he began walking toward the girls.

"Thanks," he said quietly.

"For what?"

"For listening. You're rather good at it."

She smiled. "Some of the prosecutors I battle might not agree with you."

Tiffany was holding up what looked like a backpack as they drew near, waving it back and forth excitedly. "Look what I found!"

Cole took it from her, flipping it over. It was black with a bright green stripe down the middle. At least it had been bright at one time, he thought. Now it was covered in mud and faded although the nylon was still intact. "Pretty exciting find, girls." He lifted it up and down experimentally, winking at Kat. "What's even more exciting is I think there's something inside. Wonder what it is?"

Olivia's eyes were wide. "Maybe it's another head!"

"Pretty disgusting thought but I doubt it." He offered the bag to Tiffany. "Since you found it, how about you opening it?"

The girl debated and then shook her head, taking a step back. "No, I think you should do it. After all you're the law."

Cole laughed. "Pretty slick, little lady. Okay, I'll do the honors."

Kat came forward and wrapped an arm around each girl's shoulder, joining in the excitement. "Assuming you can unzip the thing. It's pretty rusty."

"Hey, you doubt my strength?" he teased, tugging at the stubborn zipper. "Ah, here it goes." He slid the backpack open and slowly and dramatically turned it upside down, shaking it gently.

With a dull thud, the contents of the bag fell to the ground. Kat's startled gaze flew to Cole's.

"My God, it's a gun!"

Chapter Seven

"Dan, whatever you can't handle, just put aside and I'll deal with it when I get back. I'll be home in just a few days."

"Will do. How are things going there?"

"It's always great to see everyone. Aunt Evelyn and Andy send their love."

"How about the investigation?"

"Not much to tell at this point although something really strange happened yesterday." She told him about the backpack and the gun. "From the looks of the thing, it had to have been there for a long time. Cole is hoping the nylon protected the weapon enough to lift some fingerprints."

"Cole?"

"He's the new chief I was telling you about. His daughter and Tiffany Ross are best friends. That's why we were out by the old cabin. The two of them wanted to see the creek and rails. Dan, you should see what they've done to that old place. A couple bought it and completely remodeled the interior as well as the outside. It's for sale now and I've already put a bid in. It'd be a great place to spend vacations."

"From what I remember it was a real dump. They must have spent an arm and leg fixing it up."

"It appears they did. I fell in love with it right away. Besides, as run-down as the place was, I have lots of good memories there. My parents used to visit Mr. Saunders about once a week. Mom always made him an apple pie. He was a crusty old curmudgeon but I remember being mesmerized by his stories. We used to build a fire in that old fireplace and roast marshmallows. I recall being scared to death by the spooky stories he would tell and loving every minute."

"Never met him personally but I sure heard about him in town. He died a few years back, didn't he?"

"More like fifteen. Remember he was found dead in his cabin the Saturday after my parents were killed?" She paused, pushing back the flicker of pain. "He was well into his eighties." She sighed. "As strange as it sounds, I think it would have been a little less painful time for Andy and me if we had been able to sit around that fire with him just once or twice more."

"It's hard not to get sentimental when you return to your past. You sure you're okay dealing with the memories?"

"I'm sure but thanks for caring. Doesn't seem like I've done much in the way of helping with the investigation anyway since my two weeks are almost up."

"Any idea who the backpack belonged to?"

"Not yet but I can't imagine forensics won't come up with something."

"Maybe so. Remember to miss me, will you?"

"Always. By the way, how's our new associate holding up?"

"Saving my ass, to be frank. He's plowed right in and, believe it or not, we're not too incredibly far behind at the moment. Amazing, since you're away and I've been stuck for the past two weeks in court with the Delgado murder trial."

"I like him, Dan. Good judgment on your part. See you soon."

"Bye, love."

She flipped her phone closed slowly. She was going to have to get the courage to tell her partner that there wasn't going to be a future between the two of them. It had only taken one kiss to cement her decision. One kiss from a tall, slightly irritating Irish cop.

She refused to allow herself to wonder why that was. She had agreed to meet Cole tomorrow afternoon and she would do her best to tell him anything that might help. Then it was end of discussion and back to New York where she belonged.

Speaking of that, she had something she needed to take care of. She flipped her cell phone open again and scrolled down. Punching some numbers in, she tapped her fingers on the steering wheel, waiting impatiently.

"NYPD, Lieutenant Johnson."

"This is Katarina Ramon. I'd like to speak to Chief McCreary."

She waited again while he connected her.

"What can I do for you, Katarina?"

"I'm sorry to bother you, Chief, but I received a text message on my cell that has me concerned about the security at your precinct."

"What kind of message?"

She told him. "I assume you received the message Adam Frank left on my machine."

"I did. However I doubt it's possible you received any messages from our friend Frank. He was transferred to Rikers yesterday."

"Interesting. Why the location change?"

"Complaints that he was being abused by the other prisoners. Apparently your client had prison groupies and they weren't too happy with Frank trying to set her up."

"I'm sure Miss Keenan will be thrilled to hear that," she said dryly. "However, that doesn't mean that Frank couldn't have found a way to text me or get someone to do it for him. He knew my home phone so it's not beyond the realm of possibility that he knows my cell as well. I'll change my number but I'd appreciate it if you'd notify Rikers to keep an eye on our murdering friend."

"I can do that. Just watch yourself, Katarina. If he isn't the one who left that message, then someone else is out there."

"I know that. Thanks."

She flipped her phone closed again and turned into Mandy's. Smiling, she stepped out and surveyed the restaurant. Nothing had changed and that was reassuring. She couldn't begin to count the number of times she and her family had stopped here after church or for a Friday evening fish fry. She glanced at her watch. Just a little after five was early enough to beat the bulk of the dinner crowd. She opened the door and immediately saw Ellen Sulin sitting toward the back in a booth. She waved and weaved through the tables toward her.

"Katarina Ramon! When did you get into town?" Mandy asked, waving at her from behind the counter.

Kat smiled, meeting her halfway and hugging the older woman. "You mean you didn't know I was here? You're slipping, Mandy."

"Nope, but that explains why I haven't seen our chief of police lately. I've heard tell your aunt thinks the two of you would be a perfect match."

"Oh, she does, does she?" Kat said ruefully.

"Yes sir, and so do I. Man's a hunk."

Kat rolled her eyes. "Same old Mandy, I see."

She laughed, moving to greet some new customers. "Yep, and don't tell me you aren't glad."

Kat shook her head in amusement as she slid into the booth across from her friend, leaning forward to squeeze her hand. "I'm so glad you had time to meet me, Ellie. I just want to tell you again how sorry I am about your parents."

The woman's smile was tinged with sadness. "Thank you," she said quietly.

"I only wish I could have been there for you and Sam."

"You called and sent flowers," Ellie said firmly. "And you're here now."

"Yes, I am, and I'm so glad my aunt convinced me to take some vacation. I'm always more grounded after a visit home."

"Getting a little crazy in the big city?"

Kat nodded. "Crazy isn't exactly the word but hectic is. How about you?"

Ellie shrugged. "It's always busy when you're the only doctor in town. It's helped a little with the healing."

"I know." Kat surveyed the woman sitting across from her. Ellie Sulin was her exact opposite. They had been best friends in high school but while Kat had been tall and gangly, Ellie had been cute and petite with ebony hair and big blue eyes. "I loved your parents, Ellie. They managed to fill a big hole when I lost my own."

The blue eyes darkened for a moment. "I know that. It hasn't been easy for me, or Sam, for that matter. He was always so close to Mom."

"They were good people, Ellie, really good people."

"They were," she agreed. "As I said, my being so busy at the office kept me sane right after they were killed. People were wonderful around here but..." She paused, raising her gaze to Kat's. "This is going to sound awful, but for a long time afterward, I actually found myself asking patients where they were the day Mom and Dad were killed." She sighed. "Discreetly, mind you, but I hated myself for doing it just the same."

"Speaking of patients, how are things going in that direction? Still happy with small town life?"

"I am. Unlike you, Kat, I never had a desire to stray too far from home." She took a sip of her ice water, her voice just a little husky when she continued. "Dad was so proud when my shingle went up. God, I miss them!"

"I hate to ask, Ellie, but do you have any idea who would do something like this? Did your parents have any enemies? Someone that could have held a grudge?"

"Not that I know of. I've asked myself the same questions over and over. Why Dad and Mom? According to Cole, robbery wasn't a motive. Then what was?"

Kat leaned back in her chair, waiting until they gave their orders to the waitress before she replied. "This may sound strange, but for some reason I get this really strong feeling that the murder of your parents and mine are connected."

Ellie looked up, startled.

"I know. Sounds crazy, doesn't it? But think about it, Ellie. This is a small town. Everyone knows everyone and it's highly unlikely someone just cruised in here and murdered just for the fun of it. Even though it has been years, the cases are eerily similar. There has to be a motive."

"I never thought of that but you might be right, although your parents have been gone a long time. Do you really think whoever killed them is still around here?"

"It's a possibility. Let's face it, the case is as cold as ice."

"Pretty scary thought, isn't it?" Ellen broke off a piece of bread and bit into it, chewing thoughtfully. "Someone we might meet in the grocery store or on the street could be a murderer." She shivered. "Somehow that doesn't fit with the spirit of this town."

"Murder seldom does," Kat replied. She leaned forward, lowering her voice. "Ellie, I think whoever killed your parents knew them very well."

Ellie's eyes narrowed. "You mean as in a good friend?"

Kat nodded. "Remember when we were kids we used to laugh at how I sometimes could tell when something was going to happen before it did?"

Ellie smiled lightly. "If you're talking about your ESP or whatever it is, Kat, the whole town is aware of your family history."

"That figures. Anyway, Cole Collins gave me a ride home from the church social on Sunday and on the way we stopped by your parents' home. Cole thought he saw someone inside."

"That's not the first time someone has tried to break into the house," Ellen said, concerned. "I've taken all the valuables out but we haven't moved anything yet." She grimaced, lifting her shoulders. "I just haven't had the heart to go in there and deal with their clothes and personal items yet. I know it's been a while, but Cole reassured me there was no hurry." She frowned. "What has that got to do with your ESP?"

"I walked toward the back of the house while Cole looked inside and suddenly I had one of those visions. I saw someone enter the house from the back door. I didn't see his features but whoever it was instinctively jumped over that creaky step on his way inside. I saw it clearly."

Ellie's eyes widened, shock in their depths. "My God, Kat! If you're right then whoever killed them had to have been in the house enough times to know about that step."

"Question is, Ellie, what would drive someone to return to the scene of the crime?"

"They're looking for something, aren't they? Something incriminating?"

"Could be. Any idea what that might be?"

Before she could reply, the waitress returned with their food, interrupting the conversation. Kat bit into her huge burger with relish. "I've forgotten how delicious these are."

Ellie forked her salad, shaking her head. "I always hated

that in you."

"What?"

"The fact that you could eat whatever you wanted and stay as thin as a rail. I've had to work at keeping thin since I was thirteen."

"And I always envied that while I towered over everyone you were such a pretty little thing."

Ellen laughed. "Funny how adulthood tends to make you reevaluate what's really important." She stabbed a piece of tomato, frowning. "You know, Kat, maybe you're not so far off the mark about the two cases being connected after all. About a week before...before Dad and Mom were killed, he mentioned something I'd forgotten about until just now."

Her tone of voice had Kat glancing up quickly.

"Remember the classic Mustang convertible that Allie Sandoval drove around in the summer that she was here staying with her aunt?"

"I think I do. Why?"

"Dad bought it about two years ago. He saw it advertised in the paper and you know how he loved old cars. Of course it was in deplorable shape by then because the spoiled little rich girl hadn't bothered to take care of it. Dad said it was parked behind her garage in the weeds. Looked like it hadn't been touched in years. Anyway, she was asking big bucks for it. What's strange is Dad paid it. You know how frugal he was with his money."

Kat smiled. "He always told me if I'd grown up poor, I'd appreciate frugality."

Ellie's lips tilted slightly. "I only heard that about a thousand times. Yet his one weakness was always sharp cars. Mom was just as bad."

"I remember." Kat took a sip of her drink and leaned back in her chair. "So what was it that bothered you about your father buying that car?"

"It isn't buying the car that I thought was rather strange but it was something he said when I stopped by one night for dinner. He took me out to the garage to show me the finished product. The car looked great, red and white with the entire interior restored." She glanced up at Kat. "I could always tell when something was bothering Dad and I had a feeling he had taken me outside so he could talk to me."

"Were you right?"

"At the time I wasn't too impressed but now, thinking back, maybe I should have been. He told me when he took the seats out to restore them he found two vials of morphine buried underneath."

Kat shrugged. "That's no surprise. Cole told me his ex-wife was into drugs when they divorced. Chances are she started using in high school."

"There's more. You know how Dad was when something bothered him. He didn't stop until he got to the bottom of it." She paused, smiling sadly. "I can't believe I'd forgotten about this but with the shock and then the funerals and everything it just slipped my mind. He told me the vials had lot numbers and expiration dates on them so he called the pharmaceutical companies to see where they might have come from."

"Why would he go to all that trouble, Ellie?"

"I asked him the same question. That was when he told me he remembered passing Allie Sandoval driving that car in the opposite direction like a bat out of hell the night your parents were killed. What's even odder is the expiration date for those narcotics was the year your parents were murdered."

A cold chill ran down Kat's spine. "Are you telling me those vials came from Dad's office?"

Ellie shook her head. "Dad couldn't pinpoint that for sure but what he was able to find out was that some of that lot was shipped to your Dad. Of course, more of it was shipped to physicians' offices in the surrounding area as well."

"Did your father tell the police about this?"

"I don't know. What I can tell you is it was really bothering him."

"I wonder if he called Allison Sandoval and asked her."

"If he did, she wouldn't have told him the truth anyway."

Kat's mind was racing. "From what I remember about the girl, I could see her doing a lot of dumb things but murder? I don't think so."

"Maybe not, but I think it might be worth investigating."

"I agree. Aunt Evelyn asked me to come home to talk with Cole Collins." She grimaced. "You know how she can be when she gets her mind set on something. I'm meeting with Cole tomorrow so I'll tell him about this."

Ellie rolled the ice in the bottom of her glass around thoughtfully. "You know what bothers me the most, Kat? Why Mom? Dad was found in the hallway, but from what the coroner said, Mom never woke up. She was still in bed. If Dad surprised a robber, then it would be logical for him to attack and run. But why would he go down the hall and attack a sleeping woman? It doesn't make sense."

"Could be whoever killed your father was worried he shared whatever information he had with your mother. Maybe he thought he couldn't afford to take that chance."

Ellie's eyes flashed. "I want him to pay for what he did, Kat. What he took from us. Sometimes I lay awake at night and wish I could have just one more moment with both of them. I just want some closure and I have a bad feeling that won't happen until the questions I keep asking myself are answered."

Kat put a hand over hers, understanding her pain. "I intend to ask Cole those same questions, Ellie. Promise me if you think of anything else you'll call me."

"You know I will." Her expression changed, lightened. "I see you're on first name terms with our chief of police."

"Don't even go there," Kat warned. "The whole town has got me paired with him already. What I don't understand is why the two of you aren't an item. You know. The very attractive female doctor and the handsome policeman. Stuff soap operas are made of."

Ellie laughed. "Don't think I wouldn't have gone after him if there wasn't a Todd in my life."

Kat immediately leaned forward. "Okay, tell me," she demanded.

They spent the rest of the lunch catching up on each other's lives while the booths around them filled.

"You mean to tell me you're talking about Todd Austin? The Todd Austin Sandy Mallory had her claws in for most of our senior year?"

"That's the one."

Kat leaned back, replete. "Then I congratulate you. I always imagined she would have his ring on her finger before our diplomas were cold."

"She tried but he went away to college. She stayed here and married Luke Taylor. They're expecting their fifth kid next month."

"Don't tell me she still has the blonde hair and fake eyelashes."

Ellie grinned mischievously. "She does but somehow they aren't as impressive as they once were with a pregnant belly."

Kat laughed. "We're awful, aren't we?"

Ellie sighed. "I miss you, Kat. Any thoughts of coming back to stay?"

"Now you sound like Aunt Evelyn."

"Just asking."

Mandy walked over with a pot of coffee in her hand. "Any luck in convincing your friend here to pack her bags and come back home?" she asked Ellie.

Kat reached for her purse, shaking a finger at Mandy. "Not you too!" She stood, tossing some bills on the table. "I've got to run, Ellie. I'll call you after I meet with Cole."

"Don't stay away so long next time," Mandy called after her.

"I'll do my best," Kat reassured her, waving.

Ellie and Mandy watched her walk out the door, blonde hair swinging.

"Think it'll work?" Mandy asked, pouring herself a cup of coffee and sliding into the seat across from Ellie.

"If you mean pushing her and Cole Collins together, it just might. Underneath all the sophistication is a small town girl at heart," Ellie said wisely. "She just has to realize that." She glanced out the window absently. "What she really needs is what I need."

"And what is that?" Mandy asked, taking a sip of her coffee.

"Answers."

"You might not like them."

Ellie's gaze swiveled back to her. "Maybe not, but it sure beats wondering if the person I'm next to in church killed my parents."

Mandy cradled her cup and nodded. "Or if one of us is going to be next."

Chapter Eight

Kat pulled her aunt's car into the circular driveway and turned off the engine, taking a moment to survey the scene in front of her. She'd only had a quick glimpse of the property the day they had spent at the creek. Her gaze roamed from the newly blacktopped driveway to the freshly painted front steps.

Cole Collins had undertaken quite a project when he had purchased this house, she thought. Although the front had been lovingly restored, she could see scaffolding in the back along with several power saws lying on a bench inside the open detached garage. The old Leonard house, as it was called in town, had been vacant for more years than Kat could remember. As kids, they used to spin stories about the ghosts that they were sure lived inside. Jacob Leonard had made his money in timber but the general talk around town was that he had never drawn up a will. After years of family fighting over whatever money was left, the house had fallen into disrepair and none of the relatives wanted the job of fixing it up. It had been for sale for years. Kat's thoughts went to the tall Irish cop, her lips tilting. Trust Cole Collins to go where no man had gone before.

So far he had done an admirable job. The flower beds in front had been cleared, leaving the early spring flowers to bloom in a riotous blend of colors. The pillars in front had been restored back to their glistening white. Double porches running the width of the front of the house gleamed as well.

She opened the door and closed it slowly behind her, smiling slightly as she caught sight of Deanna's car parked by the garage. If she wasn't mistaken, since it was the beginning of spring break, she had a feeling Cole was being coerced by a pint-size Tiffany once again. Before she could ring the rather impressive doorbell, the front door flew open.

"You're late," Tiffany accused, hands on her hips.

"And how would you know that, squirt?" Kat said mildly, ruffling the girl's hair.

"Because you were supposed to be here at five o'clock and its five-fifteen," she tossed back.

Deanna walked up behind her, swatting her lightly. "Don't mind my obnoxious child, Kat. Cole said to come on in. He and Liv will be with you in a moment."

"Let me guess. He's helping his daughter pack an overnight bag, right?"

"Yep," Tiffany said, nodding vigorously. "But she has to ask you first if it's okay." She frowned. "Her father said it isn't polite to plan to go somewhere else when you're expecting a house guest." She glanced up at Kat hopefully. "But you're not really a guest, are you?"

"And you're not really eight years old, either?" Kat replied, attempting not very successfully to hide a smile.

"In my daughter's rather skewed way," Deanna said, "she's trying to tell you that if you okay things, Mike and I are going to take the girls camping for a few days."

"Of course it's okay with me."

"Yes!" Tiffany shouted gleefully. "Wait 'til I tell Liv!"

Both of them watched her tear up the beautiful circular stairway in search of her friend.

Kat turned slowly, eying the grandeur in front of her.

"Pretty impressive, isn't it?" Deanna said, following her gaze. "Cole's worked long and hard to get it this far. Place was a mess when he first bought it."

"I remember." Kat walked over to run her hand along the curved oak banister. "Did he do all of this on his own?"

"Most of it."

"Why?" Kat asked, turning back to her.

Deanna glanced up the stairs. "If you're asking why he's tackled such a large project, I can only tell you I believe he needed something when he moved here to keep his mind off of things. When he was elected, he was smack dab in the middle of a custody suit with his ex." Her expression darkened. "He wanted to make a home for his daughter, one that was fueled by love and not greed."

Kat's brow lifted. "Strong words."

Deanna folded her arms and leaned against the wall, her expression set. "Kat, that woman is a witch. I've been here when she's come calling. Not to visit Liv, mind you, but to see what kind of money she could get out of Cole. The last time I pulled in just as she was leaving. I've never seen him so angry. He told her he'd strangle her with his bare hands if she set foot on his property again. Poor Olivia was standing next to him on the porch, tears streaming down her face."

Pure fury rushed through Kat. "No wonder the child is confused."

"Mom, we're ready!" Tiffany said, interrupting their conversation as she flew down the stairs. Cole and Olivia followed at a more sedate pace. "I told Liv to unpack all that fancy stuff and put in old jeans and shoes. Right?"

"I hate to admit it, love," Deanna said, smiling as she reached for Liv's bag, "but Tiff's right. It wouldn't hurt to have a few hooded sweatshirts as well if you have them."

"Already packed," Cole said, his eyes moving to Kat. "Sorry we weren't here to greet you."

"Are you sure you don't mind, Kat?" Olivia asked timidly. "It's not that I don't want to spend time with you but..."

Kat put a finger to the child's lips. "Olivia Collins, if you wanted to spend an evening with me instead of spending time camping with your friend, I'd say something was seriously wrong." She tapped the tip of her nose affectionately. "Go and have a wonderful time. Just keep an eye on your friend so she doesn't drive her parents nuts."

"Too late," Deanna said dryly, waving as she opened the door. "See you Wednesday night, Cole. You've got our cell number in case anything comes up. All right, let's go, you two."

Olivia started for the door and then stopped, turning back. Hesitating for just a moment, she rushed forward and wrapped her arms around her father. "Bye, Daddy."

Kat saw him swallow hard as he lifted the girl high in his

arms, pressing a kiss to her cheek. "Have fun, my love."

"I will," she reassured him as he set her down. She skipped down the front steps to join her friend. "See ya!" she said with a grin, waving.

Cole moved to stand next to Kat, watching as they drove away. *This feels right,* she thought. *Standing next to him, being with him.*

"No chaperone after all," he said gruffly as he closed the door.

"Am I going to need one?" she asked candidly.

He considered for a moment. "Probably."

"Then I've been forewarned." She smiled up at him. "How about a tour first? I saw the outside when I met the two of you here last week. Now I'm dying to see the rest."

"It isn't completely finished yet," he warned.

"That doesn't matter. I'm already beyond impressed at what you've accomplished just in the foyer. Lead the way."

The home was truly amazing. The lower level mirrored the upper one with a huge ten-foot wide hallway traversing its length with rooms situated on both sides. There were two parlors, a butler's pantry that was the size of her bedroom at home and a kitchen that was equipped well enough to satisfy even the most discriminating cook. She sniffed at the appetizing aroma that was coming from a pot on the stove. Lifting the lid, her eyes widened.

"This smells like beef stroganoff."

"It is."

She replaced the lid. "And this is your idea of something simple?"

He grinned easily and she felt that familiar rush of attraction. He was wearing a well-worn pair of jeans and a white t-shirt. She had a strong urge to run her hands along those muscular shoulders and chest and maybe lower...

"I've kind of got into this cooking thing, to tell you the truth. I was determined Liv wasn't going to eat fast food every night. Took a few courses at the local college."

She took a deep breath, irritated at how hard it was to concentrate on what he was saying. The deep voice, those vibrant green eyes, the crooked grin. It was a package she was suddenly finding significantly distracting. *Get a grip girl,* she told herself.

"Nice kitchen," she said brightly, motioning toward the gleaming granite countertops and stainless appliances.

He nodded, glancing around. "Probably spent more than I should have on it but the kitchen was always the center of my house growing up. You know, a place to share the day at dinner, do homework and drink hot chocolate on a cold night."

"Sounds like some pretty good memories," she said, smiling.

"They are." He straightened, his expression changing, growing distant. "Come on, I'll show you the rooms upstairs. I'm still working on two of the bedrooms, but it's coming along."

She followed him up the curving stairway to the huge hallway that was a copy of the one below. The first two rooms were obviously still in the middle of being restored, with equipment and remnants of peeled wallpaper littering the floor.

"There are six bedrooms up here or there were," he corrected himself. "I combined two rooms into a master suite for me and the other a suite for Liv." He opened the door to his right and motioned for her to enter. "This is Liv's room."

Unexpected tears stung her lids as she moved inside. The room was pink and white with sparkles everywhere, in the paint, on the dresser, on the ceiling, on the fluffy white comforter covering the bed. A silky pink canopy covered the top, draping gracefully on four sides to the floor. The warm oak planks were covered by a huge oval rug with fairies and stars glittering against the dark background. A window seat faced the flower garden in back, covered with bright pillows.

"Cole, this is truly wonderful," she said softly, moving toward the series of paintings strategically placed on the wall. They were in identical frames depicting a dragon, a witch, a fairy. She moved to the other side of the room. These pictures were of castles with moats, a dark, raging storm behind a mountain, a tiny cottage. The use of light and shadow was incredible as was the choice of colors.

She ran a finger along one, raising a surprised gaze to Cole's. "These are original oils." She leaned closer. "G. R. Lane," she read aloud. "Is this the same Lane that penned *A Fairy's Triumph and A Dragon's Love*?" she asked incredulously.

He nodded.

"I remember reading every one of her books growing up but I had no idea she was also an artist. These are oils of each and every one of her book covers. Where on earth did you find them?"

He met her gaze and she saw, felt, the pain. "G. R. Lane was my mother. I wanted Liv to recapture some of the childhood she'd lost living with..." He stopped, clearing his throat. "I thought maybe being surrounded by her grandmother's art might give her back some of that innocence, that imagination again."

Her eyes widened. "Grace Lane was your mother?" She turned back to the paintings. "You must have been very proud of her."

"I was. I only wish Liv could have known her. Things might have been different then."

She glanced up at him. "Different how?"

His gaze slid to hers. "She would have seen what Allie was doing to Liv long before I did. Although she was an artist through and through, no one, including myself, managed to fool her. Allie certainly didn't."

"She didn't approve of your marriage?"

He ran a hand through his hair, his eyes looking past her. "No and she had no qualms in telling me so either. But I was so damn stubborn back then. So sure I was making all the right decisions. I didn't listen."

The pain was there just below the surface. She could feel it. For some reason, she also could feel an intense anger as well. "Beating yourself up for something you can't change serves no purpose, Cole. My mother used to say things happen for a reason and sometimes we just don't know what that reason is at the time."

He glanced around the room. "I told myself that same thing over and over again after she died but it didn't do a hell of a lot of good."

"How long has she been gone?"

His gaze slid back to her, his eyes growing cold. "She was killed right after Allie and I were married." He closed his eyes for a brief moment. "Mom wanted to develop some kind of relationship with her. She had tried on several occasions to invite her to go shopping or to meet for dinner with the two of us." He sighed, tucking his hands in his pockets. "I think Allie knew even back then that she hadn't fooled my mother like she had her parents and me."

"What happened?"

"Allie finally agreed. They were on their way to lunch when Allie lost control of the car and wrapped it around a telephone pole. She wasn't injured but my mother was killed instantly."

"Oh, Cole, I'm so sorry."

He looked down at her, his jaw tight. "At the time I was so torn up that I didn't even question the reason for the accident. It had been raining so I just assumed slippery roads caused the accident."

"She was drunk?"

His gaze shot to hers. "Yeah, only three times over the legal limit. High as a kite as well. Daddy's money managed to brush it all under the table with his high-priced lawyers almost before I was aware of the toxicology reports. Probably paid people in high places some very nice bribe money."

"Did your father press charges?"

He shook his head. "I wanted him to but he said there was no point. By then Allie was pregnant. Hell, I didn't know how I felt. On one hand, I was excited about the baby and on the other I found myself almost hating my wife." His eyes darkened. "No, I take that back. I did hate her."

"I can't blame you."

He smiled grimly. "My father warned me that there was no point in dwelling in the past and I tried to tell myself he was right." His gaze slid back to the paintings. "But when they put Olivia in my arms for the first time, all of that hate faded away. She was a miniature of my mother and I fell in love instantly. From then on I tried to make the marriage work if for no other reason than for Liv." He smiled tightly. "Pretty naïve, wasn't I?"

Just those few words and the look in his eyes touched her as nothing else could. She moved toward him, putting a hand on his chest, her gaze locking with his. "No, what you were was sensitive. I have always admired that in a man, maybe because my father was like that as well."

She was falling for Cole Collins and right now she didn't care what the repercussions might be. "Why don't you show me that master suite, Cole?"

The softness in his green eyes changed. It was replaced by a glitter that was unmistakable. He didn't say a word but simply took her hand and led her across the hallway.

This room was entirely different. The tall ceilings were there but it was definitely a man's room with an exquisite massive sleigh bed in its center. The floors were the same warm oak and the walls a serene green.

"Believe it or not, the bed was left here." He grinned lopsidedly. "More than likely because they couldn't get it out."

"It's wonderful," she said, moving closer to him and wrapping her arms around his waist.

"We don't have our chaperone," he said, running his finger along her cheek.

"No we don't, do we?"

"You don't sound too upset."

She pressed her lips against the brown column of his neck. "That's because I'm not," she replied.

He tipped her chin up until she met his gaze. "I told myself I wasn't going to get involved again, Kat. Told myself I wasn't going to set myself up for a fall. It hurt."

"I know. Life does," she said simply.

"It doesn't do any good though."

"What doesn't do any good?" she asked softly.

"Telling myself all those things when I know I'm not going to listen."

"I was hoping you'd say that." She lifted her arms from around his waist to his neck, pulling his lips down to hers. The kiss was just as explosive as before but this time neither of them pulled away.

He edged closer, his lips straying to the nape of her neck and then to a suddenly sensitive earlobe. "What about you?" he said softly.

She leaned back just enough to look up at him. "What about me?"

He trailed his hands up and down her slender back. She shivered as his fingers left a line of sensuous heat.

"You're big city, lady. I'm small town. You want this to go somewhere or am I just a diversion?"

"That's insulting," she snapped, sliding out of his arms. She felt the sting of tears and turned toward the door in an effort to hide them. "Go to hell!"

Before she could march out the door, he spun her back, crushing his lips to hers. This time, for just a moment, she fought him. However, she didn't have the will to continue fighting when his lips slid down her neck to the scented base of her throat. She found herself allowing him access, her own hands moving up and down his chest, finding their way underneath his shirt to the bare skin beneath. He trembled when she trailed her nails across his hard abdomen.

He lifted her into his arms and then fell with her onto the mattress. Blue eyes met green for one long, charged moment and then it was as if neither of them could get enough of the other. She pulled his shirt over his head while he tore at her blouse. Buttons popping, he tossed it aside, his lips replacing the material. He nibbled the side of her neck, the hollow between her breasts, her bare stomach. She couldn't stop the moan as he released her sheer bra. Letting the silk slide away, his mouth enclosed one pebbled nipple. Arching, she wrapped her arms around him, pulling him even closer as he suckled.

"Oh, God!" She moaned again as he shifted to the other breast. Reaching down, she released the snap of his jeans, her hand finding him. She saw his eyes change, grow dark. When he echoed her moan, she caught his lips, tasting the dark heat inside of him.

His hands roamed down her body, finding and tearing the silken underwear whispering across her hips off. He used his lips to nip and soothe, sending painfully exquisite sensations rushing through her. Writhing beneath him, she raked unsteady hands along his back, pulling him closer, her movements wantonly seductive.

When he reached his limit, he reared back and buried himself deep inside of her. She arched, meeting him thrust for thrust, violent sensations erupting around them.

Their lovemaking wasn't slow and it wasn't sweet. It was wild and rough, frantic almost. As if they couldn't stop, couldn't breathe until they soared together. Kat froze for one heart-stopping moment before he took her up and over. Her cries blended with his as they shared a release so strong, so intense that Kat almost felt as if she'd stopped breathing.

Spent, both of them stayed silent for a long time. Finally Cole eased up on one elbow, his eyes still smoldering. "You can use me as a diversion any time you want," he growled.

A smile played about her mouth even as she smacked him lightly on his bare arm. "You're lucky lust outweighed my being royally ticked off at that remark."

His jaw tightened. "Is that what this was?"

"Isn't that what you wanted it to be?" she countered. She pushed herself up to rest against the headboard, stretching long slender arms above her head.

He shook his head thoughtfully, frowning. "I'm not sure what I want this to be, Kat."

She appreciated his honesty. "I have to tell you, I'm not one to jump between the sheets lightly, Cole. But when I do I never regret it. My philosophy is that the future will take care of itself."

He smiled slightly, rubbing a hand along her bare arm. "You always this up-front?"

"I try to be. It works for me most times."

His gaze locked with hers again. "I like you, Katarina Ramon. I didn't intend to." His lips curved. "Evelyn's matchmaking was pretty obvious. Since I've been elected, the ladies in this town have tried everything in their power to set me up. Gets irritating after awhile."

"Poor, poor you."

He leaned forward, nipping her hand lightly. "Smart ass."

"Then I guess I have to be honored that you succumbed to my charms."

He shook his head emphatically. "It's deeper than that. If it wasn't, I wouldn't have touched you with a ten foot pole no matter how gorgeous you are."

She raised a delicate brow. "Am I to take that as a compliment?"

"No, the truth. From experience, the one thing I will never do again is go into a relationship based on sexual attraction. Been there, done that."

"Your wife?"

He nodded, easing back against the pillow. "I finished my tour of duty and college and came home from the Navy big and strong and full of myself. A friend of mine introduced Allie to me and sparks flew immediately. She was vivacious, wealthy, damned good looking and wanted me." He punched the pillow viciously. "I was young, liked the attention and was too stupid to figure out the real reason she went after me."

"And that was?" Kat asked, wrapping her arms around her knees.

"What it always was with Allie Sandoval. Prestige, looks, money. My father was a senator, my mother a well-known author. Just the kind of marriage she and her parents had always wanted."

"What went wrong?"

"Besides the drugs and booze?" He shrugged. "I guess if I'm honest I can't blame her entirely. I thought I wanted the same kind of lifestyle she did. I was wrong. What I really wanted was the kind of marriage my parents had. A relationship based on trust and mutual respect. Allie didn't even know the meaning of those words."

Kat caught the anger in his tone. "Correct me if I'm wrong, Cole, but don't you think it's time you resolve the bitterness? After all, you have a beautiful house, a great daughter and your marriage is behind you."

He threw a hand over his eyes, rubbing his temples. "You're probably right. Problem is, I have this knot in my stomach that tells me my past isn't past just yet."

Kat's senses went on the alert. She could feel that familiar rush that told her the psychic power she found so irritating was trying to gain entrance. She attempted to ignore it but to no avail. The words whispered across her subconscious

...strangle her with my bare hands...past isn't past...I could have killed her for that...the drugs and the booze...I hated her...

She struggled to push the barrage of words away along with the sensations that chilled her to the bone. That sixth sense she hated so much was trying to tell her something. And whatever it was she had a feeling it was vital not only to her but to Cole as well.

Shaking her head slightly to clear it, she reached down for her clothes with suddenly trembling hands. Damn! She hated these sporadic visions, warning whispers. She would be perfectly content to not know what the future held just like everyone else.

Impatiently, she slid her arms into her blouse and reached for the buttons. Frowning, she looked down and then relaxed, laughing.

"What's so funny?"

She turned so he could see the gaping material. "Guess I won't be wearing this home." She leaned down and grabbed his t-shirt, sliding it over her head. It settled nicely about mid-thigh. She stood, gathering the clothes strewn about the floor.

He grabbed her wrist as she reached down to pick up his jeans, his green eyes intense. "I don't do one-night-stands, Kat. There's something between us. I intend to find out what that is."

"Then you better hurry," she said lightly. "I head home in just a few days."

"You'll be back," he said confidently.

She put her hands on her hips. "Really? And how would you know this?"

"Irish intuition," he said, grinning as he grabbed her around the waist and pulled her onto his lap.

"Or Irish blarney," she tossed back. When he began to nibble her neck, she shook her head, pushing him away. "I'm starved and we've got some things to discuss. Let's go down and see if that dinner you fixed is as good as it smells."

He exaggerated a sigh. "Great, I'm spurned for damn stroganoff."

She laughed, pulling him to his feet. "Grab yourself another shirt while I make use of that fantastic bathroom you have in there. Meet you downstairs."

She took a long, hot shower and then donned Cole's shirt again, lifting it up to smell the essence of his cologne still clinging to the fabric.

This isn't going to work, Kat. His life is here and yours is in New York. You're a career woman and he's the father of an eight-year-old girl.

Even as she tried to convince herself, she knew it wasn't going to make any difference. There was a burning deep inside her that she couldn't ignore. It was a strong feeling that the two of them were in for a fight. A fight that had something to do with those prison bars she had glimpsed earlier. Cole was right, she would be back. It was the reason that she would return that worried her.

Shrugging, she tucked her blonde hair back in a simple ponytail and went downstairs to join him. He was in the kitchen setting the table, his eyes darkening again when he caught sight of her standing there, his t-shirt riding high on her thighs, her slender legs enticingly bare.

"How the hell am I going to eat with you dressed like that?" he growled.

"Like what?" she asked innocently, stretching her arms above her head so the shirt rode up even further.

Before she could lower them again, he had her against him, twin green flames flashing in his eyes. "You're killing me!"

She stood on tiptoe to brush her lips along his cheek. "Get a hold of that libido and let's eat."

Groaning, he slowly released her, the look he tossed her way promising retribution later. "Sit for God's sake. Everything's ready."

She slid into the chair, taking a sip of the wine he had poured, enjoying the slightly dry flavor. Placing a dish of rice and the stroganoff in front of her, he joined her. She didn't need to be invited to help herself. After the first bite, she closed her eyes in appreciation.

"Cole, this is absolutely delicious!"

"You sound surprised."

"I am." She took another bite. "A man who cooks like this could convince me to do almost anything."

"Is that a promise?" he asked, his lips curling.

"What do you think?" she countered.

He put his fork down and rubbed his chin thoughtfully. "I think I'm looking at a very complex woman. One who is smart, quick, and knows how to relate to an eight-year-old without missing a beat." He grinned. "And I think if said woman is so impressed by beef stroganoff, heaven only knows what she'd do for lobster bisque."

She moaned. "Now that is my idea of paradise."

He topped off her wine glass. "Can I ask you something?"

"Sure."

"Why New York?"

She shrugged. "I guess because I wanted to get away, prove myself without the support of my family and this town. My aunt wasn't thrilled and neither was my brother but I'm convinced it was the right thing to do."

His glance was shrewd. "Running away from memories?"

"I guess I could have been. Whatever the reason, succeeding in such a setting gave me a security and confidence I'm not sure I would have had here at home. Besides which, the experience of defending the kind of clients I represented was invaluable."

"Okay, how about another question? You came thinking Olivia would be here. Yet you had no problem with her leaving. Why?"

She quirked a brow. "I'm going to assume you're not just asking to pump up your ego?"

His lips twitched. "No, ma'am."

"All right then, I'll give it to you straight. Number three, you're not exactly hard to look at. Number two, your daughter needs to experience camping. She needs to be allowed to be just what she is, an eight-year-old girl."

"And number one?"

She didn't return his smile. "That's a little more complicated." Her gaze was clear and direct. "This might sound bizarre, but my instincts are telling me our futures are somehow entwined."

His lips curved. "That doesn't take a sixth sense, Kat. I'd

predict the same thing."

"You don't understand. Aside from the attraction we feel for each other, and"—she couldn't help giving him a saucy grin—"the pretty fantastic sex, there's something else." The smile disappeared. "Something's going to happen, Cole. Something terribly bad. I just don't know what that is but I do know it will involve both of us."

"Olivia?" he asked, concern lighting his eyes.

She shook her head, putting a hand on his reassuringly. "No, of that I'm certain."

"Then it has something to do with me?"

"Could be." She sighed. "I only wish I had a better handle on this darn clairvoyance thing. I don't. Things come to me when they come."

"Then I guess there's no point in worrying about something we have no control over, is there?" he said calmly. "Want another helping?"

She shook her head, watching as he rose and carried their dishes over to the sink and flicked the coffee pot on.

"You aren't concerned?"

"Sure I am," he said, turning back to her. "But I learned a long time ago that the best defense is a strong offense. My guess is whatever it is that's making you so uneasy probably has something to do with this investigation. So why don't we compare information and see what we come up with? Perhaps you'll see or sense something I haven't."

She stood, nodding. "That's what I'm here for." She grabbed the glasses and bent to place them in the dishwasher. When she straightened, he put a hand under her chin, his gaze serious.

"You have the answers, Kat. I knew it the moment I saw you."

She shook her head. "I wish I was as sure of that as you are, Cole." Reaching behind for a cup, she poured herself some of the aromatic brew. "Want some?"

He took a mug from her and they made their way into the front room. Cole put a match to the waiting wood as Kat curled up on the comfortable burgundy couch in front of the fireplace.

She looked around the room appreciatively. The walls were cream, softening the height of the ceiling, and the flames tossed a warm glow on the wood floor. Although the grouping around the fireplace was cozy, there wasn't much in the way of decoration on the walls or the mantel.

He followed her gaze. "I haven't had a lot of time to do the designer touch stuff yet. To tell the truth I'm not much good at it."

She looked up at him, a yearning inside her that was totally out of character. "I never thought I would say this, but I'd like nothing better than to scour every antique place between here and Birmingham to find things for this house. It deserves that after being neglected for so long."

"You aren't usually into that kind of thing?"

"Unfortunately I haven't had time to be into that kind of thing. When you work ten- to twelve-hour days, decorating is the last thing on your mind."

"You have a partner?"

"One partner and another we recently hired that, if all goes well, will be a third. I started on my own and then Dan Rogers joined me about a year after I went solo. He's an old friend. Grew up a few streets away from me here in Brookdale." She smiled. "I imagine that made being away from home a little less painful although I wouldn't have admitted it back then."

"Old boyfriend?" he asked curtly.

"We've dated. He'd like to take it further. I'm just not sure if I want that," she admitted.

"All right, enough about your past then. How about we get down to work?"

She glanced at him quickly, noting the change in his voice. She hadn't sorted her feelings out regarding the two of them and she had a feeling he hadn't either. Plenty of time to deal with their past relationships, she thought. Now wasn't the time.

"Where do you want to start?"

"Aside from what you told me about that reoccurring dream, what else do you remember about your parents' murders?"

"Unfortunately not much. I was seventeen at the time. I

was spending the night at Katie Waller's house and Andy was out with his friends." She closed her eyes for a brief moment, a grimace of pain flashing across her face. "It was just after eight or nine o'clock when Mrs. Waller asked me to come to the front door. She was crying. I can still remember Paul Sulin standing there, tears running down his face. He took my hand and told me what had happened." Her lashes fluttered closed for a brief moment. "He held me close while I sobbed. That's something I think I'll always remember about him. Those wonderfully strong arms."

He moved to sit next to her, touched at the emotion in her voice. "Did he say anything that would shed some light on what they discovered that night?"

"Not to me but I heard things later. The people that lived in the house in back of Dad's office noticed the rear door opened and called the police. I remember Charlie Powell telling my aunt that there was no evidence of a break-in, so either the door hadn't been locked yet or whoever broke in had a key." She caught his gaze. "If my dream is right, I'd guess it was the latter."

"It's possible. Charlie thought so anyway."

"What did he tell you?"

"Pitifully little. There were no witnesses, no fingerprints. Only motive appears to be the narcotics that were stolen. Charlie believed that the killer entered probably thinking everyone was gone for the day. That or he was high enough to think he was invincible. The gun might have been an afterthought. It's a good bet when your mother recognized him, he panicked and then there was no turning back."

"Do you think whoever this is might have had an accomplice?"

Cole's gaze shot to hers. "Why do you ask that?"

"I met with Ellie Sulin for lunch yesterday. She said the night my parents were killed her father saw your ex-wife barreling down the road in that vintage Mustang she owned back then. Right about the time the murders occurred."

His first instinct was to protest that what she was suggesting was ridiculous and then he caught himself. He hadn't known Allie back then but Barry Sullivan had evidence that she was doing drugs way back in high school. Yet his ex-wife a murderer?

She stayed silent, waiting for his reaction.

He rose and poked at the fire and then turned slowly, shaking his head. "It just doesn't fit, Kat. The woman even back then was spoiled rotten, had anything and everything she wanted, even the drugs and booze. There was no reason to go out hunting for it and certainly no reason to kill."

"Just listen to what you're saying though, Cole. Sometimes when you can get anything you want at the snap of the fingers. Taking a joy ride to steal drugs might just have been an incredibly exciting change of pace."

"Hard to believe the mother of my child could be capable of something like that, Kat, no matter what I think of her." He shook his head. "No, it just doesn't work for me."

"You might believe differently when I tell you what Paul Sulin told Ellie just a few weeks before he was killed."

When she was finished, he frowned into the fire for a long moment. "I didn't know anything about this and I'll bet Charlie didn't either. Which means your friend's father must have approached Allie first."

"And died because of it."

"We're assuming a lot," he said, taking another sip of his coffee, swallowing thoughtfully. "She could have obtained those vials anywhere. There's no way of proving they came from your father's office. As far as her being nearby the night they were killed, doesn't her aunt live just down the street from your aunt?"

"I know. Not even enough for an indictment. Yet..."

"Yet you think she's involved."

She shrugged. "Who knows, Cole? Maybe I'm just trying too hard to find a common theme to connect the deaths of people I cared so much about."

"You're not off base there, Kat. Charlie told me before he handed the reins over that he felt the same way. Only problem is, he couldn't prove it and it doesn't look like we're making much headway either."

"Any luck on that gun we found?"

"So far nothing. No fingerprints on the gun and the numbers were filed off. Suspicious in itself, but forensics tells me we might be able to get something from the backpack. They're working on it."

She drained the last of her coffee and stood. "Guess I should head back home."

He caught her gaze. "Would you stay if I asked you?"

She considered. "Do you think it's wise?"

"Probably not but frankly, Scarlett..."

"You don't give a damn," she finished smartly.

"You got it."

"No, what I've got," she said, moving to wrap her arms around his waist, "is a man who intrigues me. I've always been a sucker for mysteries."

"Do you need to call Evelyn? Let her know you aren't coming home?"

She sent him a long look. "Are you kidding? I tell her I'm staying with you and she'll have a party at her house and the whole town will know tomorrow."

"Is that a bad thing?"

She laughed. "Not for me. I'll be back in New York. You're the one who's going to have to put up with the unmerciful teasing."

He flexed his muscular shoulders. "I think I can handle it."

She eased back to look up at him. "I know you can," she said quietly. "Just don't take any unnecessary risks, will you?"

"Learned not to do that a long time ago," he said lightly.

She didn't say anything else but as she followed him up the stairs, a deep foreboding settled over her. *You just might not be able to handle everything, Cole. Not everything...*

Chapter Nine

The cigarette trembled in her hand as she lifted it to her mouth. She took a long drag and then crushed it violently.

"I'm not taking the fall for this. You either give me more money or I blow the whistle and I mean it. Cole's asking too many questions and that lawyer of his is digging into my past back to when I was a goddamn teenager."

"Calm down, Allie." The voice was soothing. "They have no way of tying you to those murders. Your ex is blowing a lot of hot air. Wants to make a name for himself and he's using old history to do it. Don't let him get to you."

She snorted a derisive laugh. "I don't know what world you live in but he's already a damn hero here. Besides which, I'm not exactly popular in Brookdale." She lit another cigarette, pulling on it and letting the smoke curl around her. "God, I need a drink. Listen, either I have cash in my hand by the end of the week, big cash, or I'll spill my guts to the local hero. Your call."

"Yes it is, isn't it?" The voice no longer was soothing but harsh, the tone sending a frisson of chills down her back.

"Now don't be that way," she wheedled. "We're in this together, remember? I just need some cash until I can get Cole to start paying child support again. He's loaded as of next week and I intend to share in that load, even if it means dragging the brat home to live with me."

"Your motherly instincts amaze me," he said dryly.

"Fuck motherly instincts. Do we have a deal?"

"I'll take care of things, don't worry."

"Good, see that you do."

She hung up the phone, smiling slyly. Blackmail was such a handy tool. Yet as she made her way to the bar and poured herself a martini, something about their conversation sent a shiver of warning through her again. He wouldn't pull a fast one...would he?

ℰↄ

He missed her. No matter which way you cut it, he missed her, Cole thought, driving through the pouring rain on his way to pick up his daughter at school. It had been a little over two months since he'd spent that night with her, shared the most incredible sex he had ever had. Yet it was the hours afterward that they spent tossing ideas around, challenging each other with theories that he thought of the most. She had been happy to let him cook and he had been just as happy letting her grab his laptop to prove something she had argued with him about. Neither of them was ready to commit to more at the moment. At least, that was what he kept telling himself.

He braked in front of the school and Olivia came skipping out with Tiffany at her side. She flung open the door and grinned up at him, raindrops glistening on her dark hair and eyelashes.

"Hi, Daddy. Happy birthday."

The words touched him deeply. The girl standing in front of him wasn't the same shy, backward child, thanks in large part to Deanna and Katarina. She had blossomed into a normal eight-year-old and he thanked God every day for that.

He ruffled her hair and smiled at Tiffany. "Thanks, munchkin. So how does it feel to be out of school for the summer?"

Tiffany slid in next to Olivia. "Fantastic. I've been counting every day for the last two weeks." She tossed her ponytail back, spraying water over the leather seat.

"Mom said I'm supposed to ask you how it feels to be one year older?"

His eyes crinkled as he leaned behind him to swat at her

legs, sending her and Olivia into a fit of giggles. "You tell your mom to mind her own business."

"You can tell her yourself. She wants to see you when you drop me off."

"Oh, oh," he said dramatically, sending both girls into giggles again.

He pulled in front of the Ross's house and the girls bounced out of the car, meeting a smiling Deanna at the door. She rushed them inside and closed the door firmly. "Quite a gully washer out there," she said, grabbing her daughter by the arm before she skidded on the wood floor. "Take the shoes off, young lady."

"Can we go up to my room? I want to show Liv my new computer game."

"Sure."

They tore up the stairs, their laughter wafting downward.

"Do they ever stop?"

Deanna lifted amused eyes to Cole. "What, the giggling?"

He nodded.

"Not for another three or four years. Wait until you get five or six of them in the room at once."

He grimaced. "I'll hold off on that as long as I can."

She patted his cheek. "I'll help ease you into it, old pal. By the way, happy birthday."

He waited. "What, no teasing about how old I'm getting, how hard of hearing I am? Come on, you're slipping," he finished, grinning.

"I would if I wasn't two years older," she tossed back, eyes brimming with laughter and something less definable. "Listen, Cole, why don't you let Liv stay for dinner? I'll bring her over afterward if that's okay. She's working on a surprise for you and I don't think she's quite done with it yet."

He shrugged. "Okay with me. I've got to stop in town for a moment anyway so that'll work. Thanks."

After calling up to his daughter to tell her about their plan, he headed back to town, stopping at the station.

"Afternoon, Betty," he greeted the motherly plump woman

behind the desk in front. Betty Wills had been with the department back when Charlie had been chief and he had seen no reason to change that. He liked the woman. He liked the quick intelligence she exuded as well. What she didn't know about Brookdale wasn't worth knowing.

"Hey, Cole. Happy birthday."

He rolled his eyes. "Does everyone in town know I'm a year older?"

She laughed. "Of course they do. Besides, it's not every day a man turns thirty five and becomes a millionaire."

"Yeah, I guess you're right at that." He met her gaze. "It won't make a difference, you know that, Betty."

She eyed him, arms crossing her ample bosom. "Some people it would but not you, Cole Collins. That's why the people in this town voted the way they did. We might not be big city folks but we know a good one when we see it."

Her words warmed him. "Thanks, Betty. That means a lot."

"Oh, by the way, Dale Cowls over at forensics just called. Wants you to give him a jingle when you have a moment."

"Thanks. I'll do that now," he said, moving to his office and closing the door.

She waited for a moment and then picked up the phone, punching some numbers.

"He's here now. Probably will be for at least another half hour. If you're going to move, now's the time." She paused, listening. "Sounds terrific. I'll be there after I close up. Can I bring anything more? Okay, see you in a bit."

She disconnected the call, grinning, and tossed a look at the closed door. Her boss was in for a big surprise, a very big surprise.

Unaware of the plotting going on in the next room, Cole eased back in his chair and dialed the phone. "Dale, its Cole."

"So how does it feel to be pushing middle age?"

Cole groaned. "Not you too!"

The laughter on the other end was deep and lusty. "Don't mind the teasing. Wish I were that age again."

"Like you're so ancient," Cole responded, an image of the man flashing in front of him. Dale Cowls was six foot five, two fifty and strong as an ox.

"Add a wife and three kids and see how you feel."

"Never thought I wanted that. Now I'm not so sure."

There was a brief pause on the other end. "That's a loaded answer."

"Yeah it was, wasn't it? What've you got?"

"The gun is a no go so far. No fingerprints, or if there were, time washed them away. Registration numbers were filed off but we're working on that. Still had four bullets in the chamber."

"Then it was fired twice."

"Yep. Ballistics isn't finished, but they're fairly certain the gun is the same caliber as the one that was used to kill the Ramons. Problem is, unless we can identify the owner, making a match with the striations of the bullets isn't going to help."

"So we're no further ahead?"

"Now did I say that? Unlike the gun, the backpack yielded a few more clues. I've got hair and blood."

Cole's chair straightened with a snap. "From the Ramons?"

"No such luck. Both belonged to an old hermit who used to live down by the creek. He died right after the Ramons were killed. Had some DNA from the original investigation but the general consensus at the time was the old coot keeled over and hit his head on the fireplace."

"Clay Saunders," Cole said, his mind racing.

There was a surprised pause. "Figured you wouldn't know about that."

"Katarina and I were out at his old place a few months back. New owners had it for sale and she was interested. She told me the story."

"Looks like the old theory just got shot to hell. My guess is we've got the murder weapon especially if that gun was inside. Wouldn't take too much to knock out an old man like that."

"Question is why."

"Robbery?"

Cole leaned back in his seat, frowning. "Or maybe it was something more sinister. Like maybe he witnessed something someone didn't want him to see or talk about."

"You suggesting his death might have something to do with the Ramon murders?"

"Right time frame. Do me a favor, Dale. Call me the minute you've got anything more. I've got a strong hunch we find the owner of that backpack and we find our killer, maybe to both sets of murders."

"Think it ties into the Sulin case?"

"It's a possibility. I've thought that all along but damned if I can find any proof. That is until Ellie Sulin dropped a bombshell." He relayed what she had told Katarina.

There was silence on the other end for a moment. "I remember that summer well, Cole. Used to hang around with a crowd that included your ex even though we were a hell of a lot older. Excuse me for saying so but she was a real bitch even back then. She liked a good time as in sex and drugs and we small town boys were intrigued. She was snooty, threw her money around but I just can't see her committing murder. Too messy."

"Same thing I'm thinking. That doesn't mean, however, that she might not have been involved in some way."

"You're not exactly open-minded about the woman, Cole."

"You're right, but I lived with her long enough to recognize when she's hiding something. I approached her with some questions a few weeks ago. She spit like a cat but I saw the flicker of fear in her eyes. She knows something, either about the Ramon case or the Sulins. I'll stake my life on it."

"Just watch your back, pal. She knows people in high places."

Cole laughed grimly. "Now that, my friend, isn't news to me. Thanks for the info."

"No problem. Take my advice for what it's worth, Cole, and forget things for a little while and simply enjoy your birthday."

"I intend to. See you soon."

Cole hung the receiver up thoughtfully. There was no doubt in his mind that he was looking at four people murdered by the same person, perhaps five with Clay Saunders. But murder weapon or not, they still didn't have the person or persons responsible and that irked him. He wasn't letting his ex off the hook that easily either. He fully intended to pay her another visit, press a little harder.

He glanced at his watch and rose. It was time he headed home. For just a moment, he felt lonely for the first time in a long time. More than likely there was a message from his father on the answering machine wishing him a happy birthday. They kept in touch and he and Olivia had visited him a few weeks back. His mother had always been the one who was into his birthday big time. His lips curved slightly. She had overdone it every year. Balloons, party hats, a huge cake with never-ending candles. Even when he outgrew that, she always found a way to make the day special. He rubbed a hand through his hair. God, he missed her! He could only imagine how his father felt.

Resolutely, he grabbed his car keys and opened the door. Betty was still typing on the computer. She glanced up, a suspicious twinkle in her eyes. "Going home?"

"I am unless you need me for something."

She shook her head. "I don't and even if I do, I'll call Jerry first. This is your night so enjoy it!" She tapped her computer. "Of course, if you're feeling generous with all that money you could spring for a new computer. This one's almost as old as I am."

He leaned down and surprised her by planting a kiss on her cheek. "Consider it done."

She raised a brow, blushing slightly. "Damn! I should have asked for more if you're feeling that benevolent."

He laughed as he opened the outer door. "See you on Monday, Betty. Have a great weekend."

"I will." She grinned after the door closed, reaching in the desk for her purse. "You'll see me a lot sooner than that."

Cole locked the cruiser then slid into the Corvette. The rain had disappeared and the late sun filtered through the trees. Opening the windows, he enjoyed the feel of the wind on his face as he headed home. He stretched, leaning against the backrest, waving at people as he cruised down the main street. More than a few of them mouthed happy birthday and he grinned to himself, appreciating the fact that he had been accepted in this town. Along with that acceptance came the realization that his private life was no longer as private as it had been. Oddly, he didn't mind that anymore.

Relaxed, he drove passed the Sulin house, glancing at it as he always did. Suddenly he had a strong urge to stop. His foot hit the brake and he pulled to the curb. Frowning, he scanned the house. The no trespassing sign was long gone and a large for sale sign sat in the front lawn. Yet his gut and experience told him there were answers here. He had missed something vitally important. No matter how many times he had searched the house, he couldn't rid himself of that thought.

He turned the car off and climbed out. But instead of going toward the house, he headed toward the free-standing single car garage. Almost as if he was being guided in that direction mentally. The doors were unlocked as the vintage mustang Ellie had mentioned was now in Sam Sulin's garage in town. He wandered in instinctively. Something was pushing him...something was telling him...

...he isn't what he seems...

Cole jerked, glancing around, seeing no one. What the hell?

...he'll kill again...she is in danger...remember the knife...it holds the key...

Cole could feel the muscles in his shoulders and neck tense. He might not possess that sixth sense Katarina had, but he was as sure as he could be that he had just been given a message. Only problem was he hadn't a clue as to who the she was or what knife...

He closed the garage door, walking rapidly back to his car. He slid in, flipping open the glove compartment. He had forgotten about the damn knife he had found behind the house. Stupid!

It was still wrapped in the napkin he had placed it in. He lifted it up to the light. He recognized the make. Nice piece but not unusual. Maybe Dale could lift some fingerprints off of it. His eyes went to the worn initial carved in the base. Sure would be nice if he had a suspect that had a name that started with the letter R or L, if that's what the faint initial said. Or at least one he could nail with more than just suspicion. Disgusted, he rewrapped it and put it back in his glove compartment. He'd drop it off at forensics on Monday but he had a feeling it wouldn't yield any more than they already had. He started the car and put it in gear.

The knife is the key...the key...the key...

A tingle slid down his neck and he glanced in the rear view mirror. Okay, he told himself, maybe he did have that sixth sense after all. He put his foot on the accelerator and sped away, but a deep sense of foreboding followed him.

She is in danger...

He was starting to push the envelope and it wasn't beyond the realm of possibility that someone might be getting just a little nervous. And in his experience nervous people did stupid things. Like kill again.

His thoughts were deep and dark as he pulled into the driveway and it took a moment for him to recognize the fact that a car was parked in front of him. His father's Chrysler to be exact. He grinned, letting his dark thoughts disappear for the moment. He bounded up the front steps just as his father opened the door.

"Happy birthday, son," Jared Collins said, embracing him in a strong bear hug.

Cole stepped back and took a good long look at his father. While Cole had his mother's dark hair and green eyes, he was built much the same as his father. Jared was still lean and muscled and the only concession to his age was the streaks of gray at his temples. The lines that had formed after his mother's death were still there but not as deep as they had been and there was life in those deep brown eyes once again.

"I had no idea you were coming, Dad. If I had, I wouldn't have let Liv stay with her friend."

Jared's brown eyes glinted with humor. "No problem. She's already here."

Cole frowned. "That's strange. Deanna told me she was going to have dinner with them."

Jared stood aside, motioning for Cole to precede him. He stopped dead in his tracks at the sight that greeted him. Balloons were everywhere, along with a huge banner that stretched across the foyer that said, HAPPY THIRTY-FIFTH, COLE!

"Surprise!" Deanna said, Tiffany and Olivia dancing at her

125

side with excitement. Behind her stood Evelyn, Andy Ramon and Betty, along with half the town, among them Barry Sullivan and his wife as well as Mandy Stanislaus.

Cole reached down and pulled his daughter up in his arms while she squealed with delight. "Did you plan this, young lady?"

She nodded coyly, her dark curls bouncing. "Me and Tiff and Deanna and Kat and just about everybody."

Cole's eyes immediately swung around the room. Kat was standing at the back, her blue eyes focused on him, smiling. He returned the smile, amazed at how much brighter the day suddenly seemed.

He tweaked his daughter's hair and set her down. "Well then I guess I have to thank everyone, don't I?"

"You won't thank us when you see the gifts we brought," Barry teased.

Olivia tugged at his arm, pulling him into the huge kitchen where a table fairly groaned with food. "Mrs. Ross said we had to eat first before you can open your gifts." She looked up at him, her face lit with impatience. "So hurry up, Daddy."

Mandy laughed, shoving a plate at him. "I suggest you start like your daughter said, Cole. The rest of us are starved, and since yours truly made the food, I know it's good."

"Then I'll just dig right in," he retorted, his stomach suddenly growling at the delicious smells.

A line formed behind him and he moved into the front room where tables had been set up throughout, settling next to Katarina.

"Why didn't you tell me you were coming home?" he asked, unable to resist running a finger along her bare arm. She looked incredibly sexy in black stretch pants and an off-the-shoulder sleeveless turquoise shirt. He saw the reaction in her eyes, felt her quick intake of breath as his thumb brushed her soft skin.

"That would have ruined the surprise," she said, smiling.

"I've missed you."

Her gaze shot to his. "I know. It wasn't supposed to be that way."

He knew exactly what she was talking about. "Doesn't matter, it's a fact, Kat. We need to talk about why that is."

She leaned forward, kissing him briefly. "Later," she whispered.

Soon the house was full of people eating, laughing and teasing him unmercifully. He found himself ushered to the chair of honor beside the fireplace, a mound of brightly wrapped packages piled in front of him. Most of them were lighthearted things like a subscription to Senior Life and arthritis medicine. It was only when he reached the bottom of the pile that his daughter walked toward him, shyly handing him a nicely wrapped package.

"This is for you, Daddy. I made it." She perched next to him on the floor, gazing at him expectantly.

Cole gazed down at her, marveling at how much she had changed. There was a sparkle in her eyes and a bounce in her step that had been missing when she first moved in with him. He had this town to thank for that. They had enveloped her in their collective arms and made her feel welcome. Made both of them feel welcome.

He shook it lightly, frowning. "Hmmm, I wonder what it could be?"

"You're not going to find out unless you open it," Tiffany spouted.

"Good point," he admitted, reaching over to pull one of her pigtails. "All right, let's see what's in here."

He tore through the bright green paper and found himself holding a small photo album. He flipped it open and immediately was overcome with emotion. The first picture was a newborn photo of his daughter, even then dark curls framing her tiny head. The next several were pictures of her as a toddler. There was a photo of her first grade school picture, looking so solemn, followed by several that he recognized had been snapped the day he and Katarina had taken the girls to the cabin.

Olivia's expression grew more serious, insecure. "Do you like it? Kat and Mrs. Ross helped me and Grandpa Collins gave me stuff to decorate the front cover."

He leaned down and pulled her into his arms. "It's the very

best present I could possibly have," he whispered, hugging her close, "because you made it."

She ran a hand along his cheek. "I love you, Daddy," she whispered.

"Well, isn't that just the sweetest little old thing," a deceptively sugared voice said from in front of him.

He looked up. Allie was leaning against the wall just inside the foyer in a tight red sundress and high heels, a cigarette hanging from lips slashed a violent scarlet.

The change in Olivia was immediate. She shrank against Cole, her small hands clutching his arm, her gaze going from her mother to her father and back again. "Why is she here, Daddy? Don't let her take me away," she whispered. "Please!"

"That's not going to happen, munchkin," he said, rising and tucking his daughter behind him.

Deanna, sizing the situation up quickly, ushered both girls away with a glance back at Cole. The room went quiet, everyone waiting for whatever was going to happen next. Kat walked to Cole's side, slipping an arm through his.

"I don't believe your name was on the invitation list, Miss Sandoval," she said coldly.

Allie waved her hand in the air, the smoke curling around it. "Probably not. But then again, I don't need an invitation to see my child, now do I?"

"As a matter of fact you do," Kat returned, feeling Cole's arm tense against her.

The blue eyes flashed venom. "And who the hell do you think you are?"

Kat fought the very strong urge to slap the arrogant expression off the woman's face.

Cole's eyes were a glacial green. "She's a friend, Allie, a very close friend. Now, I suggest you turn around and leave before I do something I'll regret."

Allie laughed, her expression tight and hard. "Like what? Kill me? You'd like that, wouldn't you? Get me out of the way so you can have our daughter to yourself along with all that lovely money." She threw her cigarette on the gleaming wood floor, crushing it with her foot, and strode forward to stand in front of him.

Cole's fists clenched at his side. Underneath the heavy makeup and chic clothing, he could see the toll the booze and drugs were taking on her. The skin wasn't as taut and young, the fine wrinkles splaying across the corners of her eyes and discontented mouth. The blue eyes were already cloudy with something, probably the booze he could smell on her breath.

"What do you want, Allie?" he muttered harshly.

Her smile was ugly. "What do I want?" she repeated, her gaze scanning the room. "I want my daughter back with me. A girl belongs with her mother growing up, not with a man who"—her glittering gaze settled on Kat—"has a *very close friend.* After all, it's so important for her not to be exposed to immorality at such a young age."

Cole's reaction was explosive. He straightened, grabbing her arm and spinning her toward the door. "That's enough." She uttered a little shriek as he yanked her forward. "Now get the hell out of here. The next time you set foot anywhere near me or Olivia, I'll have you arrested. Understand?"

She grabbed the edge of the door, steadying herself. When she spun back, her face was an unbecoming red, her lips trembling with rage.

"I either get half of what you just inherited or I take Olivia," she spat, eyes shooting daggers at him. "Either way, you're going to pay."

Jared and Barry stepped forward to stand by Cole. Jared's brown eyes were just as hard as his son's. "I suggest that you leave now, Alison."

Her smile was laced with bitterness. "Or what? You going to attack poor, defenseless me? Oh, I'm going, but make no mistake, I'll be back either for the money or my precious daughter."

Barry shook his head. "Not going to happen, my dear. We've got enough on you to insure that no court in the land would award you or your parents custody. So I suggest you mosey on home and leave us to celebrate."

"You think you're so damn smart, don't you?" she shouted at Cole, swaying slightly. "This isn't over by a long shot."

"It is for now," Mandy said, shoving past the men and

taking Allie's arm firmly in her strong grasp. "Time to say goodbye, Alison."

Andy moved to her other side and, between them they pushed her out the door amid a stream of vulgarity that would make a grown man blush. Moments later, tires squealed as she roared away.

Mandy shook her head as she and Andy walked back inside. "Well now, that was pleasant." She glanced around at the stunned faces and put her hands on her hips. "Don't tell me you're going to let one spoiled and slightly drunk woman ruin our party? Come on, everyone! I've got a cake back there just waiting to be eaten. Now move!"

Immediately the atmosphere changed and people headed toward the kitchen although there was still hushed conversation among them.

Mandy reached over to squeeze Cole's hand. "Just let it go, Cole."

He nodded, but the tense expression remained. "Thanks for getting rid of her."

She grinned. "I enjoyed it. Chances are she won't be back after she realizes what a fool she made of herself."

"Don't bet on it," he said darkly.

Evelyn's eyes were flashing with temper. "I'd like to slap that woman silly!" She tossed Cole a look. "What I want to know is how in the world you managed to marry that witch?"

Jared chuckled. "Looks like you have quite a support group, son."

Cole relaxed enough to smile lightly. "Yeah, I do at that."

Evelyn slipped an arm through Jared's. "How about escorting this supportive person back for some cake and coffee?"

"I'd be delighted," he said, bowing.

Kat didn't miss the way his gaze skimmed the slim woman by his side. There was more than mild interest there, she thought.

Evelyn tugged Jared toward the kitchen. "Come on. Let's grab some dessert before it's all gone."

He raised a brow. "With Mandy Stanislaus cooking? I don't

think so."

She laughed. "Maybe you're right at that. Humor me anyway."

Kat smiled as she watched them leave. Jared Collins was a perfect match for her aunt. She and Cole's father had been able to talk during the afternoon while they were preparing for the party. The qualities she admired in Cole, the strength of character, obviously had been an inherited trait. There was pain, a sense of loss, she could sense underneath but she also sensed great pride and love for both his son and his granddaughter. The way the little girl had thrown herself in his arms when she walked in told her everything she needed to know.

She heard her aunt laughing at something Jared murmured in her ear as they moved down the hall and smiled. Evelyn deserved happiness and she had a very strong feeling Cole's father could very well be the one to provide that.

Her attention turned back toward the man standing next to her. She should have expected the ex-wife's visit yet she hadn't. She glanced toward the front door, eyes narrowed thoughtfully. It had taken her longer to react because of the vibes that had literally sizzled through her when she first caught sight of Alison Sandoval. Yet they hadn't been the ones she would have expected. Instead of anger and jealousy, she had sensed, actually seen, an aura around the woman, a dark one as she stood there in the foyer. It had only lasted for a moment but it had been enough to chill her to the bone. What it meant, she hadn't the slightest idea.

Cole walked toward the window, gazing out, his jaw tight. "Damn it! When is it going to stop? I've half a mind to sign my whole bank account over to her just to get her off my back."

"Do you really think that would work?" she asked pointedly. "It might for maybe a year or so, and then she'd run through the money and be back. Unless you've got more millions stored somewhere, it will never be enough, Cole."

He swung around impatiently. "Then what do you suggest? Killing her?" he said dryly.

Jerry Landers chose that moment to knock on the still open front door, a package in his hand. Cole tossed Kat a surprised look and motioned for him to come in.

"Problems, Jerry?"

The older man shook his head, looking a bit uncomfortable. "No, everything's fine although I just passed your ex tearing down the road. Wasn't going to waste time chasing her though." He smiled slightly, his gaze flicking toward Kat. "Figured she wouldn't cause an accident because most of the town is already here."

"Please come in," Cole invited. He was still trying to get a handle on his emotions. On top of that, he was concerned that Jerry had overheard his conversation with Kat. He should have known Allie couldn't resist the chance to make a scene. It was typical that she didn't give a damn the entire town saw her for what she really was.

Jerry continued to stand there, his plump face perspiring slightly. "I'm on duty so I can't stay long, but I thought I'd drop this off."

Cole shook his head, eying the plainly wrapped object he held in his hand. "You were in on this too?"

Jerry grinned, nodding. "Sworn to secrecy by Betty and Evelyn." He held out the package again. "Happy birthday, Cole. I've got to run."

"Well, at least have something to eat," Cole insisted. "Mandy has enough back there to feed an army."

A look of yearning came over the deputy's face. "Okay, I guess I can manage a quick bite." His gaze slid to Cole's. "About that," he said, pointing to the gift in Cole's hand. "Take it for what it is." He cleared his throat and lumbered past him, a faint hint of red sliding up the back of his neck.

"Well, it looks like today is full of surprises," Kat said softly.

Cole ripped the wrapping off and fingered the desk plaque. It was in rich mahogany, the letters in gold. He handed it to Kat, pleasantly surprised.

"CHIEF COLE COLLINS," she read aloud. She flipped it over and raised warm blue eyes to his. "Cole, he made this. It's signed underneath."

He ran a hand through his dark hair. "He and I have had some long talks recently. I value his smarts and told him so. There isn't much he misses." His lips curved slightly. "I'd say from that we've come to an understanding of sorts."

She shook her head. "Jerry Landers isn't one to make friends indiscriminately." Her expression hardened. "Probably because his ex-wife was a bitch of the worst sort and raised her son to be just like her. He doesn't trust easily, Cole, so value this. He means it."

He smiled, pulling her into his arms. "I intend to. Now why don't we talk about how you managed to pull this off without me knowing about it?"

She shimmied out of his arms. "That would be rude. You have guests to entertain. Come on. Let's go get some of that cake and coffee."

It was a long, hectic time later that it was finally just Cole, Kat and Olivia left curled up in front of the fire. The unexpected coolness of the evening was just chilly enough to warrant the spitting flames inside. Cole ran an arm along the back of the couch, liking what he saw in front of him. Kat's blonde hair glowed golden in the firelight. Olivia was curled in her arms, dressed in a cotton nightgown, freshly bathed. Kat was reading aloud from one of his mother's books, both of them entirely enrapt in the story.

Thanks to Mandy and a score of helpers, the house was back to normal, the tables and folding chairs outside waiting to be picked up in the morning. He stretched his feet in front of him. He owed this town big time. Only way to repay was to do his job and that meant finding the killer among them. And he was convinced that was the case. One murderer, five people dead, and it was up to him to find what or who connected them. He frowned darkly as an image of his ex-wife found its way inside his thoughts. He'd like to...

"Daddy?"

"Yes, munchkin," he said, tossing his thoughts aside as she curled up next to him on the couch, her green eyes big and serious.

"Why did my mother say she wanted me?" She put a chin on her knees, wrapping her thin arms around them. "I don't think she ever really liked having me around even when I was little. She told me so."

Cole's anger matched the furious flash he could see in Kat's eyes. He ran a finger along the silken cheek. "Honey, there are some things you have to understand about your mother," he said carefully. "Sometimes she doesn't mean what she says. It's just that..."

"She drinks too much." The tone was simple but the gaze she lifted to his was much more adult than it should have been. "I used to hear what Grandfather Sandoval said to her. They thought I couldn't hear but I could." She moved closer to him, her arms unwrapping from around her knees and curling around his neck. "I don't want to ever go back to that house, Daddy. I want to stay here with you for ever and ever."

He couldn't speak, the emotion was so strong. Instead, he buried his face in her dark curls, holding her close. "I'm going to see that you do just that," he said gruffly when he had control of his voice.

"She just wants money, Daddy. She always wants money. If you give her some, then she'll leave us alone. I know she will." She glanced around the house. "I could sell my bike and maybe you could sell your car. That would be enough for her, wouldn't it?"

Anger like he had never known tore through him. No child should have to justify staying with a parent by selling what she loved. What in God's name had Allie done to their daughter?

"Daddy," she said timidly, pulling his attention back to her, "I've been thinking about something. I don't think she would want me if I was adopted by a new mother." She clapped her hands delightedly as the idea took hold. "Why don't you marry Kat?" She launched herself from her father into Kat's arms excitedly. "I'd love it if you were my mother, Kat! It would be so cool!"

Kat's amused eyes found his but underneath the amusement he could see something else, something that had his heart beating faster.

She lifted the child up on her lap. "I think I'd love having you call me mother. But it's just a little more complicated than that, my love." She pushed dark hair back from the child's forehead and pressed a kiss to the smooth skin. "Why don't you let your father and I talk about it? Unless I miss my guess it's time for bed, isn't it?"

Just for a second there was mutiny in the green eyes followed by speculation that had Kat biting her lip to keep from laughing. "I guess so. Can you read me another book though?"

Kat shook her head, glancing at Cole. "I think you're seeing a Tiffany clone."

He groaned, rising to lift his daughter high in the air, swinging her until she shrieked with laughter. "Nope, it's just Olivia Collins being very, very clever and avoiding bedtime."

Kat held out a hand. "Come on. One more story it is."

Olivia happily skipped by her side as they climbed the stairs, her hand firmly clasped in Kat's. She scrambled into bed, tilting her head to look up at her, eyes narrowed. "Tiff says you should wear more eye makeup and let your hair hang loose." Before Kat could prevent her, the child had her braid loose, allowing the thick strands of gold to cascade down her back. "There, that's perfect!" She cocked her head to the side. "Nope, I don't think you need any more eye makeup. You have really neat blue eyes. Dad'll be a goner."

Kat couldn't help the laugh that escaped. She reached underneath the covers and tickled until the child giggled helplessly. "I was wrong. You aren't Tiffany's clone. She's turned you into a monster. Just for that read your own story, young lady."

Liv lifted mischievous eyes to hers. "It's okay, I can read it myself."

Kat shook her finger, reaching down to plant a kiss on the tip of her nose. "Goodnight, little terror."

She flicked on the small lamp by her bed before turning off the main light and blew another kiss.

"Kat?"

She paused in the process of closing the door and turned.

"Tell Daddy I love him."

"I will. Night."

"I love you to, Kat. Really and truly. It would be so great to have you for my mom. I'd be just like normal kids at school."

Kat's fingers fisted at her side. "Sweet dreams, my love."

She closed the door softly, all the while wishing she hadn't resisted the urge to slap Alison Sandoval. It might have been childish but she would have enjoyed it tremendously! Slowly she made her way back downstairs, pausing at the bottom to look at the front room, firelight making the large space warm and cozy. Since she had been here last, Cole had finished most of it save for the work he was still doing on the back porch. It was a good house, a house made for a family.

"She tucked in?" Cole asked, catching sight of her standing there.

Kat nodded, moving into the room and putting her hands up to the flickering flames. "I don't know what you've done with that shy little girl I left a few months back. There's no trace of her in that little scoundrel upstairs."

He laughed, reaching over to run his fingers through her hair. "What's this?"

Her eyes brimmed with laughter. "According to your daughter and Tiffany, I needed to let my hair down, literally. Tiff thinks I need more eye makeup but Liv disagrees. She said, and I quote, you'll be a goner when you see my long tresses."

"She's absolutely right," he muttered, his lips brushing hers as he tucked her against him, his thumbs caressing the slender line of her neck. "I think I was a goner the first time I saw you."

She looked up at him for the space of a moment and then fisted her hands in his hair, pulling him down to her, taking his lips. The smoldering fire flamed once again as it always did when their lips touched. He yanked her closer, taking what she offered, plundering her mouth. She threw her head back, allowing him access to the soft tender skin of her shoulders. She gasped, arching, when his lips moved lower, taking her taut nipple through the thin material of her blouse. Summoning a will she wasn't sure she had, she put her hands up, moving him back a step. They stared at each other, both of them breathing hard and fast.

She glanced up the stairs and shook her head. "Don't assume that daughter of yours is asleep yet," she whispered huskily. "She sees something she shouldn't and tells Tiffany, half..."

"...the town will know," he finished, groaning.

She tossed him a look of sheer sex. "Sixty days or so does seem like a rather long time, come to think of it."

"You're pushing it, Kat. I only have so much self control."

She settled on the couch tugging him down next to her.

Leaning into his wide chest, she could hear the rapid beat of his heart, enjoying the power she had to make it so. "Well, let's give it about an hour or so and you can give in to your urges," she said, smiling. "I suggest you make the most of it because I've got an afternoon flight back to New York tomorrow."

He frowned. "Why so soon?"

She pushed the hair back from her face, looking up at him. "Because I've already had my vacation, remember? It was just fortunate that your birthday happened to fall on a Friday. I flew in late morning today. I'd love to stay longer, but I've got court Monday morning bright and early."

The frown didn't disappear. "Any suggestions?"

She raised a brow. "About what?"

"About how we're going to handle our future?"

The subject had been uppermost in her mind almost every day since she'd left Problem was, she didn't have an answer. It was out of the question to ask Cole and Olivia to move to New York. That only left one other option and that would take a firm commitment from the man sitting by her side. Too many people depended on her to pull up very secure stakes and move back and start all over again without marriage being part of the plan. Only that was something she didn't feel comfortable discussing with him yet. The passion was there, the respect. Yet, in reality, they really didn't know each other that well. She decided to opt for honesty.

"I wish I knew the answer to that, Cole," she said simply. "There are so many things to think about. My relationship with Dan, not only business-wise but personally as well. You, Olivia, the people who work for me and the clients I represent. Let's just let things move forward and see what happens."

He sighed, tucking her next to him. "I don't think I like that answer."

"Then what do you suggest?"

The frown disappeared and a wicked grin took its place as he pushed her against the cushion, glancing at the clock on the mantel. "I suggest we live dangerously and assume my angelic daughter is asleep."

She sighed dramatically. "I love a man who throws caution to the wind."

He bent his head. "Then you're gonna love this..."

Her laughter was muffled by his lips and rapidly turned to a moan as his mouth moved to the soft flesh of her shoulder, his hands moving the neckline of her blouse downward. His mouth replaced his hands, nipping and tasting, moving torturously toward her firm breasts.

Ripping his shirt out of his pants, she raked her nails along his muscled back as he bent his head, his lips sliding along the curve of her breast. Impatiently she tugged at his pants and then her own, wanting to feel flesh against flesh. Finally there were no more barriers. Nothing to keep them apart.

She felt the trail of heat as his tongue slicked her stomach and the soft skin of her inner thigh. All the while his fingers caressed and teased. When he slid one inside her moist heat, she shuddered, arching.

"Oh, sweet Jesus!" she muttered hoarsely. She writhed beneath him frantic with need. Their eyes locked again for a long, long moment. She felt the heat shimmer between them, the sexual need, and yet there was more. So much more.

Heart pounding, she watched him rise above her. Unable to wait, she wrapped her hands around him, guiding him inside her. She threw her head back, her breath coming in short hard gasps as he filled her, moved with her, each thrust harder and deeper than the one before. The air almost sizzled with heat as they challenged each other, tortured each other, touching, retreating and plundering. She buried her face against his neck, moaning as he pushed her higher and higher.

Yet, just before they plummeted together Kat sensed something dark, something thoroughly frightening. It wasn't so much a visual as a certainty that their immediate future was murky, cloudy. As if one thing, one event might change it forever. And amid the explosion of sensations and the heat, she found herself shivering uncontrollably.

Chapter Ten

"We, the jury, find the defendant, Timothy J. Carson, not guilty," the jury spokeswoman said, smiling at the man who stood beside Katarina.

A cheer echoed throughout the courtroom. The judge hammered his gavel, shushing them. "Thank you, madam floor person. The defendant is hereby released and is free to go."

Katarina found herself wrapped in an enthusiastic bear hug. "I can't begin to thank you, Kat. I never thought this day would finally come."

She smiled down at the short slightly balding man as he stepped back.

"You were innocent and the jury saw that, Tim. It wasn't hard convincing them."

He shook his head. "I'm glad you were so confident because I sure as hell wasn't."

Kat put a reassuring hand on his arm and began gathering the mounds of paper in front of her. She eyed the irate woman across the aisle that was in the process of arguing with her attorney.

Her client followed her gaze as he reached down to pick up his briefcase. "My father-in-law's death was tragic enough but to accuse me of coercing him into writing his will the way he did was despicable even for her. It wasn't my fault the man finally saw her for what she really was. A bitch of the worst sort. Then to convince the prosecutor to indict me for something I had nothing to do with..." His brown eyes were indignant. "Imagine having the audacity to think I had anything to do with his death. He'd had a bad heart for years and she knew that." He glanced over at the jury as they filed out. "I'm glad they had more sense."

"Ex-wives can be vicious," Jack Steinman murmured as he lifted another box of evidence. "Especially when they've lost a loved one and all that lovely money one right after the other."

Tim's lips curved. "Sounds like you speak from experience."

"Not personally," Jack said, returning the grin as they made their way down the aisle. "But I've defended enough women scorned to get the gist."

Their client held out his hand when they walked into the lobby, shaking both of theirs. "Anytime the two of you need my expertise feel free to call. I'll put you at the top of my list."

Kat raised a brow. "No offense, Tim, but I'm not exactly champing at the bit to elicit the use of a serial profiler no matter how much I like you."

He turned to her in amazement. "You're a noted criminal attorney and you haven't defended a serial killer yet?"

"No, thank the Lord. I pride myself on my objectivity but I'm not sure I could manage that one."

Tim's attention turned toward the woman who was rushing across the marble floor, her arms outstretched. He caught her in a bear hug, swinging her around and then thumbed the tears away as he murmured softly to her.

"I think this is our cue to vacate the premises," Jack said aside to Kat.

She nodded, moving toward the wide front steps that led to the street. "Thanks for all your help, Jack. With Dan gone I'm not sure I'd have been as ready as I should have been for this trial."

"Thanks, but I know you too well by now, Kat." His voice lowered in exaggerated adoration. "You're my hero."

She laughed, giving him a shove. "Lay it on a little thicker and I'll let you treat me to dinner." She immediately noticed the faint blush. "A date with Alicia Keenan again? Do I sense a hint of serious here?"

He shrugged. "You might. We'll see."

She didn't push further, respecting his right to privacy. Jack had become invaluable to her in the past six months. The problem was Dan was taking advantage of Jack's junior status. To the point where she had a feeling she was going to have to step in.

She waited until they had stuffed the box and her briefcase in the trunk of her car and then put a hand on his arm. "I want you to know I mean what I said back there, Jack. I'm impressed with your skills in the courtroom. I also know Dan's been letting you handle a lot more than you should on his end." She opened the car door and leaned against it, speaking above the crowd and traffic din. "Don't let him use you. He's a terrific attorney but I think sometimes he forgets you're a soon-to-be partner."

His eyes lit. "You're serious?"

"Absolutely." She slid into the car and smiled up at him. "I've already had the paperwork drawn up. Congratulations."

He leaned inside the window when she slid it down. "About Dan, Kat. He's all right. I guess when I've been in practice as long as he has I'd look for someone to do the busy work as well."

She didn't respond but waved as she cut into traffic. Always the diplomat, Jack wasn't going to admit what she knew to be true. It was time she had a heart-to-heart talk with her partner. As she fought her way through midtown traffic, she reluctantly glanced down at her cell phone. There were messages blinking and the familiar feeling of dread crept inside. The phone messages had continued, threatening messages that remained untraceable according to the police. She hadn't mentioned them to Dan or to Jack, reluctant to open that can of worms. Adam Frank was safely incarcerated so it was unlikely the calls were coming from him unless he had someone on the outside making them, which was a possibility. What was more likely, she told herself, was some harmless nutcase was getting his jollies out of frightening her.

And doing a damned good job of it.

Braking in front of her condo, she pulled into the garage and grabbed her briefcase. Not willing to struggle with the box of papers, she left them in the trunk. Unlocking her door, she dropped her keys on the foyer table. Sliding out of her high heels, she stretched, the now familiar dissatisfaction invading her thoughts. Her sleek condo no longer appealed to her and, if she were honest, neither did her job. She pulled pins out of her hair as she made her way to the bedroom, shedding her jacket as she went. Court had lasted until well after six and it had taken over an hour for her to get home. Stupid taking the car today, she thought, but between her briefcase and the other evidence she had had no choice. Moving back to the front room, she uncorked a bottle of wine and poured herself a glass. She took a sip, appreciating the dry flavor. The answering machine blinked but, before she could push the button, the doorbell chimed. Frowning, she glanced at her watch, not happy with the interruption. She longed for a hot bath and maybe a disgustingly fattening pizza. She definitely wasn't in the mood to entertain.

She peered through the peephole and then smiled, flinging open the door. "Dan! When did you get back?"

"Just came from the airport," he said, dropping his suitcase on the floor. He tugged her into his arms while he kicked the door closed. "Miss me?"

"I always miss you when you're gone," she said truthfully and then immediately regretted the words at his change of expression. She knew he was going to kiss her and didn't try to stop him. It was time to find out if her feelings for the man were as platonic as she thought they were.

He leaned down, settling his lips on hers. It was pleasant and nothing more. When he finally lifted his head, she could see the regret in his eyes.

"You haven't changed your mind about us, have you?"

She shook her head. "I wish I could say yes but I can't."

He sighed, loosening his tie. "I guess I've known that for a long time."

She reached in the cupboard, found a wine glass and poured him some of the Chablis she had opened. "So how are your parents?"

He acknowledged the change of subject with a wry smile. "They're great. Loving retirement."

"Was the cruise as wonderful as they advertise it to be?" She eyed his skin color. "Doesn't look like you spent too much time in the sun."

"Cursed German/English skin. I burn like hell if I'm out for any length of time. As far as the cruise, it was great. Lots of food, drink, and fast women."

She laughed, curling on the sofa next to him, tucking her legs underneath her. "So tell me where you went, what you saw."

He shook his head. "I'll fill you in when I print the digital pictures up. Suffice it to say we had a great time and it was good to get away for awhile."

"I know the feeling." She sipped her wine again and then set it down and turned to him. "Dan, I want out."

The shock in his eyes mirrored hers. What in the world had made her say something like that? And just as quickly she knew the answer. Because it was what she had been thinking about for six or seven long months. Since the day a certain sexy chief of police and one sweet eight-year-old girl had entered her life.

"You can't be serious, Kat!"

She took her time answering because she wanted to be as open with him as possible. Knowing her partner, she was aware he wouldn't accept her decision easily. "I am, Dan." She glanced around the room, comparing it briefly to another room full of firelight. Best she stay away from those thoughts, she reminded herself. "I think I've been feeling this way for a long while but just now had the courage to admit it." Her gaze slid back to him. "It's not fun anymore and to be successful in this town it has to be." She sighed, putting a hand on his. "I can remember rising every morning jacked up about whatever challenge I was going to face that day. Fighting to get to the top and then stay there. I'd say we succeeded."

"And you want to give all that up?" He shook his head. "Come on, Kat, think about it. You've got it all. A fancy condo, a hot car, the respect of the legal community, notoriety. What do you hope to gain by leaving all of that?"

She shrugged, standing to pace the room. "I know. Sounds kind of silly, doesn't it? But I've been back to Brookdale several times the past six months. Every time I get ready to come back, it feels more and more like I'm visiting New York and leaving home. I'm ready for a change, Dan. Is that so hard to understand?"

He eyed her for a long moment. "Biological clock ticking?"

The way he said it irritated her. "Maybe it is. That's really not your concern." She saw his hurt expression and immediately was ashamed. "I'm sorry, Dan. That was uncalled for. I guess I'm having some issues with my decision as well. Either way, I'm certainly not going to leave you in the lurch. I've already informed Jack we're offering him a partnership. My suggestion is that you begin looking for another associate while I'm still here. I'll give you six weeks, longer if necessary. That should be sufficient time to transfer cases and tidy things up."

"Does this sudden change of heart have something to do with Cole Collins?" he asked harshly.

She arched a brow. "Partly," she answered honestly. "I've grown close to his daughter, Olivia, and I'm not sure what my feelings for her father are but I intend to find out." She again sat next to him, wanting him to understand. "It's more than that, though, Dan. I thought I'd finally resolved the issues I had with my parents' death all those years ago but I've discovered I haven't. Especially after Paul and Marie Sulin were killed in a similar way." She ran a hand across her forehead, leaning back against the cushion. "I keep getting visuals, sometimes in my dreams. Other times they just appear. I close my eyes and I can remember someone carrying a backpack just like the one we found in the woods. I hear a voice in my dreams I think I recognize but when I awaken I can never place it with the person." She shook her head in exasperation. "The clues are there. I simply need to put them together."

He eyed her over the rim of his wine glass. "Kat, be reasonable. You know when someone is emotionally involved with a murder case objectivity flies out the window."

"I know." She frowned. "And that is exactly why I have to do this, Dan. Besides, I realized I miss small town life. Don't get me wrong, New York has been good to me. I've loved every minute of the time I've spent here, even the lean ones." Her eyes caught the blinking light on her answering machine and walked toward it. "This is what I'm not going to miss." She pushed the button.

"*Ten new messages,*" the mechanical voice said. She let it play, pouring herself as well as Dan another glass. All of them were in regards to cases they were presently working on until the last one. Color drained from her face as the familiar muffled voice filled the room.

"Every morning I wake up and think of you, Kat. Ever hear the term 'let sleeping dogs lie'? You keep your pretty nose out of the past or someone just might get killed. Just like your parents did. Have a nice day."

The machine clicked off and she jerked involuntarily at the sound.

Dan stood abruptly, his gaze shooting to hers. "What the hell was that all about?"

She looked up at him, taking a deep breath before she answered. "At first I thought it was just someone out to scare me but..."

"At first?" he interrupted. "You mean this has happened before?"

She nodded. "Actually for about six months now."

"And you didn't say anything?" he accused. "I'm calling the police right now," he insisted, lifting the phone.

She put a hand on his, replacing the receiver. "Don't bother. I already have, although I'm sure they'll want to examine this tape."

He put a hand under her chin, scanning her face closely. "It's obvious whoever made that call wants you to stay away from Brookdale. Why don't you listen? Let your chief and his deputy do the investigating. Christ, Kat! It sure as hell sounded to me like whoever that was wasn't playing games."

Anger helped put the color back in her cheeks. "Whoever that was is getting nervous, Dan. That means we've got something he thinks might identify him." She reached for her wine glass again, her hands remarkably steady. "There were no fingerprints on the gun but forensics is sure the backpack with that weapon inside was the murder weapon that killed old Clay Saunders."

He eyed her silently for a moment. "Now you're beginning to babble, Kat. What has Clay Saunders got to do with all of this?"

He listened intently while she explained. "Forgive me but it sounds like you're going around in circles here, Kat." He reached down to pick up his suitcase and then paused, gazing at her for a long moment. "Do me a favor?" he said quietly, sliding a finger along her cheek. "Sleep on this decision for a little while, will you? Jack Steinman is good but he isn't you."

She smiled, warmed at the sincerity she saw in his eyes. "I appreciate that, Dan, but my mind is made up." She reached up to kiss his cheek. "Want to join me for some pizza?"

He shook his head. "Thanks but I need to get home and unwind a little. See you on Monday."

She nodded, leaning against the closed door for a moment after he left. She had been perfectly honest about her decision but that didn't mean it would be easy. There were clients she had a responsibility to, cases she needed to divvy up among Jack and Dan and whoever they hired. She sighed, acknowledging the beginning of a headache as she rubbed her temples.

The phone rang at that moment, startling her. Heart thudding, she glanced at the clock and then relaxed as she saw the number on the caller ID. Eight p.m. sharp. Right on time as usual.

"Hi, Kat!"

She found herself smiling as she curled into the sofa. "Hi, yourself, sweet pea. How was school?"

"I got an A on an English test today," Olivia's voice said proudly on the other end. "Daddy said I could go to DQ after dinner and order anything I wanted."

"I'm proud of you. See, your English teacher isn't so bad now is she?"

"She's not so nice either. I think she was disappointed I did so well."

Kat had to suppress a laugh. "Don't you think you're being just a little unfair, Liv?"

"Nope."

She couldn't prevent the laugh this time. "How's Tiff?"

"Grounded again. She got a D. But I get to stay there tonight because I promised to help her study for a math test we're having tomorrow. Mrs. Ross says I'm the only one that can make her sit still for more than five minutes. She's coming to get me soon."

"Sounds typical. How's Ringer?"

"Growing big. Daddy says he's going to be huge because his paws are like ten inches wide or something."

"Did you tell him I wasn't the one who picked him out of the litter?"

"Yep. He gets mad at him when he pees on the carpet but I think he loves him anyway."

She heard giggling on the other end and Olivia's childish voice was replaced by the deep one of her father.

"I'm raising a rotten child," he quipped. "So how's the attorney today?"

"Missing you and Liv." She hesitated for just a moment. "I told Dan I'm leaving today."

"You sure about this, Kat?"

"As sure as I've been about anything. Don't take this as any kind of pressure on my part, Cole. You're still footloose and fancy free as the saying goes."

"I haven't been that way since, oh, I don't know, about half a year ago," he replied, the nuances in his gruff voice sending shivers of sensation through her.

"Someone isn't as happy about me coming home as you are," she confessed, telling him about the most recent phone call.

"How is this idiot getting hold of your cell and unlisted number?"

"I can't figure that one out, Cole. The calls stop for a few weeks when I change my listing and then it starts all over again." She rubbed her arms, subconsciously attempting to ease a sudden attack of chills. "I keep on thinking Adam Frank has something to do with this and I know that doesn't make any sense. Yet sometimes I catch an inflection in the masked voice, a turn of word that makes me think he's the caller."

"Have you told the police about your suspicions?"

"More than once. They can't find anything that confirms he's the one. In fact, he's been transferred to a minimum-security prison because of good behavior. Chief McCreary told me according to the prison psychiatrists he's making remarkable progress. Since he pled guilty by mental defect, there's a good chance he could be out in a matter of months."

"You don't believe those psychiatrists?"

"Not a chance, Cole. I saw the expression in the man's eyes

when he admitted killing Grady Jackson. He isn't stupid and I think he's just manipulative enough to put on quite an act when he wants to. I'm not exactly his favorite person."

"I don't like where this is going, Kat. I gather you think he's managed to secure background information on you?"

"It wouldn't be hard. The inmates have access to the internet. He's a computer programmer so he's got the skill to find out anything he wants to if he puts his mind to it. Multiple homicides in a small town like Brookdale make headlines."

"I've got one more to add to that," he said grimly. "Liv," he called out, "why don't you go see what that dog is up to now?"

There was a pause and then he was back. "Sorry, had to get her out of the room. Dale just finished the autopsy on Clay Saunders's exhumed body today. No question, he was murdered and from the positioning of the blood and hair the backpack was the weapon of choice."

"Obviously the backpack alone couldn't have killed him."

"No but whacking him with the gun still inside multiple times would. Skull showed blunt trauma, repeated blunt trauma."

"Any tie-in to my parents' murders?"

"Not yet but there has to be one. I keep thinking that maybe the killer panicked and instinctively drove toward the cabin knowing it was the most secluded place to toss the gun. Could be Saunders surprised him and he knocked him over the head with it."

She contemplated that for a moment. "But why not just toss it in the creek? Chances are it would never have been found. The coroner might have missed the mark as to the cause of death back then, but I know Charlie would have done a thorough investigation. If Mr. Saunders was killed where we found the backpack, wouldn't there have been signs of a body being dragged back to the cabin where he was found? Mud or blood on the porch steps, fabric caught on the wood?"

"Not if whoever did the deed was strong and the killer was high on drugs or alcohol or both. From the description, Saunders was no more than five foot five or six and weighed about one twenty or so. Dead weight is dead weight but it wouldn't take much to fireman carry him to where he was found. Even make sure to knock his head against that fireplace to finish the set up."

"I see you've given this some thought."

"Haven't been able to do much else with you in that big city and me here."

She laughed. "Poor lonely you."

"I am," he said. "At least I was until you came into my life."

"I think the man has a smooth tongue," she teased.

"I mean it, Kat," he said quietly.

"I know." She was silent for a brief moment, wishing he was standing next to her instead of miles away. "I've given Dan six weeks. I'll try to sneak away in the next week or two for a long weekend but I can't guarantee anything. I've got loads to do before I hand over the reins."

"Let me say goodnight," Liv interrupted, the puppy barking loudly in the background. "Mrs. Ross is here. I've got the portable phone so Daddy can say goodnight too."

"Night, my love."

"Was that directed at my daughter or at me?" Cole asked.

"At both of you," she answered, pressing a kiss into the receiver before hanging up.

She treated herself to a thick-crust pizza dripping with cheese and polished off another glass of wine. Feeling pleasantly full and just a little tipsy, she crawled under the covers, looking forward to sleeping in. The sheets were cool and crisp and smelled fresh from the softener she used. Smiling sleepily, she let her mind go blank, refusing to dwell on today or that disturbing message. Drifting off, her lips still curving, she slid into the subconscious and horror...

...the blue eyes were wide and staring, lifeless, the blonde hair matted with congealing blood. A knife was lying by her motionless body, the scarlet from the deep slice in her neck marring its gleaming blade. The lips were opened as if in shock, still painted a deep pouting pink, the only color in an otherwise ghostly paste-like complexion. Allie Sandoval!

Even in sleep she could feel her heart beating so hard it felt like it would break free of her chest. Fighting for breath, she shot up in bed, flailing to free herself from the tangled sheets. Finally she sank back, putting a trembling hand to her face, surprised to find tears. She reached for the phone but before she could dial, it rang. She started violently, glancing at the illuminated clock by her bed. Who was calling at two in the morning?

And then she knew.

"Kat, something terrible has happened." Her aunt's voice was shaking. "Cole has just been arrested. They found Allie Sandoval dead in his garage not an hour ago, her throat slit with a knife from his kitchen drawer."

"I know," Kat managed through a throat constricted with fear. "I just saw the whole thing in a dream."

"You what?"

"I saw her, Aunt Evelyn. Lying there with the knife on that cement floor." She closed her eyes, tears pricking her lids. "Tell Cole I'll be there as soon as I can. Where's Olivia?"

"She's still with the Rosses. She doesn't know anything yet."

Kat was already throwing things in the suitcase she had pulled from her closet. "Just keep it as quiet as you can until I get there and call Jared. He'll have the funds to pay for the bail."

"I will." There was a short pause at the other end. "Did you see who murdered her in your dream?"

"No and I wish to God I had. There is no way Cole killed anyone."

Evelyn's voice was stronger, steadier. "Jerry told me as much but he had no choice but to take Cole in. The evidence was stacked against him. I don't have the same kind of sixth sense you do, Kat, but I know a set up when I see one."

Kat was struggling into a pair of jeans, the phone balanced against her shoulder. "Someone stacked that evidence, Aunt Evelyn. Someone who wants Cole off the job. Put the chief of police in jail and the pressure's off."

"I gather you aren't going to let that happen?"

Kat threw on a t-shirt, wriggling her head around the collar and the phone. "You're damn right I won't. It's even more personal now. I have to go. I've got to find a flight as quickly as I can. I'll phone you when I have a set arrival time."

She contemplated calling Dan, then decided against it. She could call him at a more reasonable hour since it was the weekend anyway. She didn't bother with her computer but phoned the airlines direct and was able to arrange a flight at five a.m. The fare was ridiculous but she didn't care.

By noon she was rushing out of the terminal, scanning the parking lot for her aunt's car. Instead of the sedate four-door sedan Evelyn drove, Cole's red Corvette squealed to a stop in front of her. When he unwound his long length from the driver's side, she simply walked into his arms. He pulled her close and held her, ignoring the impatient horns and cars zooming past.

Finally she lifted her gaze to his, noting the exhausted eyes and hint of pallor under the tanned skin. She probably looked even worse with two hours' sleep. "We better move before we get hit," she said huskily.

"Not before I do this," he said hoarsely, bending his head. The kiss was long and desperate and settled her as nothing else could have.

She touched his lips with her fingers after they left hers. "You okay?"

He shrugged. "As okay as I can be. Let's go."

He shoved her cases in the back of the 'Vette. Just before she slid in, she noticed the car parked behind, a familiar figure in the driver's seat.

"What's Jerry doing here?"

Cole glanced at his deputy, his expression grim. "Even though I'm a free man at present, trotting off to the airport isn't exactly acceptable behavior for a suspect. Jerry was nice enough to allow me to drive my own car."

"I gather your father put up bail? I told Aunt Evelyn to make sure she called him."

"He didn't need to. After Jerry asked his questions, he didn't have enough evidence to hold me."

"I thought the murder weapon came from your kitchen."

He rubbed a hand across his eyes. "It did. What the killer

didn't know was that I never touched that knife. When Evelyn was preparing for my party, she said she couldn't find a decent knife in the entire place so she bought a set that included that particular one. She told me to consider it a birthday gift. Although the final fingerprint results aren't back yet, it's fairly obvious the ones that are on the knife aren't mine."

"You could have worn gloves."

"Yeah, I could have, but since they didn't find any, that theory didn't wash. On top of that, I've been leaving the house unlocked even when I'm gone because I've got some men finishing up work on the back porch. Anyone could have entered and I'd never have been the wiser." He glanced over at her. "I only lock the doors when Liv and I are home. A competent prosecutor could probably build a damn good circumstantial case but right now I'm a free man."

She leaned her head against the headrest, settling her gaze on him. He guided the car effortlessly around the heavy traffic. There was a sense of power about him, a sense of purpose, even after the hellish night he had just had. Beneath the Irish good looks and the muscular physique, those were the qualities that had really attracted her to him.

"I love you." She said the words almost defiantly, challenging him.

His lips curved although his eyes remained hidden behind the sunglasses he had on. "You make it sound like a confession you didn't particularly want to make."

"I'm not sure I did but somehow circumstances have changed things just a little."

He removed his sunglasses, his gaze finding hers. The expression in them had her swallowing hard. "You realize you've just confessed to loving someone who could very well end up in jail for murder?"

She shook her head. "No, what I did was confess to falling in love with a man I admire, respect and frankly is rather spectacular in bed."

Her response got the desired reaction. He swung the car off the freeway and into a fast food parking lot, slamming it out of gear. "Come here."

Unmindful of the console between them, he hauled her

onto his lap, crushing his lips to hers. She fisted her hands into his hair, touching and tasting with abandon. When her backside slammed into the gearshift, she grinned against his mouth.

"That's going to bruise."

He grinned back although the smile didn't quite reach his eyes. "Sorry. I guess I got a little carried away."

"Don't you dare ruin things by apologizing. That was rather wonderful. Of course I bet Jerry is blushing right to the roots of his hair right about now."

He glanced in the mirror and shook his head. "He's parked across the street. The man might feel the need to keep an eye on me but he knows how to be discreet."

"Well, that's a relief," she said, moving toward her side of the car.

He stopped her with a hand on her arm. "Kat, you know the first thing I thought of when I found Allie lying there, God help me?" His fingers tightened on her briefly. "Right in the middle of all the shock and horror, my initial reaction was that I couldn't have handled it if that had been you. I'm not proud of that, given the circumstances, but it's the truth." He reached for her hand, his thumb rubbing across the soft skin. "I think I've loved you since that day at the cabin. What took longer to realize was it's more than that." He traced her lips with slightly unsteady fingers. "I need you, Kat. Liv needs you. Can you handle all that baggage?"

Whether it was his words or exhaustion or both, tears began to run down her cheek. Tears she didn't even try to wipe away. "Just try and stop me."

"No way," he said, raising his hands. "Chances are good I might need your legal expertise as well," he said dryly as she eased herself into a more comfortable position. "I'm still the prime suspect."

He had to resist the impulse to drag her back in his arms at the change in her expression. Her eyes turned from soft aqua to steel blue. The woman had no idea how amazingly attractive she was even with her hair raked back in an untidy ponytail and remnants of those tears still on her cheek.

"I'm not sure it would be ethical for me to take your case.

That doesn't mean that I don't want you to tell me everything you can about the last twenty-four hours."

"Which isn't a hell of a lot. The most damning part is that Allie paid me a visit yesterday afternoon. It just so happened at the time Tom and Joe Peterson were both there helping me finish up the back porch. Deanna had just dropped Liv off after soccer practice when she came roaring up the driveway in that sports number she drives...drove," he corrected himself grimly.

"I gather you had a confrontation?"

"That's a mild word for it. She grabbed Liv's arm and threatened to throw her in the car and kidnap her unless I gave her money. She was wild, drunk and high. I could smell the weed even before I got to her. Liv was sobbing, Deanna was furious and so was I." He glanced over at her. "I grabbed the keys to her car and called Jerry on my cell. During the time it took for him to arrive, she screamed, ranted and raved and managed to slap me in the face just as Jerry pulled in. It took him, Joe, Tom and I to get her in the back of the squad car. She fought like a damn wildcat." He lifted an arm, showing her an ugly long scratch. "I drove her car back to the station and called her father. Told him either he dealt with her drug and alcohol problem or I would and that's an exact quote."

"What did he say?"

"The same thing he's always said when I've confronted him or Sonya in the past. His daughter was certainly not an alcoholic and he stood behind her one hundred percent. He also made it clear they were still pursuing custody of their dear granddaughter so I'd better be prepared to hear from their lawyer in the very near future."

"What is that saying about ignorance being bliss?" she said dryly.

"In this case it wasn't ignorance. It was blatant denial."

"Well that won't work anymore because they've denied their daughter right into her grave."

He was silent for a brief moment while he put the car in gear again. "This wasn't just a set up murder, Kat," he said quietly as he accelerated into traffic. "Whoever killed her almost cut her head off."

"Could it have been a dealer she owed big time?"

"I thought of that, but if it was a professional hit it was damned messy. The autopsy results will tell us if she put up a fight but I've got a feeling she was taken by surprise. I'm sure that she was killed elsewhere and moved to my garage. There wasn't enough blood for it to be the scene of the murder."

"Unfortunately I'm willing to bet she had enemies, not to mention those her father might have. Rumor has it he's an unscrupulous businessman." She frowned thoughtfully. "When did you find her?"

"About midnight. Ringer suddenly went crazy, barking and scratching at the back door. I figured it was an animal of some sort so I grabbed a flashlight and did a quick once around the backyard. That's when I noticed the garage doors open." He paused briefly. "I flicked the lights on just to make sure everything was secure and...I found her," he finished gruffly, his jaw tight.

"I know this sounds kind of silly but I'm sorry, Cole," she said softly.

He reached over and squeezed her hand. "Thanks. There were a few good years at the beginning and I wouldn't have Liv if it weren't for her. Still, I can't find it in myself to be truly sad. She had become a vicious addict and I still can't forgive her for what she almost did to our daughter."

"That might be but no one deserves to die that way." She looked out the window at the passing scenery. "The only thing that makes sense is that she was killed because she knew something, Cole. You just told me how desperate she was for money. Maybe she was blackmailing our killer and he got tired of it. That would explain the viciousness of the murder."

He nodded. "I've thought of that. It would also explain why I was being set up. We're close, Kat. The answer is right in front of us if we can put the pieces together."

She yawned hugely, covering her mouth apologetically. "Sorry, I know you're just as tired as I am."

"I'm beyond tired right now," he agreed. "I guess numb is a better word. Deanna is keeping Liv for the weekend. I stopped by before I came to pick you up and told her about her mother. The poor kid didn't know how to react."

"She's stronger than you give her credit for, Cole. She'll

deal with it as long as she has you."

"Assuming I'm not in jail."

"That isn't going to happen," she said firmly.

He sent her a narrow look. "You haven't asked me if I killed her," he said flatly.

She swung around, eyes blazing. "That's the most ridiculous thing I've ever heard you say."

"I've killed before."

"If you're trying to piss me off, you're doing an admirable job. Your skill as a Navy Seal has nothing to do with this."

"A court might make it an issue," he muttered, swinging the car into his driveway. He braked in front of the yellow police tape that surrounded most of the front yard. Several squad cars were parked at various angles beside it.

"Number one, you won't be in court," she snapped. "Number two, quit feeling sorry for yourself and be prepared to help me find who it is that is responsible for Alison's death. And number three..."

He arched a brow. "Number three?"

"I suggest you back out of this driveway and take me to the cabin. I need some time to think and I desperately need to jump your bones."

She would have laughed at his expression if she hadn't been perfectly serious. She was punch tired and wasn't in the mood to deal with the police and forensic crew that were working behind that tape. What she was in the mood for was rough, mind altering sex. She had a strong feeling it was what both of them needed.

"Let me tell Jerry where we're going," he said gruffly. He opened the door and stepped out. "Just don't change your mind while I'm gone."

She couldn't help the laughter that bubbled out. "I promise."

Moments later he backed out of the driveway, gravel spitting.

"Jerry okay with us leaving?"

He nodded. "Said to tell you welcome home." He glanced over at her as he changed gears. "He believes I'm innocent."

"That's because you are," she said simply. She reached inside her purse for her cell phone. "I better let Aunt Evelyn know I'm home and where she can reach me."

The phone rang just once before her aunt picked up.

"Are you and Cole okay?" she asked immediately.

"We're fine," Kat reassured her. "We're heading to the cabin to regroup. Best way to reach me is on my cell. I promise we'll stop by tomorrow after we've had a chance to go over everything."

"Just be careful, Kat," Evelyn warned. "Three murders in less than a year in a place like Brookdale mean somewhere there's a killer with an agenda. He won't have any qualms murdering again if he's threatened with exposure. That cabin is extremely isolated."

"Oh, my God! You're right. No matter what the motive he *is* a serial killer. Thanks, Aunt Evelyn. I'll call you."

Before her aunt could reply, she disconnected the call, her gaze flying to Cole's. "I can't believe I didn't think of this sooner," she said, digging in her purse and coming up with a small card triumphantly. She punched some numbers in.

"Tim, it's Kat. You know that favor you mentioned? Well, I'm calling you on it. Can you give me your personal fax number? I'm going to send you everything I've got regarding an ongoing investigation in my hometown. See if you can see a pattern for a profile?" She reached in her purse again and pulled out a pen and paper. "Go ahead." She jotted a number down. "I really appreciate this. I hate to push a favor but could you make it as quick as possible? I owe you big time. Thanks."

"Care to share what that was all about?" Cole asked, braking in front of the cabin.

"Maybe later," she said, reaching behind her to grab her suitcase. He followed while she unlocked the door. Dropping the case on the floor, she spun, yanking him inside. She kicked the door closed behind her and turned the lock.

"Kat, I'm not sure what you're..."

She didn't give him time to finish but simply fastened her mouth on his. Wrapping her arms around his neck, she pressed against him. He tasted hot and sweet and she feasted on his sensual lower lip and the strong brown curve of his neck, her hands splaying across his chest. She wasn't exactly sure when he took over, didn't much care. His kisses were deep and searing, his hands ripping at her shirt, the zipper of her jeans. Hers were just as busy searching then finding bare skin.

The wood floor was cold as they sank down, neither of them caring that they had barely crossed the threshold. They made love hard and fast, not allowing for anything other than the mindless release, the roaring sensations that ripped through both of them. She arched to meet him time after time, their breathing harsh, gasping as the blood sang through them, within them, until they shuddered in mirrored release.

He finally managed to lift his head, gazing down at her. The early afternoon light shimmered across her face and hair, highlighting her still-heated skin and the stormy blue eyes that stared up at him. Her breasts rose and fell against his bare chest as she reached up to run her hand along the stubble of beard on his face.

"You haven't shaved."

He captured her fingers, nipping at them lightly. "Wasn't a priority this morning."

"I guess it wouldn't have been at that," she said lightly, stretching, the movement threatening to arouse him once again.

Smiling wickedly, she looked up at him. "I'm impressed."

"I aim to please," he drawled, stilling her with his legs as he stretched and yawned. "The body might be willing, however the mind is almost asleep."

Laughing, she shoved him to the side and rose gracefully, gathering their clothes. "I can think of a better place to sleep than the floor."

"Do tell," he challenged, his hands sneaking around her waist.

Shaking her head, she ducked free, grabbing his hand. "Forget it. Come on. Let's go get some shut eye."

It was the better part of two hours later that she stirred. Cole was sleeping soundly next to her on the big antique bed, his arm flung across her. Quietly making her way to the bathroom, she took a fast hot shower, the water serving to push the remaining drowsiness away. Tiptoeing out, she slipped on a robe she unearthed from her suitcase. Closing the door quietly behind her, she shivered slightly as the cool air of the bigger room touched her skin. Touching a match to the waiting wood in the fireplace, she padded her way into the kitchen, stopping to spin around and admire her new home. Although the furniture had been included in the price, she had added a few touches of her own. A favorite seascape over the fireplace, a bright blue afghan on the sofa, fat jewel colored candles on the mantle.

Her gaze moved to the floor-to-ceiling windows that reflected the trees surrounding the cabin. They were breathtaking with the gorgeous orange and yellow of early fall.

Her stomach rumbled, interrupting her thoughts. Realizing she hadn't eaten for a very long time, she rummaged through the cupboards and the freezer. Silently thanking her aunt for providing her with a carton of frozen homemade soup, she got busy. Soon she had the broth bubbling nicely and a batch of biscuits she had mixed herself baking. Fixing a cup of hot tea, she reached for the phone.

"Andy, Cole and I are at the cabin. Think you can round up Ellie, Sam and Jerry Landers and meet us here about seven o'clock or so? Good. I'll fix something for dinner if you bring drinks. Okay, see you then."

Cole wandered in about an hour later, looking entirely too sexy with his bare hair-roughened chest and well-worn jeans. He smelled of aftershave as she smiled up at him.

"The stubble is gone. Shame. I kind of liked it."

He sniffed the air and stretched. "Something smells good."

"A late lunch," she said, rising and ladling some soup into a bowl. Putting the biscuits between them, she settled across the table, pleased at the clear gaze he directed at her. "Feeling better?"

His lips curved as he reached for the butter. "A long sleep after sex with a hot woman does that to me."

"I better be the only woman you're having hot sex with."

"You're the only woman I want to spend the rest of my life with," he drawled.

Her gaze shot to his. "Is that a proposal?"

"Not a very romantic one, is it?"

"It doesn't have to be," she reassured him.

He leaned back, his eyes somber. "You deserve romance, Kat. I intend that you have it once this mess is over with."

Her gaze moved to the floor in front of the fireplace. "Oh I don't know. I'd say there was plenty of romance just a little while ago."

He laughed, the worry lines in his face disappearing. "You're something else, you know that? I still haven't heard an answer."

"Do you really need one?"

He contemplated for a moment. "I think I do."

She rose and tipped his chin back, her lips finding his. "Is that a sufficient answer?"

"It'll do for now," he grinned, smacking her silk-covered backside as she turned.

"Now eat before it gets cold because we've got some work to do."

Four hours later, both of them were sprawled on the couch comparing notes. Kat tucked her hair behind her ear, frowning as she tapped her pen against the paper she held in her hand. "I keep coming back to Paul Sulin discovering those vials in the Mustang. It's the only thing that ties the two sets of murders together. Ellie said her father practically obsessed about it so I have a feeling he suspected Allie knew more than she was willing to tell him."

Cole glanced out the window and rose. "Maybe we'll get more answers from the crew. They just pulled in."

"Good, because I'm beginning to get a headache here. You go greet them and I'll check on dinner."

He nodded but when she rose, he turned her into his arms, his eyes dark and serious. "I love you."

"It's about time," she said, lips curving. "I don't seem to remember those three little words as part of that marriage proposal."

He released her, nudging her toward the kitchen. "I figured it wasn't necessary since you've got that sixth sense thing."

She smiled but the light in her eyes dimmed. "It sure hasn't been much help so far, has it?"

He put a hand on the doorknob, raising a brow quizzically. "Then I guess we'll just have to do things my way. You know, evidence, fingerprints, investigation. Not all of us can cheat like you."

She grinned, shaking a finger at him. "Stuff it, cop."

"Seems I've heard those words before," he teased as he opened the door.

By the time she'd checked on the lasagna she had thawed from her well-stocked freezer and was contented it was bubbling nicely, Cole had everyone seated around the fireplace while Andy served drinks.

"This cabin is wonderful," Ellie exclaimed, her gaze roaming around the soaring ceiling and the warm wood floors. "Andy said the people who owned the place after Mr. Saunders remodeled it but I had no idea they *really* remodeled it." She smiled at Kat. "I can tell you right now if I'd known what a showplace it was I'd have snatched it myself."

Kat accepted a glass of wine from Andy and curled next to Ellie on the sofa. "Then I'm glad it was a well-kept secret. Hi, Sam," she said to the bear of a man that sat across from her. She still marveled at how much he resembled his father both in looks and personality. "How's Connie?"

"Sick of being pregnant and cursing our family history of twins. Luckily it won't be much longer according to our resident doctor. Right, sis?"

Ellie winked at Kat. "Don't let him fool you, Kat. My brother is the classic first time dad. He calls her five times a day."

"Lies, all lies," he denied sheepishly.

Andy slapped him on the back, handing him a beer. "Tough imagining my best friend the father of twins." He shuddered. "I'm not sure I've got that much imagination."

"All right, enough teasing," Kat said firmly, taking another sip of her wine. "Leave the poor man alone." She set her glass down on the end table. "I hate to change the subject but I called this meeting so we could meld minds or at least share ideas. I want to thank you for coming on such short notice, especially you, Jerry. I know with Cole still a suspect, this whole thing has fallen directly in your lap so I appreciate any time you can give us."

The older man was standing by the fireplace, staring into the flames. He slowly turned, meeting her gaze steadily. "Cole isn't a suspect in my book, Kat. Of course that doesn't mean I don't have to dot the Is and cross the Ts." He glanced at Cole. "I have to warn you the Sandovals are already gathering forces. I hate to say it, but Dallas Sandoval spent more time grilling me about when I was going to arrest you than grieving for his only daughter." His lips thinned. "Never did like that family."

"Thanks for the support, Jerry," Cole said sincerely.

"Jerry, this meeting might be crossing some ethical lines so it's up to you as to how much you want to tell us," Kat said frankly.

"Not much to tell at this point if you're talking about Allison Sandoval's murder. Coroner places time of death between one and three in the afternoon. Rigor mortis was well established by the time we arrived on the scene."

Kat's gaze snapped to Cole's. "Is he sure? Because if that's the case, I imagine you could verify your whereabouts, Cole. That would immediately eliminate you as a suspect."

"No such luck," he replied. "Liv was at soccer practice with Deanna and Tiffany that started right after school and ended around five." He rubbed a hand across his chin thoughtfully. "Come to think of it, I got a call around that time yesterday complaining about kids parking up near the old Campbell farm. Betty said the caller wouldn't identify himself. Said he didn't want to cause trouble but just wanted the kids out of there."

"Let me guess," Andy said. "No one was there?"

"Not a soul. I spent the better part of an hour cruising around the back roads making sure there was no one hanging around or vandalizing. Even went up to the old abandoned farmhouse. Didn't see a thing. I checked in with Betty about five o'clock and then went home because I knew Liv was due back."

"You told me Tom and Joe Peterson had been working on the back porch when Alison arrived earlier yesterday afternoon," Kat said thoughtfully. "What time did they leave?"

"About half an hour after I left on that call, according to Tom. They stored the tools in the garage but couldn't lock the side entrance because I had the only key on me. I told Tom I'd lock it when I got home."

"Did you?"

"I intended to but with Liv hungry after soccer, it slipped my mind. The only reason I lock it at all is because I've acquired a fair amount of tools with the renovation and I store them in there."

"Doesn't matter," Jerry added, "because forensics determined the garage wasn't the scene of the murder. Not enough blood." He tossed Cole an apologetic look. "We put both the squad car and your 'Vette through a very complete once over. Found nothing. No blood, hair, nothing."

"Of course they didn't," Ellie said indignantly.

"Any tire tracks or blood outside the garage?" Cole asked Jerry.

He nodded. "Tire tracks might have done us some good if there hadn't been so much activity with workers going back and forth and such. Contaminated the scene. No blood except on the floor of the garage."

Cole glanced up at him speculatively. "With that kind of wound there should have been more blood. Unless..."

Jerry's eyes met his. "Unless that slice was made after she was already dead."

"What about that, Ellie?" Cole asked, shifting his gaze to the woman across from him.

"You're probably on to something there, Cole," she agreed. "Let's assume several hours elapsed between the time she was killed and she was moved to your garage. There would have been congealing and significantly less blood if that wound was made after death."

"Which leads us right back to someone setting you up," Kat said.

"We'll know more when we get the final autopsy results," Jerry added absently.

Kat eyed him, sensing there was something else on his mind. "Is there something you see that we don't, Jerry?"

"Yeah and it just hit me a little while ago." He watched Cole take a sip of his scotch. "Killer was left-handed."

All four of them stared at him. Cole was the first to speak.

"Forensics tell you that?"

Jerry shook his head. "They didn't have to. Something about that knife wound bothered me from the get-go." He moved to the empty chair by the fireplace and settled his bulk in it. "When I was first out of the academy, I went to a seminar that included evaluating stab wounds at the scene of a crime." He reached in his pocket and pulled out some photographs. "These aren't pretty," he warned.

He spread them on the coffee table. Kat leaned forward curiously. All six of them were close-ups of the wound itself.

"I never liked the woman," Ellie murmured softly, "but to die like that..." She shook her head.

"What is it you see that would indicate which way the wound was made?" Kat asked.

Jerry leaned forward, picking up a photograph and turning it toward the group. "A wound has to have a start and stop point unless it's a stabbing kind, which this one isn't. See the way the slice starts deeper and then gets shallower toward the left? That indicates that that the knife was moved from right to left. That would be totally unnatural for someone who is right-handed."

Kat frowned, picking up one of the pictures and studying it closer. "That's assuming the killer was standing behind her."

"He would have to have been to make that kind of slice," Cole said, eyes narrowed thoughtfully. "It would also explain why it's so deep. A dead person doesn't fight."

Kat ran a finger along the rim of her wine glass. "Cole and I have spent the better part of three hours tossing things back and forth and have come to the conclusion that these murders are all related. The question is how?"

"It starts with Mom and Dad," Andy said. "It has to."

"Okay let's begin there. Ellie, you and Sam already know about my clairvoyance but Jerry probably doesn't." She turned her attention to the man sitting across from her. "After my parents were killed, I had the same dream over and over. Still have it on occasion. It's always the same." She closed her eyes briefly, steeling herself for the emotion that was never far away when she relived the scene. "Whether the killer thought they were gone or he was high enough not to care, I always see the same thing. He comes in the back door of the office and opens the medicine cabinet. Mom finds the door open turns and..." She stopped, swallowing hard. "She knows him, that I'm sure of. She says something like what on earth are you doing here and he panics. Dad hears the gunshot and..." Her gaze shot to Cole's. "The backpack! Now I know why it looked so familiar. It's the same one the killer was stuffing vials into that night right before Mom caught him."

"And vials just like those that your father had in his office were found in the Mustang Dad bought from Allie Sandoval," Sam added, frowning. "Andy, didn't we see Allie the night your parents were killed?"

"No I don't think..." Andy began and then paused, rubbing his jaw, brow furrowed. "It's been so long ago. I do remember a group of us were out earlier cruising but a whole lot of that night is hazy. I can't even remember who all was with me but come to think of it I'm pretty sure Allie was in the car. She was really hot back then." He shot Cole an apologetic look. "Sorry, Cole, that was rather tasteless."

Cole shrugged. "No apology necessary."

"I think we stopped for pizza, didn't we?" Sam asked. "Drank some beer?" He paused and then nodded. "Now it's all coming back. Allie was close to being plastered by the time we dropped her off at her aunt's house."

"What time was that?" Kat asked.

Sam considered for a moment. "Must have been around seven or so because I remember we went back to my house and watched a movie."

Andy's expression tightened at the memory. "You're right because I had just arrived home when the police came to the door around ten o'clock."

"Anyone else get out with Allie?" Cole asked.

Sam shook his head. "I can't remember, to tell you the truth. What I do know is that Allie was thick with one of us back then or at least for that summer. Remember who that was, Andy?"

"Wasn't it Brian, Jerry?" Ellie asked, turning to him. "I remember seeing him and Allie speeding up and down Main Street and thinking how cool they looked in that sharp red car of hers."

"It's possible," the deputy admitted. "Brian was pretty rebellious back then. I wasn't exactly thrilled with him hanging around that girl. She was older and more street wise than he was at the time but his mother didn't feel the same way."

"Then we need to talk to Brian," Kat said, sensing the undercurrents. "If those vials are from my father's office, she could very well have been in the car with whoever killed my parents. Ellie, you said your father saw Allie driving later that night around the time Dad and Mom were murdered. I'd be willing to bet there was someone else in that car. Could be she found herself someone to blackmail."

"Jerry," Cole said, "did Paul Sulin tell you about those vials?"

The older man shook his head. "Nope. Didn't know a thing about them until now."

"Then he must have approached Allie directly." He stretched his long legs out. "That would explain why she was so twitchy when I threw some questions at her about them. Knowing her as I do...did...she wouldn't have hesitated to up the ante if she thought she had a bargaining tool."

"And that very well might have been the final straw, sealing her death," Andy speculated. He glanced over at Cole. "That would explain the severity of the wound. Could be she threatened him with exposure and paid for it with her life. Strangling her might not have been enough to appease him. So he slit her throat."

"Which served two purposes," Ellie added. "One, he vented his anger and secondly, it was a way to put the blame squarely on you, Cole."

"Okay, people, what we've got so far," Kat said, "is a left-handed murderer who, at some point, probably was in Allie Sandoval's car the night Mom and Dad were killed." She uncurled and stood, moving toward the kitchen to check on the food. "Now all we have to do is round up the people Allie hung around with back then and ask some questions."

"Brian is left-handed," Jerry said quietly.

The room was suddenly still as all eyes turned to him.

"We weren't suggesting Brian was involved," Cole said.

"I know you weren't." His eyes met Cole's, a look of understanding passing between them. "He's my son and I love him but I put away those blinders awhile ago. Do I think he killed John and Emily Ramon? No. But that doesn't mean I don't think he wasn't capable of being involved if he got high or drunk enough, especially if Allison Sandoval urged him on. He was pretty infatuated with her that summer." His expression darkened. "Kid didn't drink or dabble in drugs until then. He was always a follower and Allie Sandoval was mighty enticing with her blonde hair and fast car. I didn't like it and told him so more than once. His mother thought differently. It's one of the reasons we ended in divorce court." He grimaced. "Sorry, you didn't need to know that. Either way, it's time I have a long talk with him."

"Forgive me, Jerry, but I think it would be better if I were the one to do that," Kat said, removing the lasagna from the oven. "Primarily because, if he isn't involved, I don't want you taking the brunt of his anger."

Jerry's gaze locked with hers for a long moment. "All right, if you think that's best." He shrugged. "He's a mean cuss when he wants to be, Kat, but I'd like to believe he isn't capable of murder even under the influence. At least I hope not."

"Then that's good enough for me," she replied. "That doesn't mean he might not know something about that night that could help us."

Ellie walked over to the cupboards at Kat's direction and began setting the table. "That smells wonderful," she said, inhaling as Kat placed the pan in the center.

Cole brought over the salad that had been chilling in the refrigerator and they all dug in. It was only later as they were sharing after-dinner coffee that he turned to Ellie and Sam. "Kat said she felt whoever murdered your parents knew your house very, very well."

Sam raised a brow in surprise. "How would you know that, Kat?"

"Because when I walked the yard with Cole, I found myself remembering the good times in that backyard and suddenly I had this vision. I couldn't see who the person was other than it was definitely a man. What struck me is that when he went up the back porch steps, I saw him hop over that squeaky one.

That means he knew about that step."

Sam ran a hand through his hair, scowling. "Damn! If your instincts are right, and they usually are, that also means someone we know or knew intimately killed Mom and Dad. Terrific."

Cole felt his pain, felt Kat's as well. They were talking analytically about people who had been loved dearly. He couldn't entirely repress the feeling that he had failed all of them. His ex-wife was dead and yet he found himself feeling more deeply saddened about the deaths of four people he had never known. God help him for that.

Andy tapped the side of his glass with his finger. "Okay, so let's gather this information in a timeline. We've got Allie Sandoval driving the Mustang around the time of night that Mom and Dad were killed. We've got several vials of morphine found under the seat fifteen years later that might or might not be the same vials as those stolen from dad's office. We've got a backpack that Kat says is similar or identical to the one she sees in her dreams and a gun inside that might or might not be the murder weapon that killed our parents. Finally, we have Allie Sandoval murdered and Cole set up for that murder." He looked at Kat. "Put it together like that and it makes a neat circle of suspicion."

She nodded. "Jerry, since you were involved in the original investigation, could you summarize what the police found?"

"Sure you want to dig all that up now?"

"No," she admitted, "but we have no choice, do we?"

"Time of death was approximately between seven-thirty and eight-thirty in the evening on a Friday. Probably closer to seven-thirty because they had reservations at Kleinman's for eight. Single shots, one for each victim. Never found the gun. Weather had been dry so we got nothing in the way of footprints. No sign of forced entry either."

"Which means either his nurse didn't lock the door like she assured Charlie she did or the killer had a key," Cole added. "I went over the old records and before Charlie left he brought me up-to-date on what he had. Problem is there were only a few people who had keys to both the doors and the narcotic cupboard." He ticked them off on his fingers. "John Ramon, his wife and his nurse."

"I had a set as well," Andy said. "Dad wanted to have a spare just in case." His eyes darkened in memory. "I kept them in the console between the front seats. Once in awhile I'd go get a file for him from the office when he forgot one."

"Were they there after your parents were killed?"

"I know they were there a week later when Charlie asked me if there were any more sets. With the nightmare of that week, looking for a set of keys was the furthest thing from my mind."

"Did Brian know you had those keys?" Kat asked, knowing the question had to be asked and hating that she was hurting Jerry in the process.

Andy thought for a minute and then nodded. "I guess he could have. However, although I might have been only nineteen at the time, I knew enough not to advertise something like that." He frowned. "I do know that almost everyone I hung around with back then had been at Dad's office at least once or twice." His gaze moved to Kat. "There's a good chance any one of them could have seen Dad unlocking that narcotic cupboard."

"Including Alison Sandoval?" Jerry asked, glancing at Cole.

Andy shrugged. "Maybe," he said, glancing at Cole, "but it's unlikely."

Cole took his plate over to the kitchen counter and then turned to look at the four of them. "My ex-wife was an addict. Addicts do stupid things, including breaking and entering. As you said, Jerry, at nineteen Allie was sexy, rich and spoiled. Pretty potent combination for an in-lust seventeen- or eighteen-year-old boy," he said, his eyes finding Jerry's. "Brian wasn't the only one she had on a string back then, including boys that weren't from Brookdale. I gather you've got someone checking her phone records?"

Jerry nodded, pushing his chair back. "It'll take some time but I'm working on it."

Sam leaned back in his chair, rubbing his coffee cup between his hands. "You know what I'm thinking? I'm thinking that Dad called Allie and probably got nothing so he went further. He was damned tenacious when he set his mind to something. Could be he suspected someone and, if this someone was a close friend of the family as Kat thinks he was, he might have approached him first." Pain flickered in his eyes briefly. "He was that kind of man."

"Then it wouldn't hurt to look at his phone records again as well," Cole said, rinsing his dish and placing it in the dishwasher. "I just gave them a cursory once-over initially because they didn't enter into the investigation."

Kat motioned for the rest of them to sit while she and Cole made short work of clearing the table.

Finally Ellie stood, stretching. "Lord, I'm full. That was wonderful, Kat, but I've got to get home. Hospital rounds tomorrow before office hours." She put a hand on her friend's, glancing at Cole. "Either of you need anything, you call." She shivered slightly. "You know this is the kind of stuff you see on *Forensic Files* or *FBI's Most Wanted*."

Jerry opened the door for her. "I've got to get back as well. Thanks for the food, Kat," he said, smiling slightly. "Not that I needed it."

Cole extended his hand and Jerry took it. "I owe you, Jerry, big time."

The older man shook his head. "No, you don't owe me a damned thing, Cole. Just watch your back, will you?" He grinned wryly. "Somehow taking over as chief doesn't have the appeal it once did."

Cole returned the grin. "I'll do that."

Sam followed Ellie out. "Keep us informed and if I think of anything else I'll let you know."

Andy was the last to leave. He waited until the others were gone, pouring himself another cup of coffee. Kat knew he had something on his mind so she busied herself wiping counters and restoring order until he was ready to tell her what that was.

Cole glanced at the two of them and tactfully went outside, closing the door behind him.

Andy leaned against the counter, frowning. "Did you notice there are a lot of coincidences here, Kat? Vials in a Mustang, a backpack you just happen to find out of the blue, visions of someone leaping over a squeaky step. Doesn't it make you wonder?"

"Wonder what?"

"That someone is trying to tell us something."

"Like for instance our parents?"

He nodded morosely. "I never knew what people really meant when they talked about needing closure until Mom and Dad were murdered. Now I know." His gaze found hers. "I've got this bad feeling that the reason they are trying to reach us, as crazy as that sounds, is not because of what happened to them but what might happen to us."

She wiped her hands on a towel and nodded. "That's why we need to press as hard as we can right now, Andy. This isn't going to stop even if we ease up on the investigation. Sooner or later, someone will remember something and it will start all over again. I don't want that on my conscience. Do you?"

"I'm not worried about me, Kat. Just do me a favor and don't stay out here alone until this is resolved. Same thing goes in New York. It'll give me some peace of mind, okay?"

Cole overheard the last comment as he came in, dropping several big logs by the fireplace. "I'm with Andy on that, Kat. Wrap things up as quickly as possible and leave New York for good."

Andy's expression lightened. "Am I hearing right? You're moving back home?"

Kat gave Cole a dark look. "That wasn't supposed to be made public quite yet."

"And why not?"

Cole strolled over to put his arm around Kat. "Because, that would lead to questions about why she was leaving a successful big city career and a partner behind."

Andy sent Kat a speculative look. "I could ask the same question."

She groaned. "Cut the male bonding crap. You'll get your answers, big brother, when I'm willing to give them." She looked pointedly toward the door. "Now don't you have a house to sell or something?"

He put his hands up in mock protest. "Okay, I can take a hint." His gaze slid to Cole. "You have any idea what you're in for?"

"I'm beginning to," Cole said tongue-in-cheek and then

doubled over when Kat rammed an elbow in his stomach none too gently.

"See what I mean?" Andy retorted, hastening to the front door at the look Kat gave him. His expression sobered as he opened it however. "I meant what I said, Kat. Be careful. I didn't inherit the family talents but I trust my gut instincts and they're screaming right now."

"I know," she said softly, moving forward to kiss his cheek. "I'll keep in touch, I promise."

Both of them watched him leave, their arms wrapped around each other. Cole inhaled the scent of her hair and pulled her close. The love he felt for this woman was stronger than anything he had ever felt for another person save his daughter. To compare her with his ex-wife was almost laughable. His gut clenched at the last picture he had of Allie lying there rigid, the look on her face one that was permanently engraved in his memory. It disturbed him that he couldn't find it in himself to grieve for her.

Kat ran gentle fingers along his brow, smoothing the lines away. "Don't."

He captured her fingers and squeezed. "Don't what?"

"Don't blame yourself for things that aren't your fault. She had your love and she preferred the lure of drugs and alcohol."

He kissed the top of her head. "Maybe, but I wonder if I had been more understanding, seen more, whether she would be on a slab right now."

She spun in his arms, looking up at him, impatience flickering in her eyes. "Listen, Cole, Allie had you, she had a wonderful daughter, was secure financially and had two parents who doted on her. To take the blame for her choices is egotistical. You didn't have that much power."

He felt a spurt of anger and then immediately a feeling of release. "You're too damn smart for your own good, you know that?"

"Oh, I don't know," she replied, coyly wrapping her arms around his neck. "I went and fell in love with a smooth-talking ex-Seal who's convinced me to do something my aunt has been trying to get me to do for years."

"Yeah, but your aunt can't do this," he murmured, bending

his head and nipping her lips. "Or this," he added, easing her against the counter, lowering his mouth to the curve of her breast, tasting the scented skin he exposed with his roaming fingers. When his teeth slid across an erect nipple, she drew a sharp breath, her fingers grabbing his shoulders as she arched toward him.

Almost frantically, she tore at the buttons on his shirt. Emotions riding high, the turmoil, the anxiety of the day made their caresses more urgent, more desperate. Clothing was dispensed with quickly, impatiently.

He watched her eyes grow cloudy with need, her breathing become shallow and fast. She groaned as his fingers trailed lower. Suddenly he lifted her onto the counter's edge with her legs wrapped around his waist. He ran fingers through her silken hair, massaging, caressing until she moaned with the pleasure of it.

"Kat," he rasped, "look at me."

She raised her gaze to his and held it for a long, charged moment. "I'm looking," she whispered.

"I want to see your eyes when..."

"When what?"

"When I do this," he growled, lifting her toward him and burying himself deep inside her with one powerful thrust.

"Oh, sweet Lord!" she gasped, exposing the tender line of her neck as she moved with him. He feasted on the exposed skin as he thrust once again.

"Don't stop," she begged, fisting her hands in his thick dark hair, yanking his lips to hers again when he lifted his head.

"I couldn't if I tried," he muttered, nipping her lower lip.

She moved against him, with him, the warmth of the fire no competition for the heat building between them. Her nails dug into his back as she writhed, pulling a groan of pleasure from his lips.

She caught the groan with her mouth and he almost lost whatever control he had at the taste of her, the dark heat. He gazed down at her for one brief moment, noting her flushed skin and golden hair spilling over his arms, her lush breasts brushing his chest provocatively.

Then very slowly he moved deeper inside as he bent his head and laved one erect nipple.

"Cole!" she sobbed, throwing her head back as he began to suckle. When he couldn't wait any longer, he lifted her hips to his and rocketed them both into the atmosphere with one final plunge.

Long moments later, he still held her close, reveling in her warmth. "I've missed you."

She smiled sleepily. "I like the way you showed me," she murmured. Abruptly, she lifted her head, her expression changing.

"What is it?"

"Don't you smell it?"

"Smell what?"

"The cigarette smoke." She slid off the counter, grabbed his shirt and wrapped it around her. Moving to the window, she stared into the darkness. "Someone's out there, Cole."

He slid into his jeans quickly and joined her. "You sure?"

She closed her eyes, frowning, and then shook her head. "No, I'm not." She rubbed a hand across her eyes. "Maybe I'm just imagining things. It's been that kind of a day."

Smiling up at him reassuringly, she tucked an arm in his and guided him away from the window. But, as he reached down to pick up his shirt, she casually walked toward the door and slid the deadbolt home.

Chapter Eleven

"Suffocation, Cole. That's the final say-so from the coroner. Throat was slit post mortem."

Cole leaned back in his chair, eying his deputy just as Mandy poured them both another cup of coffee.

"Thanks," he said, smiling up at her.

"No problem." She put the pot down and crossed her arms. "How are you two holding up?"

"Surviving," Cole said grimly.

Mandy glanced around the almost empty restaurant and then slid her gaze back to them. "Dallas Sandoval has been shooting his mouth off to the local newspapers. Rick Lawyer over at the Post was in here earlier. He's trying damn hard to blame you for his daughter's death, Cole, and he doesn't particularly care how he goes about doing it."

"I know," Cole said resignedly. "He made how he felt about me pretty obvious at Allie's funeral." His jaw tightened with remembered fury. "I got Liv out of there pretty fast but not fast enough."

Mandy's eyes flashed. "I heard. That man should be horsewhipped, rich or not."

Cole's lips curved. "I can always trust you to tell it the way it is, Mandy."

Jerry took another sip of his coffee, his expression relaxed. "Don't worry, Mandy, he's running out of gas. Even the circumstantial stuff isn't enough to do anything with. A little bird told me Sandoval's lawyer has already advised him to turn his focus elsewhere."

Cole took a sip of his own coffee, appreciating his deputy once again. Their friendship had evolved slowly and, as it did, his respect for the man increased. Jerry Landers might be ponderous and slow but there was solidity about him that Cole had come to rely on. He noticed things, little things that others missed. His suspicion that Allie's throat was slit by someone left-handed had been corroborated by several professionals and that alone had helped to eliminate Cole as a suspect.

Unfortunately, the same couldn't be said about his relationship with Jerry's son, Brian. The man still remained confrontational and defiant. He had refused to meet with Kat as well as Cole. Since they didn't have enough to bring him in, nothing had been accomplished in that direction. It was obvious he resented his father and Cole's friendship. He could see it in his eyes and in his demeanor.

His cell phone rang, interrupting his thoughts. He glanced down and eased away from the table. "Excuse me for a few. I've got to take this call."

"Problems?" Jerry asked, moving to rise.

"No. It's Dale Cowls. I asked him to notify me when he got the toxicology results from the autopsy back."

Jerry settled back, motioning to the coffee pot. "In that case, I think I'll have a piece of that apple pie up there and some more brew."

Cole answered as he moved outside. "Afternoon, Dale. Got something for me?"

"What I've got is proof your ex was loaded when she was murdered. Just got the final blood and alcohol levels back. She was well over the legal limit booze wise. On top of that she had cocaine in her system."

"Unfortunately that's not a surprise, Dale."

"Yeah, but the other results were."

"What other results?"

"The ones that confirm your ex-wife was about twelve weeks pregnant."

"What?"

"I know. Shocked the hell out of me."

Cole was silent for a moment, his mind racing. "Any chance

of a DNA match?"

"Take a while for that but we should be able to get one."

Cole ran a hand through his hair, frowning. "Allie pregnant? Something doesn't jive. God knows who the father might have been but I know for a fact she had no intention of having any more children."

"Accidents happen."

"Not that kind. Not to Allie. Only way she got pregnant was if she wanted to."

"You suggesting blackmail?"

"Could be. She might have been desperate enough to resort to something like that. It might also give us a suspect if we can find out who she was with."

"Then good luck. Got something else as well. Our backpack was sold between the years of 1991-1992. Special design by Nike for their commercials that year. Sold by most local as well as international vendors."

Cole waved absently at some people driving by. "Who sold it around here?"

"The big department stores in Birmingham as well as Tucker's in town."

"Then I'll see what we can come up with although after so many years our chances aren't the greatest."

"No, but I've got something else. We found hair in the zipper, and if you can come up with someone to match it, you just might have your killer. I've eliminated your ex as well as the old man."

"You've just earned your salary for the week, Dale. You keep working on your end and we'll see what we can come up with on ours."

"Will do."

Cole flipped his cell closed thoughtfully just as Jerry ambled out. "Give me a minute to pay the bill and I'll be right with you."

Jerry waved a hand. "I got it." He motioned to the phone. "Dale come up with anything?"

Cole filled him in as they walked to the squad car.

"Damn! Know anyone Allie was thick with recently?"

"No, but I'll be willing to bet Dallas or Sonya Sandoval might."

Jerry shook his head. "Approaching them isn't such a hot idea, Cole." He rested his weight against the side of the car. "Don't underestimate what those two are capable of, especially Dallas. Man throws his power around big time." His gaze found Cole's. "Rumor has it he has some strong arms on his payroll. Can't prove it but that's the talk. You're not one of his favorite people right now."

"I haven't been for a long time," Cole replied grimly, glancing at his watch. "I've got to get a move on. Liv is at Deanna's finishing up some school project."

Jerry opened the car door. "I'll drop you off at the station then. I've a mind to mosey on over to Tucker's and see what I can find out in that direction if that's okay with you."

Cole eyed him steadily. "You don't have to ask my permission, Jerry, you know that."

A faint hint of red tinged the older man's jaw. "Old habit I guess."

Cole was about to respond when Brian roared up beside them on his motorcycle. He was wearing a Harley logo on his shirt and no helmet. It wasn't hard for Cole to read the resentment in his eyes as he surveyed the two of them.

"Finished at the shop?" Jerry asked, his gaze moving from one man to the other.

"Yeah, about half an hour ago."

"Rough day?"

Brian shrugged, scowling. "What do you care?"

"I've always cared," Jerry said quietly.

"Pretty shitty way of showing it, getting thick with the enemy."

"Cole isn't the enemy, Brian. Don't you think it's time you let that chip on your shoulder fall off already?"

Brian's eyes shifted to the man standing calmly on the other side of the car. "Nah, I like that chip just fine." He revved his bike. "Just watch yourself, Cole. There are a lot of people around here who still aren't too sure you didn't have something to do with Allie's death. I sure as hell have my doubts."

The motorcycle sprang forward, just missing the car as he tore past them and disappeared around a curve in the road.

Jerry shook his head as he levered himself into the driver's side of the car. "Sorry about that, Cole. I'm fighting a losing battle with him, I think."

Cole silently agreed as he eased his long frame into the passenger seat. He wouldn't be at all surprised if Brian was fueling the fire that Dallas Sandoval had started. He was lucky the support of the town was on his side.

Jerry dropped him off in front of the station, waving as he drove away in the squad car. Cole checked with Betty and then headed for his car. His cell phone rang just as he started the engine.

"Cole, it's Deanna. We've got a minor crisis here. The plaster of Paris dried too soon and we had to go out and buy more. It'll be another hour or so before we're done. Okay if Liv stays for dinner and I'll bring her home around eight?"

"You want me to come over and help?"

"Lord no! As it is, I'm ready to strangle my darling daughter. I think there's more plaster on her than there is on the project. I've banished her to doing the report on the computer while Liv and I redo the mountains."

"Then I'll make a deal with you. I'll grab some hamburgers and fries and bring them over about six or so as long as Mike doesn't care about not eating homemade food. That way you won't have to drive her home."

"Mike would eat a burger and fries twenty-four seven," she said dryly. "Sounds great." She paused for a moment. "Liv's been kind of quiet lately."

Cole fought the now familiar anger. "I know it. She's still shook up about her mother's death and Dallas Sandoval sure didn't help things."

"What astounds me is how someone who has just lost his only child could be so vindictive. Accusing you in front of Liv was inexcusable no matter how upset he was."

Cole suddenly felt incredibly tired and fed up. "It's about time I deal with them face to face. I think now's as good a time as any since you're keeping Liv."

"Just be careful, Cole. I don't like those people."

"I will. See you in a few hours."

He backed out of the parking lot and headed north, determined to settle things once and for all with his ex-in-laws. Jerry and he were making slow progress in their investigations but he didn't appreciate Dallas Sandoval putting road blocks in their way. It was time to clear the air once and for all. He didn't hold much hope of getting through to the man, but at least they'd know where each other stood. He grimaced at his reflection in the rear view mirror, not looking forward to the confrontation.

Because he was lost in thought, it didn't register immediately that the car behind him was approaching at a high rate of speed. His gaze sharpened, a tingle of warning centering between his shoulder blades. He squinted behind his sunglasses, focusing on the license plate, memorizing it, frowning. He'd seen that plate before but he couldn't place where.

He was in a passing zone. However, the car made no move to go around but simply drew closer. He sped up slightly, testing, but the distance remained the same. His fingers tightened on the wheel. There was a large sharp curve ahead and unless he missed his guess there was a good chance his pursuer intended for him not to make that turn.

Grateful for the power and steering of the 'Vette, he increased his speed, once again hugging the center. There weren't many cars that traveled this road. Most people preferred the more direct route of the freeway. He sincerely hoped it stayed that way.

He glanced in the rear view mirror. The distance between the two cars had widened somewhat. He grabbed his phone.

"Betty, run license number BF2137 for me. ASAP."

"You caught me leaving, Cole," Betty said on the other end. "Give me a minute to reboot the computer. What's going on?"

"Got a black Pontiac GT tailing me toward Roaming Hills on Rt. 45. Two-door with a spoiler on the rear. Relatively new with a sun roof,and a raised hood."

"That sounds like Tanner Gordon's ride. You know, the Tanner that has been Brian Lander's cohort in crime since grade school."

"I know who he is," Cole said curtly, fighting to keep the car centered as the Pontiac began to gain on him again.

"And I was right. Car's registered to Tanner just like I thought."

"Thanks, Betty," he said, flipping the phone closed before she could respond. It was then his training kicked in. His hands were steady on the wheel as he babied the car around the first sweeping part of the curve, his eyes flicking to the mirror. He glanced at the speedometer. The needle was edging around eighty. He didn't dare go any faster, even though the sports car was handling the curve admirably. He glanced behind him again, watching the car careen around the start of the curve. The driver was having difficulty keeping it on the road as he skidded toward the edge and then overcorrected, skidding the other way.

Cole's eyes narrowed thoughtfully. It was time to see just how good a driver his pursuer really was. He waited until he eased the car around the second curve and was briefly out of eyesight. Quickly glancing both ways, he jerked the wheel hard and did a one eighty, fighting to keep the car steady. Just as he gained control, the GT came roaring around the curve. For a split second he caught sight of Tanner's shocked face as he whipped by him. He felt a momentary satisfaction that was quickly replaced by concern when he heard the sharp squeal of tires.

He hoped Gordon wasn't foolish enough to slam his brakes on going as fast as he was.

His fears were confirmed when the tires squealed again and kept right on squealing. Slowing, he spun the car around just in time to see the Pontiac's wheels catch the soft edge of the road, throwing dirt up in the air as it spun toward the guardrail.

He threw the 'Vette into park, praying the rail would hold. Jumping from the vehicle, he saw just a glimpse of Tanner Gordon's white face moments before there was a scream of metal against metal. Then, as if in slow motion, the car hurtled over the edge and into the valley below.

He called 911 before he even reached the torn rail, realizing it would do little good. The smoke from the blazing car was already making its way upward. Jaw tight, he ran back to his car and retraced his route, screeching to a stop minutes before the fire and ambulance arrived. It only took a few moments for them to put the fire out but Cole knew it was too late even before they dragged Tanner Gordon from the smoldering wreckage. It was more than likely the impact had killed the man before the fire.

Even though EMS worked on him for well over half an hour, it was obvious their attempts at resuscitation weren't going to work. Easing to his feet, one of them walked over to Cole, shaking his head. "Nothing we could do for him, Cole. You see the accident?"

"I did, Larry. He lost control on that big curve up there."

The fire chief turned back to survey the scene, wiping an arm over his brow and graying hair. "I knew that kid would end up dead the way he drove that car. Always was a speed demon."

They watched the body being lifted onto a gurney and the ambulance drive away, lights flashing without the noise of the siren.

"Does he have any family around here?" Cole asked.

"Only a mother that's in a nursing home in Bainbridge County. Last stages of Alzheimer's."

Cole notified the nursing home anyway and then called the local towing company. "Do me a favor, Larry, and tell them to tow what's left of the car to the impound lot until I have someone go over it. Make sure there wasn't any tampering with the brakes or steering."

"You got it."

It was another half an hour before things were cleared away and Cole was back in the 'Vette heading toward the Sandovals. His shoulders were tight with tension and the anger was a living thing inside of him. If Dallas Sandoval had anything to do with Tanner Gordon's ultimately fatal plan, he was going to haul him in for accessory to murder.

He drove into the long driveway and curved around the carefully landscaped yard, slamming the car into park. He climbed the steps to the impressive double front doors. Ringing the doorbell he waited, arms crossed, trying to keep his anger at bay.

A uniformed maid answered, her eyes widening as she

recognized him. "Mr. Collins, I don't think..."

"Who is it, Janie?" Sonya Sandoval called from the front room.

Cole moved passed the maid and into the foyer. "It's me, Sonya. We need to talk."

He had to admire how she hid the quick flash of irritation behind a façade of composure. She looked every inch the rich man's wife, dressed in linen pants and silk top, diamonds glistening at her ears and wrists, her blonde hair sleek and smooth. Her face was unlined and the expression haughty.

"I fail to see what we could possibly have to talk about, Cole. Don't you think you've done enough damage to this family?"

He leaned against the doorjamb. "Is that what you call yourselves? A family? Odd, that wouldn't be my choice of words."

The anger was there a little longer this time. "How dare you speak to me in such a manner!" She looked behind him at the maid who was nervously standing there, not sure what to do. "Get Mr. Sandoval, immediately."

"Excellent," Cole drawled, moving into the large room. It was decorated to perfection, each pillow and picture in perfect symmetry, giving it the look of an exquisitely designed museum with its white walls, white ceilings and lush white carpeting. He remained standing when Dallas Sandoval stormed in.

He wasn't a big man but there was steel gray in his hair and in his eyes and not an inch of fat on his disciplined body. He was ruthless and unbending and not afraid to use his wealth to get exactly what he wanted. Yet, for the brief time Cole had seen him at the funeral, he had also seen something else in the man's eyes. Grief, strong and violent grief. He just hoped that grief hadn't translated into being an accomplice to murder.

He strode up to Cole, eyes blazing. "Get the hell out of here, Collins!"

"Or what? You'll call the police?" Cole tossed back, moving to sit on one of the wing chairs by the fireplace and crossing his long legs casually. "I figure it's about time we had a heart to heart. After what happened today I know we do."

Dallas remained standing. "What are you talking about?"

"Tanner Gordon was just hauled away in an ambulance, dead. Seems he was interested in making sure I didn't make that big curve right before your house. I made it, he didn't."

"Shame, but what has that got to do with me?"

Cole eyed him silently for a long moment. Unless Sandoval was a very good actor, it appeared he had no idea why Gordon had been following him. "It's no secret you hate my guts, Dallas. It's also no secret that you wouldn't be above hiring someone to either put the fear of God in me or worse." He held the older man's gaze, his own unflinching. "If I find out you had anything to do with Gordon's high speed chase and death, I'll haul your ass in so fast you won't know what hit you."

"That's damned ridiculous," Dallas snapped. "You don't have a clue who you're dealing with, Collins. I don't like threats."

Cole stood, towering over him. "Oh, that wasn't a threat. That was a promise."

"Get out!"

"Not until I say what I've wanted to for a very long time now." Cole could feel the anger building, forced it back, knowing he would accomplish little by losing his temper.

"Did you have any idea how insecure Allie was? Why do you think she relied on the booze and the drugs? Because she craved the power, the strength that those substances gave her. What she really needed was your love but you were too busy to give it to her, weren't you?" He jabbed a finger toward Sonya who was sitting rigidly in her chair. "Both of you."

He saw nothing but hatred in Sonya's eyes but there was a flicker of something more in Dallas's.

"Dallas, tell him to leave!"

Cole smiled derisively. "That's the way you handle everything, don't you, Sonya? Ignore it and it will go away." His gaze slid back to her husband. "It's too late for recriminations now. Hell, I've got a whole load of my own to deal with. What matters is that I won't have you doing to Olivia what you did to her mother. I'm telling you right now to back off on the custody suit or my lawyer will start delving into things you just might not want made public."

Sonya stared at him, her blue eyes cold. "Your threats mean little. We loved our daughter, Cole. It was you that ignored her, left her alone so often that she came home crying. Now she's dead and it's your fault. Even if you didn't actually kill her, you might as well have."

Because the guilt was still there, her words stung. He nodded. "Maybe you're right, Sonya." He took a long deep breath. "Maybe I didn't love her enough."

"No." Dallas slumped onto the couch wearily. "I saw the signs. Saw her going downhill and I did nothing. We did nothing," he said, giving his wife a hard look. He rubbed a hand across his forehead, closing his eyes briefly. "No matter what you think, Cole, I loved my daughter. Now it's too damned late."

"Dallas, I can't believe you're saying such things," Sonya said furiously. "Allie was a vibrant, vital woman before you"—she pointed viciously at Cole—"came into her life. It's all your fault!"

"Allie was an addict," Dallas said flatly. "It's time to face facts, Sonya."

For a long moment she stared at him, her face a mask of fury and then she sagged against the back of the chair and began to sob. Dallas jerked as if he'd been struck and then moved to comfort her.

"No! Don't touch me!" she spat, eyes swimming. She lifted a trembling hand to swipe at the tears streaming down her cheeks, their wet path ruining the perfectly made-up face. "You know that's not true!"

"You know that it is," he countered. A muscle flickered at the base of his throat. "Cole's right. We were too damn busy to notice and when we did, we denied what was obvious."

Surging to her feet, she shook her head violently. "That's a lie!" She shoved past him and out of the room but not before Cole saw the pain in her eyes.

Dallas sighed, looking back at Cole. "She hasn't cried since Allie died. I guess she needs to."

Cole's gaze was steady. "I didn't kill her, Dallas."

"I know that." He rubbed his eyes wearily. "You're a man of principle, Cole. I believed that when you married Allie and I believe that now." His expression grew tighter. "It's a pretty pathetic man who blames someone else for his own faults."

For the first time, Cole felt a kindred spirit to the man standing in front of him. "We all make mistakes," he said quietly. "Allie loved both of you in her own way but the addictions became her life."

"I should have been more proactive. Should have put her in damned rehab."

Cole shook his head. "You're not alone in the blame. I lived with her, slept with her and yet I ignored those things as well." He moved to the front door and then turned. "I want you to be part of Liv's life, Dallas. She needs her grandparents."

He saw the hint of tears, of pain. It was a long moment before Dallas spoke, his voice husky. "I appreciate that, Cole. God knows there's not much of a relationship there right now."

"Then work on it."

A small fire lit the older man's eyes. "Is that an order?"

"No, just a request."

Cole put a hand out and, after a small hesitation, Dallas took it. "We've got some issues to deal with but I think we can sort them out."

"Agreed."

"There's one more thing I need to ask you, Dallas. Do you know if Allie was involved with anyone recently?"

"Why?"

Cole debated and then opted for honesty. "Because she was about three months pregnant when she was killed."

"Christ!" Dallas swore softly. "You sure about this?"

Cole nodded.

"She didn't keep us informed of her love life but I do know she flew out of town several times to meet someone. I took her to the airport myself on a few occasions."

"Any idea of the destination?"

"Not off hand." Dallas's gaze shot to Cole's. "You're not thinking she was murdered because of the pregnancy?"

"That's a possibility but I doubt it. What plays better is that the killer was her supplier. She didn't pay and he made her pay."

Dallas's eyes dulled. "Not something I want to think about right now."

Cole opened the door. "You straight with me about not having any dealings with Tanner Gordon?"

Dallas nodded. "Never even talked to the man." His jaw tightened. "I might be an unscrupulous businessman, Cole, but the rumors are false about me doing things illegally. I don't operate that way."

"That's all I need to know."

Gray eyes met green. "We did love her, Cole. Believe it."

"I do." He walked out onto the porch and then impulsively turned back. "Liv turns nine on December twenty-fourth. Why don't you come over for Christmas Eve? I think she'd like that."

Dallas smiled sadly. "I'll run it by Sonya."

"Good."

Cole walked down the elegant steps to his car, unable to resist a glance backward. Dallas Sandoval still stood in the open doorway, his features in the shadow. He started the engine and drove away, his heart heavy, feeling the older man's pain, acknowledging it.

&)

Much later, as he was warming some milk for hot chocolate, Olivia wandered into the kitchen dressed in her pajamas.

"Daddy, can I ask you something?"

He turned the burner on the stove off and nodded. "Of course you can, love." He poured the steaming milk into matching mugs and carried them over to the table, waiting until she slid into the chair across from him.

She looked so very serious, he thought. It was a look he had seen entirely too often since Allie's funeral. She took a sip of her chocolate and primly set the cup down, her big green eyes finding his.

"Why did Grandfather Sandoval blame you for killing Mommy?"

He didn't answer immediately, trying to choose his words with care. She didn't give him the chance.

"Kat says it's because even if they didn't know it they loved Mommy very much, and sometimes when you love someone that much and something happens to them you want to find someone else to blame. Is that right?"

Thank God for Kat, he thought gratefully. "She's exactly right, Liv. Grandma and Grandpa are very sad right now, just like I would be if something were to happen to you."

She put her small hand on his, her sweet face earnest. "Sometimes at night I wake up and I try to miss her, Daddy. I really do. But I can't."

Good Lord, he thought, how do I handle this one?

"Kat says Mommy loved me in her own way but that she wasn't thinking right because she was drinking and doing those drugs. She told me not to worry about not feeling sad but that I should say a prayer for her every night instead." She smiled angelically. "I've been doing that and I feel better."

"Come here, munchkin," he said gruffly. She moved around the table and he lifted her onto his lap, hugging her close. "I love you, sweetheart. Very, very much and I promise you I'll always try to be the best father I can possibly be."

She smiled, her dimples deepening. "I know that." She looked up at him, the expression on her face changing, growing sly as she took another sip of her chocolate. "Tiffany says that girls our age need a mother figure, someone to talk to about clothes and makeup and stuff. She says Daddies aren't very good at that kind of thing."

Trust Tiffany, he thought in amusement.

"So..." she hedged.

"So what?"

"So don't you think it's about time you ask Kat to marry you?" She scooted off his lap excitedly. "I know she'd say yes. It'd be so cool to have her for my mom."

He grinned, tapping her nose. "Are you trying to manage your father's love life, young lady?"

"Tiffany says someone has to," she said pertly as she wrapped her arms around his neck. "You could get married on my birthday right before Christmas."

He stood with her in his arms and tickled her until she was giggling helplessly.

"You tell your friend she's next if she keeps sticking her nose where it doesn't belong," he said, easing her to the floor and spinning her toward the stairway.

She scooted around the table still giggling and then turned. "Just promise me you'll think about it?"

He shook a finger at her. "I'll consider it. Now off to bed. You've got school tomorrow."

She took a few more sips of her chocolate, her eyes alight with excitement, and then flew around the table and into his arms. "I love you, Daddy," she said breathlessly, whispering a kiss along his jaw.

He watched her fly up the stairs, his chest tight with emotion. His memories of Allie weren't good but he would always be grateful to her for giving him his daughter. She could easily have made a different choice when she had discovered she was pregnant.

He leaned against the counter morosely, his thoughts going back to when they had first been married. He remembered those few months when both of them were enthralled with each other, in love with being in love. She had been enchantingly beautiful and, because things were going the way both of them had wanted them to go at the time, life had been good. The sex had been great, the candlelight dinners in expensive restaurants romantic and reality was something neither of them wanted any part of. He, because he'd seen enough ugliness and pain overseas, and Allie simply had continued to live in the ivory tower her parents had erected for her. Both of them had been so young and so unprepared for how totally opposite they really were.

He slowly walked back to the table and took a sip of the chocolate, grimacing at the cool taste, his thoughts dark and bittersweet. She had looked incredibly beautiful on their wedding day, the ravages of the alcohol and drugs not yet taking their toll. Before he could prevent it, another memory surfaced, one he'd had nightmares about since that night. Over and over he saw her sprawled on his garage floor, that golden hair stained with blood, the look on her face one of total shock and horror.

It was then he did something he hadn't been able to do for weeks. He lowered his face to his hands and, for the first time, shed tears for the mother of his child. He grieved not for the woman she had become but for the one he married. In his heart he knew she deserved that much.

Chapter Twelve

"Finally," Kat sighed, sliding into her desk and pushing the hair back from her damp forehead. "I think that's the last of it."

The tall, thin brunette across the room stacked another box and nodded. "I'll move these into Jack's office tomorrow."

"I'm going to miss you, Jenny," Kat said, smiling up at her secretary.

"I'll bet I miss you more," the girl replied, her long dangling earrings swinging as she shook her head. "I'm not so sure about this new partner you and Dan hired. She's just a little too high maintenance for me."

Kat laughed. "Come on, Jen. Just because she likes bottled water instead of the drinking fountain and certain kinds of coffee doesn't make her high maintenance."

"No, but demanding I keep her cup separate from the men's does."

"Don't worry, you'll whip her into shape before the month is out."

It was Jennifer's turn to laugh. "I'm serious though, Kat. Things won't be the same around here without you." Her eyes grew dreamy. "Of course, if I was moving home to be with that hunk of a policeman of yours, I'd be out of here pronto too."

"Is this a girl thing or can I join in?" Jack said from behind them.

Kat grinned, stretching her legs out on one of the boxes. "Of course you can come in, Jack. Just don't stumble over the mess."

"I've got some work to do myself," Jennifer said, smiling at Jack. "By the way," she continued slyly, "speaking of love lives, how are things going with yours?"

Kat hid a grin at the hint of red that always tinted Jack's face when he was asked about his relationship with Alicia Keenan. She knew things were getting serious and she was happy for both of them.

"Actually, they are going rather well. So well, in fact, that she accepted my ring last night."

"Jack, that's wonderful!" Kat said, jumping to her feet to give him a big hug. "Congratulations!"

Happiness shone from his eyes. "To tell you the truth, I was shaking like a damn leaf when I popped the question. I'm pretty lucky."

"I think she's the lucky one," Kat responded sincerely. "You're a great catch in my opinion, Jack Steinman."

"So when's the wedding?" Jennifer asked, stacking another box.

"Believe it or not, she doesn't want anything fancy so we're getting married next month in Boston where her family is from. I already called my side and they're okay with that."

Jennifer propped the door open as she grabbed two of the boxes nearest to her. "Just let me know when it is because I definitely want to buy a new outfit." She lifted a brow. "Assuming we're invited?"

"You are."

"Good, because I've always wanted to see Boston. All those preppy men with their sexy accents." She tossed a look over her shoulder. "On second thought, maybe I'll buy two or three of those outfits. I'm dropping these on the floor in your office, Jack. Let me know what you think needs to be filed elsewhere," she finished as she breezed out.

Kat laughed up at Jack. "Her life is clothes first with men a close second." She walked over to the portable fridge in the corner and pulled out two Cokes, offering him one. "Any ideas on the honeymoon?"

"Actually we're thinking cruise. Maybe one of those Windjammers or something."

"Ask Dan about that," Kat said, taking a long appreciative sip. "He and his parents were on one about a month ago. He might know the ins and outs of the best way to book."

"Not a bad idea." He glanced around the room. "Amazing what can accumulate over a decade, isn't it?" His gaze moved back to Kat. "Going to miss it?"

She shrugged. "Probably for a little while. The pace in Brookdale is just a little slower." A loud horn sounded outside followed by cursing loud enough to echo into the room through the closed window. Grinning up at him, she motioned outside. "That's probably an understatement. It's a lot slower."

He put a hand under her chin and tipped it up to study her face. "You sure about this move, Kat?"

"Positive." She squeezed his fingers lightly. "Besides, you're not the only one who has a love life."

He grinned, lifting her left hand. "I don't see a ring there yet."

"Not all of us need a ring to commit," she said loftily.

He shook his head. "Tell that to someone who doesn't know you. You can handle the big city personae, Kat, but underneath all of that there's still a woman who wouldn't mind having the white picket fence at the end of the day."

"Now *you* I'm going to miss," she murmured, touching his cheek lightly, true affection in her voice.

He captured her hand, his expression serious. "I like your Cole, Kat. He's the kind of man you need. Someone who will keep you on your toes, challenge you."

She raised a brow. "And you got all of this from one dinner at a restaurant?"

"Hey, you're the one who taught me to fine tune my instincts. He's a good guy, Kat." He moved to the window that framed a sweeping view of the city. "Are you going to set up shop in your hometown?"

"I haven't finalized anything yet but I think I will. The only lawyer in town is a tax attorney so there's a need. I'm ready to slow down, Jack. I've done the high pressure stuff and enjoyed it." She smiled up at him. "Now I'm leaving that to you and Dan."

Jack's expression changed. "You know he isn't thrilled about your decision."

She sighed. "I know and I feel badly about that considering I was the one who encouraged him to join me here in the first place."

"He'll survive," Jack said lightly. "Between you and me I think he's just a little bit intimidated by our new associate."

Kat lifted a brow. "You're kidding?"

He shook his head. "She's a lot less subtle than you, Kat." His lips curved. "I'm thinking that might not be such a bad thing Don't get me wrong. Dan's a hell of an attorney but he likes to run the show. Delegate, if you know what I mean. I've got a feeling she might take exception to that eventually."

Kat took another sip of her Coke, eying him thoughtfully. "Then I'm glad you're as easy going as you are, Jack. If what you say is true, you're going to be the mediator."

He shrugged. "Been there done that before."

She nodded. "I don't doubt it."

Jennifer popped her head in the room. "Phone, Kat."

"Thanks, Jen." She moved some papers and found her portable. "Send it in here, will you."

"Sure thing."

Moments later, the phone beeped.

"Hello?"

"You don't listen very well, do you?"

She could feel the color drain from her face at the now very familiar voice. "I beg your pardon?"

"I warned you to keep your nose out of things that don't concern you. Now it's too late. For you and for that lover of yours. You should have listened, Katarina. You really should have."

"Who the hell are you, damn it?"

The only response was a dial tone. She clicked the disconnect button numbly.

"Kat, are you all right?" Jack asked. When she didn't answer, his expression changed. "It's him again, isn't it?"

She nodded, taking just a moment to gather herself. When

she turned to him, there was fury in her expression and determination in her eyes. "This has gone on long enough." She grabbed the phone and put up a finger for Jack to wait.

"Let me speak to Chief McCreary," she demanded impatiently, waiting until she was connected.

"Chief, this is Katarina Ramon. I just received another one of those phone calls. This has got to stop. If you can't find this nutcase, then find someone who can. Good, I'll be there. See you soon."

She disconnected the call. "I've just about had it with the threats, Jack, and to be honest, I'm beginning to get spooked and I don't spook easily. This guy knows too much about me, about my home life, my hometown."

"A dissatisfied client?"

"No such luck. The calls are always regarding the investigation I told you about in Brookdale." She frowned. "What bothers me is that the voice sounds familiar although it's disguised. At first I even thought it was Adam Frank but that doesn't make any sense."

"Maybe it does, Kat. That's actually why I stopped by. Got a call from someone I know at the minimum-security prison Frank was incarcerated at. Our crazy friend was released last week to a halfway house. According to my friend, the shrinks are convinced he's on his way to recovery."

Kat groaned. "That's just terrific. You've got to love our system. Someone who kills a cat is set up for more time than a man who committed murder."

"Can't disagree with you on that point. Maybe I'm just naïve enough to think I can change that."

She smiled. "No, I'm just becoming more and more jaded. That's probably why this move works for me."

He took one of her hands in his own. "Just be careful, Kat. Those calls might not be from Frank but he poses a threat if he violates probation and leaves the area. I hear anything about that and you're the first person I call." He shook his head. "Remember, he's smart and he's an expert with computers. It wouldn't take much for him to dig up what he needed to threaten you. Maybe even hack into the phone system to find your private numbers. He's pathological no matter what the psychiatrists say. I saw the look in his eyes just like you did."

She squeezed his fingers reassuringly. "Chief McCreary says he has something for me regarding those threatening phone calls so maybe our friend will be behind bars again before he knows it." She bent to grab her purse and keys. "I hope so because enough is enough. Things are moving forward at home, Jack, and I think whoever this person is knows that. Used to be they were just mild warnings. Now they're much more threatening. What I really want to know is how it is he finds me. I've changed cell phone numbers, my home is unlisted but still the calls keep coming." She slid into her coat, shouldering her purse. "I'm ready to bring in the FBI if something isn't done soon, no matter whose feathers that ruffles."

"I'm all for that," Jack said, lifting two of the remaining four boxes. "Call me before you leave, will you? Alicia and I would like to treat you to dinner."

"That sounds great. I've got a flight out day after tomorrow so how about tomorrow evening?"

"I'll make reservations at Santini's. I know it's one of your favorites."

She reached up to brush a kiss along his jaw, smiling her thanks. "Just call me with the time and I'll be there."

She waved to Jennifer as she walked out. She made her way down the hallway to the plush lobby with its thick carpet and leather chairs. Classical music was discreetly playing in the background, softening the ring of the phone at the receptionist's desk. She looked around with fresh eyes, feeling a rush of satisfaction at what she had accomplished over the past ten years. There were things she was going to miss about this city. Things like the constant motion, the excitement, the ethnic variety, even the sidewalk hot dog vendors. It was a hard place to succeed in and she had done just that. She'd bow out gracefully, leaving room for another young, hard-headed attorney to push his or her way to the top.

Pushing open the glass door, she walked out into the brisk late October day, pulling her collar closer around her, grateful for its warmth. There was a hint of snow in the air and the newly hung Christmas decorations along the bustling street made the walk to the police station festive. The wind played with her hair and tinted her cheeks a rosy pink as she took her time window-shopping, her thoughts straying to Cole and Olivia. She missed both of them. She had managed brief trips home, and each time it took everything in her to say goodbye. Soon she wouldn't have to.

The precinct was a madhouse as usual when she walked in. The air was thick with smoke, noise and the occasional swear word. A man, a hood over his head and eyes downcast, was led past her in handcuffs. A leggy brunette leaned against the wall, a cigarette balanced between her bright red nails. Her thigh-high skirt, tight top and heels proclaimed the costume of her trade.

Kat stopped, raising a brow. "Arrested again, Julie?"

The sultry look the girl gave her didn't fool Kat. The kid was barely twenty and her background was ugly like so many of the prostitutes that made a living on the streets. Abuse, incest, drugs, it was a common theme. One she wished she had some power to change. It was a goal she felt strongly about which was why she had offered her services gratis to some of these girls over the years. Julie had been a pretty teenager when she had been arrested the first time. The stunning face had only grown more attractive over time but the expression hadn't nor had her lifestyle.

Maybe she couldn't cure all ills but she might be able to help with this one, she thought. Reaching in her purse, she unzipped her wallet and handed the girl a business card.

"What's this?" Julie asked, blowing a puff of smoke in her direction, just a hint of curiosity in the startling aqua eyes.

"The number of a modeling scout I know. I left word on the street for you to call me. You haven't."

The girl shrugged, taking another puff of her cigarette. "What's the use?"

"You want to stay on the strip, that's your business," Kat said briskly. "I just hate to see beauty and talent thrown away." She pointed to the card. "My friend likes your look. He thinks you've got potential." She began walking away. "Of course, he won't know that until he sees you in person. Only so much you can glean from a mug shot and your vital stats."

"Hey, wait a minute." Julie grabbed her arm, spinning her

back. "You're not serious about this?"

Kat met her gaze steadily. "I am."

The girl's eyes went from her to the card and back again. "He really thinks I might have something?"

"He does. Don't wait too long to grab that brass ring though, Julie. He's a busy man, so if you don't want to take the chance, then let him know up-front. It's a tough business so there's a good chance you won't make a go of it anyway."

"Says who?" the girl shot back, eyes flashing resentfully.

Kat grinned. "That's the spirit. Now go pay whatever fine you have to and see the man." She glanced at the high heels and length of leg. "What I wouldn't give for those pair of legs and that color of eyes." She moved to the side as a couple in a heated argument strode passed her. "Good luck," she said, rolling her eyes as she began walking down the corridor.

"Hey."

Kat turned back, waiting for the girl to walk up to her, seeing just a touch of vulnerability play across her face.

"Thanks."

"You're welcome." Kat laid a hand briefly on the girl's arm. "The rest is up to you."

Don McCreary motioned for her to come in when she knocked on the open door of his office. He was a tall, thin man with dark hair and a no-nonsense demeanor. They had crossed paths many times in the past and she liked the man. Liked that in the toughest precinct around, he had managed to keep from becoming jaded like so many in his field. He demanded respect and got it from those he worked with.

He motioned toward the hallway. "I overheard the conversation. Still not giving up on lost causes, I see."

She took a seat across from him. "I'm hoping she isn't one yet. We'll see."

"We've got a few things on your stalker. The calls are being made from a cell phone. Unfortunately, it's a track phone and they're a hell of a lot harder to trace. What we do know is they have been made locally, somewhere in the city."

Kat frowned. "That's odd, because the call I just received this morning referred to an ongoing murder investigation in my hometown. One I'm personally, not professionally, involved with."

"Which brings me to the second piece of information I have for you. It's a very good possibility Adam Frank could be making those phone calls. He's being monitored at a halfway house but is being eased back into the work force. He's wearing an ankle bracelet, but that doesn't stop him from making a phone call from his place of employment."

Kat's eyes narrowed angrily. "That's just terrific. Find any evidence he bought a phone like that?"

"No, but that doesn't exclude someone purchasing it for him. I've already got a man reviewing the calls from his desk space, but so far nothing."

"For two cents, I'd confront him myself. I've entertained that thought for quite a while."

He shook his head. "You know better than that, Kat. He's smart enough to sic his lawyer on you for harassment. Besides, you've got nothing on him at this point."

"So what are you going to do about this?"

He sighed, leaning back in his chair. He rubbed a hand over his jaw. "Listen, Katarina, we're doing what we can with the people I've got at my disposal. I'm not taking this lightly, but until we can find something to tie Frank into all of this, we'll just have to bide our time."

"It could be someone else."

He nodded. "It could."

Kat stood, not satisfied. "I've got some contacts with the Feds. You have any objections to me talking to them?"

"Nope. Go for it." He stood as well. "Calls getting more threatening?"

"They are and I don't like it," she said honestly. "Frank isn't the first stalker to resort to violence and I don't intend to become another victim."

"Just know we're working on it at our end." He eased back in his chair. "I hear you're heading back to Alabama permanently."

"I am. Day after tomorrow."

"Then that's a good thing. Smaller town means easier

protection. Rumor has it you've got yourself a big, strong cop to do that."

She raised a brow. "I'm surprised at you, Chief. Since when do you keep track of other people's love interests?"

"Since half the men in this place have a crush on you. They've been moping around since they heard the news."

Kat laughed. "I don't think so but thanks for the boost to my ego anyway."

He stood, extending a hand and grasping hers in a firm handshake. "I'll miss you," he said sincerely and then smiled teasingly. "At least I'll get more production out of my officers now that you won't be distracting them."

"Thanks, I think," she tossed back. "You have my cell phone number. Once I'm settled, I'll give you my home one as well. Keep in touch."

"I will. Good luck."

She could feel him watching her as she walked out. Although he was a good deal older than she was, it wasn't hard to feel the same age when it came to experience, she thought. Both of them knew the thrill of those early days when ideology was the driving force. She glanced around the crowded, noisy surroundings. At the drunks, the prostitutes, the arguing couples. This was the reality of it all. You did your best and found a way not to let the ones you couldn't help get to you.

And yet, even as sure as she was about her decision to leave, she would miss all of this. She turned for a last glimpse and spied McCreary still standing at the door. Blowing him a kiss that she knew would cause some ribbing from those who dared, she jauntily lifted her hand in a salute. Shaking a finger at her, his lips curving reluctantly, he waved back.

She walked outside again, her heart just a little lighter. As she made her way back to the office, her thoughts sifted through the last minute things she had to take care of.

That night and the next day flew by as she dealt with arranging for her furniture and a fair amount of her personal items to be put in storage. She also spoke with her real estate broker finalizing things for the sale of her condo. She would contact a moving company to transfer her belongings once she decided where that would be.

Jack had called her with the reservation time. By evening, she was more than ready to take a break. She took a long, hot shower and then put on her favorite black dress and heels, slipping into her fur coat. She was grateful for its warmth when she walked out to the waiting taxi, the crisp fall air chilling her cheeks.

Her cell phone rang just as she settled in the back seat. Hating the fact that her heart pounded every time it went off, she glanced at the number and relaxed.

"Evening, Cole."

"I miss you," he said, his deep voice calming her as nothing else could.

"I'll be home tomorrow."

"Everything okay?"

She debated on whether to tell him about the most recent phone call and then decided against it. "Just wrapping up last minute stuff. I'm on my way to dinner with Jack and Alicia. He proposed yesterday and she accepted."

"Good for him. Looks like all of us are biting the bullet."

"Stick it, cop," she said, laughing into the phone. "Dan is joining us, as well as our new associate. I've got a feeling she'll keep Jack and Dan on their toes."

"Is that a good thing?"

"Don't know yet. She's a competent attorney, that I do know. How's Liv?"

"Missing you as well. She and Tiffany are already plotting our wedding."

"Don't you mean planning?"

"Come on, you know Tiff. They're plotting."

Suddenly, out of the blue, she felt the hair on the back of her neck rising. She glanced behind her and saw nothing other than a mass of car lights blurring together. Her fingers tightened on the phone.

"Kat, you there?"

"I'm here. I just wish you were."

"Me to," he drawled, his deep voice sexy with suggestion. "If I were, you wouldn't be going to dinner."

She laughed, the images his words brought making her forget her unease. "Give Liv my love and I'll see you tomorrow afternoon."

"I'll be there waiting."

She disconnected the call just as the taxi slid to a stop in front of the restaurant. She stepped out of the car, noting the appreciative look the driver gave her long legs. Her lips curved as she gave him a larger than normal tip. She'd needed that lift.

"Thanks, lady!"

She smiled. "You're welcome."

The smile disappeared abruptly as she mounted the steps to the restaurant, that feeling sliding over her again. She stopped and turned, scanning the street and seeing nothing. Impatient with herself, she spun back and briskly made her way inside. She was being ridiculous! Yet...

Alicia and Jack were already seated when she joined them. Even with the dim lighting of the restaurant, the glow surrounding the two of them was unmistakable. Alicia had her hand on Jack's, the diamond solitaire on her finger catching what little light there was.

Kat didn't sit but moved around the table and hugged Alicia. "Congratulations. Jack told me the news yesterday."

"Thank you," Alicia said quietly, happiness making her even more beautiful.

Kat lifted Alicia's hand to the light, admiring the ring. "The man has taste, I see."

"Of course," Alicia responded, glancing at the man at her side. "After all, he chose me."

Kat moved to the other side of the table, laughing. "Evening, Jack."

"Evening, Kat," he responded, moving to stand just as the waiter appeared and pulled her chair out. He settled back, smiling. "You look damned good for someone who's been running around all day."

She winked at Alicia. "Why thank you, kind sir! You're lucky your fiancée knows I don't have any designs on you or she might take exception to that comment."

The other woman's smile was serene. "No, I'd simply

scratch your eyes out," she said and then ruined the drawling response by laughing.

Jack poured a glass of wine from the carafe on the table and handed it to Kat. "I have to admit I kind of like that thought."

Alicia gave him a shove but refrained from responding when she caught sight of a woman walking toward them. "I believe your new associate has arrived."

Kat followed her gaze. Candace Knott wasn't pretty in a classical sense but she had a presence about her that exuded confidence. She wore her dark hair short, stylishly cut to accent her big brown eyes and rather angular face. Her slacks and tailored jacket flattered her thin build, accentuating her slender waist and narrow hips. Kat had been impressed with her immediately but Dan had been slower to come around. In the end she had prevailed and the woman had been hired. She had observed her in court on several occasions and was very impressed.

"Evening, everyone," Candace said, slipping into one of the seats. "Sorry I'm late but my client and I had a celebratory drink." A flicker of triumph lit her eyes. "He was acquitted."

"Congratulations," Jack said, doling out another glass of the Merlot.

She took an appreciative sip and then turned to Kat. "You look very relaxed. It's obvious you don't have any reservations about this change."

Kat shook her head, smiling. "Not a single one, Candace. Especially now that I feel I'm leaving Jack and Dan with a very competent partner."

"I'm glad you feel that way," the other woman said ruefully, "because I'm not so sure Dan is convinced of that just yet."

Probably because you won't let him get away with what I did, Kat thought.

She hadn't realized how much weight she had shouldered in the practice until she had eased back. Before they hired Candace, Dan had become increasingly moody and irritated and she had a feeling he wasn't happy with the sudden increase in workload. On top of that, even though he hadn't said anything, she could tell he was still somewhat upset about her leaving. He wasn't exactly thrilled about her relationship with Cole as well. He had joined Jack and Alicia and herself for dinner the weekend Cole had flown to New York. Although he and Cole had appeared to get along well enough, afterward the easy friendship they had enjoyed wasn't there. She regretted that but she had a feeling it wouldn't take long once Candace became more comfortable in her new position for him to return to his normal easygoing self.

"Speaking of Dan," Candace said, "he just walked in."

"Damn cold night out there," he said as he joined them, rubbing his hands together. He ordered a martini from the hovering waiter. Pulling a chair out, his glance slid to Candace and Kat saw his jaw tighten. "I thought you told me you weren't going to be able to make it tonight."

She didn't back down but met his gaze squarely. "As luck would have it, my client was acquitted rather quickly so here I am."

"I'm so glad," Alicia said smoothly, "because we want to take this opportunity to tell you Jack and I are getting married."

Amid the congratulations, Kat ordered a bottle of champagne to toast the engaged couple and then talk became general as they waited for their entrees.

"How did court go today?" Kat asked Dan. He looked every inch the well-heeled attorney, she thought. The Armani suit was perfectly cut, the Rolex on his wrist shining as he reached for a roll and buttered it before answering. He hadn't always been as worried about his appearance. Those first few years he'd spent more time in his jeans than a suit. He'd worked harder back then as well, almost at a frenzied pace. So had she. She sighed quietly. Things never stayed the same and maybe that was a good thing. Her thoughts returned to the present when he answered her question.

"Not well. Rachel Browning is as guilty as hell. She knows it and I know it and I've got a bad feeling the jury knows it as well," he admitted. "She carved her husband up for the money. Prosecutor's got a damn good case."

"What's your angle?" Jack asked.

"No witnesses. No fingerprints and no bloody clothes." He shook his head. "To tell the truth, I kind of admire the lady. The circumstantial evidence is fairly damning, but if the jury sticks to the facts, it's going to be hard to convict her on that alone."

Kat felt a twinge of irritation. "If you thought she was guilty, Dan, why did you take the case? You know my feelings on that subject."

He gave her an impatient look. "Because she's loaded and didn't bat an eyelash when I doubled my normal fee, that's why. Since I'm the senior partner now, my philosophy has changed slightly. Frankly, I don't believe in kicking a gift horse in the mouth." He paused, obviously seeing her reaction to his words. "Hell, I'm sorry, Kat. That was totally off-base."

She shrugged off the hurt. "I guess I can't take offense at the truth."

"How are things going on that case you're involved with in your hometown?" Candace asked, tactfully moving the conversation in another direction.

"Moving along, Candace," she replied, deliberately turning away from Dan and smiling at the other woman. "Although I'm not acting in a professional capacity at this point. I do know Cole was eliminated as a suspect in his ex-wife's murder. Several experts ascertained that the knife wound in her neck was inflicted by someone left-handed."

"How in the world did they make that determination?" Alicia asked curiously.

"From the angle and depth of the wound. According to several forensic specialists, it would have been totally unnatural for someone who is right-handed to have moved the knife in that direction."

"Do they have any suspects?" Dan asked, loosening his tie.

"Not yet, but Cole firmly believes my parents' murders are connected to the others," she said coolly, her gaze moving back to him. "Dale Cowls found a hair in the backpack I told you about. Now that they have DNA, all we need is a suspect. We find the right one and we'll have our killer."

Dan took another sip of his martini. "You're not talking about the same Dale Cowls who used to drive his four-wheeler through the corn just for kicks?"

She smiled at the memory. "It appears he's settled down a bit. Has a wife, kids and is, according to Cole, very good at what he does." She leaned back as the waiter placed a sizzling steak in front of her, smiling her thanks. She waited until everyone was served and then continued the conversation. "What's even more shocking is that Allie Sandoval was about three months pregnant when she was killed."

Candace forked her linguine and closed her eyes briefly, clearly savoring the delicious flavor. "Lord, that's good. Any idea who the father is?"

"No, but the lab sent cells from the fetus for DNA. They should have the results very soon. If they find the man that matches it, my guess is he will have some very serious questions to answer."

"What makes Cole think whoever the father was has anything to do with these murders?"

"He says there is no way Allie got pregnant unless she wanted to which means we're probably talking blackmail."

"I can't imagine someone being cold enough to use an innocent unborn child as the means for something so ugly," Alicia said, shuddering.

Dan shook his head. "Come on, Kat. What was she going to do? Sue the guy for more child support? Unless the father was some bigwig or married that doesn't constitute a motive for murder."

"It does if she knew something and already had him on a string."

"Sounds like you suspect that's the case?" Jack observed.

"Cole does." She cut another piece of steak and smiled apologetically at Alicia. "Sorry. You get a bunch of lawyers together and inevitably shop talk sneaks in. Now, why don't you tell us more about the plans for your wedding?"

They ended the evening with everyone more relaxed, the earlier discord forgotten. Jack and Alicia said their goodnights, deciding to walk to Jack's apartment.

Dan raised a brow. "Hiking almost half a mile in sub-zero weather? They must be in love."

Kat laughed as a cab pulled up. "Care to join us in the taxi?" she asked Candace as she slid in the seat and Dan followed.

"No thanks," she declined, smiling. "I'm meeting friends for after-dinner drinks at Cromwell's." She bent down to catch Kat's eye. "If I don't see you before you leave, Kat, good luck and keep in touch. I promise I'll do my best to fill your shoes."

"I know you will, Candace. Good night."

Dan slid his arm along the back of the seat, glancing out the window at the woman's retreating figure. "She isn't you," he said dryly.

"She's good, Dan. Just give her a chance to get her feet wet and I have a feeling she'll fit right in."

"If you say so."

She was feeling pleasantly full and warm in the darkness of the cab and didn't feel like arguing with him so she let it go. "I'm going to miss you, Dan. We've had some good times, haven't we?"

"We have," he murmured, fingering a blonde curl. "I remember how small town and innocent I was when I first arrived. I guess I can admit it now but you damned near terrified me when I arrived and saw you at work."

She smiled. "Come on, Dan. You had about as much experience as I had at the time."

"Yes, but yours was in the big city. I was practicing in a small town near Birmingham. We were worlds apart."

She turned to look up at him. "I never would have been as successful without your help, Dan. I might have had the experience but you brought back the familiarity I had been missing. That touch of the South I hadn't realized I longed for." She glanced at the diamond ring winking on his finger and the expensive watch. "Now you're the big city lawyer and I'm headed the other way." She put a hand on his arm. "I owe you more than I can tell you, Dan, and now you owe it to yourself to give your new partners a chance to do what you did for me."

The cab stopped and Dan leaned forward, asking the driver to wait for a moment while he walked her up to her apartment. They rode the elevator in a relaxed silence, which continued until they stood in front of her door.

"I'll say goodbye now, Kat," he said, his brown eyes serious as he looked down at her. "Care to kiss a former partner for old time's sake?"

"No, but I'll kiss an old friend who I hope makes a point of visiting often," she responded, standing on tiptoe to press her lips to his.

The kiss was quick and easy. She sighed as she wrapped her arms around his neck. "Be happy, old friend."

He kissed her forehead and backed away. "Night, Kat."

She leaned against the door and watched him walk away, her eyes filling with tears. Why did change have to be so darned painful sometimes? Unlocking the door, she tossed her keys on the table and slipped out of her shoes. Stretching, she moved to the bedroom and stripped, hanging her dress in the closet and grabbing her favorite robe.

It suddenly occurred to her that she wouldn't be here much longer, that her entire life was about to change dramatically. She walked to the big front window, enjoying the view as she always did. The city spread before her, sparkling like diamonds, and she leaned her forehead against the coolness of the glass.

Am I doing the right thing walking away from all of this? From my associates, my work, the life I've known for ten years?

A vision of Cole and Olivia flashed in front of her. That quickly she had her answer. None of this meant anything without the two of them.

Yawning, she washed off her makeup and climbed into bed, suddenly exhausted. She relaxed, fluffing up her pillow as she turned on her side.

"Katarina, it's too late. I warned you but you wouldn't listen..."

She shot straight up in bed, heart pounding. She reached for the lamp with shaking hands. The warm glow immediately dispelled the shadows. She glanced wildly around the room and saw nothing. She knew that awful rasping voice, the one that had been torturing her for so long. And this time it wasn't a dream.

She threw the covers back and rose, scanning the road and sidewalk below, the dark preventing her from making out any one figure. She didn't have to see to know. He was down there. She could feel him, sense his thoughts, disturbing thoughts that bordered on maniacal. Disjointed words came through...

...can't stop now...have to finish it...they're too

close...threats aren't working...should have known...bitch was too smart...

She backed away from the window until her legs came in contact with the bed. She could almost see him in her mind, almost. She found herself fighting the image, not wanting to see the face. Terrified she might be looking directly into Adam Frank's psychotic eyes.

Shaking, she rushed through the dark rooms, turning lights on as she went until the entire apartment was ablaze. She checked the locks, sliding the deadbolt home again just to make sure it was secure. Walking swiftly to the windows, she lowered the shades she seldom pulled in the front room. Only then did she feel some semblance of safety. She chastised herself for being every kind of fool but she knew better than to ignore her instincts. Yet she couldn't call the police. What would she tell them? She had a feeling there was someone down there watching her? They'd think she was crazy.

She curled up in bed, yanking the covers over her cold skin and instinctively reached for the phone.

"Hello?" Cole's deep drawl answered.

"Hi."

"What's wrong?" he asked immediately.

"Now why would you think something is wrong?" she said lightly, silently cursing her inability to stop her voice from trembling slightly.

"Because it's midnight, that's why."

"You don't sound sleepy."

"That's because I'm still working. Don't tell me you are."

"No. I'm lying in bed wishing you were holding me, that's all."

He groaned. "Now how am I going to get the rest of my work done with you putting thoughts like that in my head?"

"You aren't," she teased, already feeling better, happier.

"You'll pay for that tomorrow."

"Lord, I hope so," she said fervently.

"You sure you're okay?" he asked suspiciously.

"I will be tomorrow. Night, Cole. I love you."

"Want me to talk dirty to you?"

She laughed, feeling herself beginning to relax. "Nah, I'll just wait for the real thing. Night."

"Sweet dreams."

She hung up the phone, a smile playing about her lips. She couldn't think of anything better to drift off with than the thoughts of what that man could do to her, she thought drowsily. To her lips, her body, her mind... Moments later she was sleeping soundly.

ଙ

He leaned against the telephone pole, smoking and watching as the lights came on one by one and then were switched off. He could see her up there, the sheerness of her robe doing things to his imagination, to his loins. The lady had a body a man could bury himself in, eyes he could drown inside. It was really a shame he couldn't let her live. It was her fault, he thought grimly. It really was.

He ground the cigarette into the pavement and turned away, the streetlight highlighting his face for one brief moment. The woman who was walking by glanced at him, his handsome features catching her attention. She smiled, tossing her hair back alluringly. Yet, when his gaze met hers she found herself shivering and hurried away, glancing over her shoulder nervously.

Enjoying the moment, he watched her walk away. Then, with one last look upward, he slid into the darkness.

Chapter Thirteen

Cole was leaning against the 'Vette, his long jean-clad legs stretched in front of him, sunglasses in place when she walked out the sliding glass doors of the airport. He needed a haircut, she thought, but liked the way his thick dark hair curled just a little against his neck. He didn't see her immediately. She took just a moment to enjoy the sight of him, the broad shoulders beneath the jean jacket, the sense of lean power, the way the women passing swiveled their gaze in his direction.

"You're drawing attention," she teased as she walked up to him.

He straightened quickly, gathering her in his arms, suitcases and all. "Welcome back," he murmured against her mouth, nipping her lower lip lightly.

She inhaled his unique male fragrance, savoring his arms around her. Lord, she needed this man. He made her feel complete. She reached up and slipped his glasses off so she could see his warm green eyes. "If that's the kind of homecoming I can look forward to, I'll have to do more traveling," she said huskily.

He laughed, grabbing her suitcases and tossing them in the back seat. "Not without me, you won't." He opened her door and closed it behind her, striding to the other side. The car started with a roar and he eased out of the parking space, not bothering to slide his glasses back on. He sent a glance her way, examining her features closely.

"What happened last night?"

Because the question came out of nowhere, she didn't have time to think of an excuse. "What do you mean?" she hedged.

He glanced at her. "You were upset when you called me, Kat. You might be able to hide it from others but your voice does this thing when you're ticked or frightened. Now tell me."

"You're going to think I'm nuts," she said.

He leveled his gaze at her. "You know better," he said quietly.

When she was finished, his expression was tight and angry. "Damn it, Kat, this has gone on long enough."

"I agree," she replied, feeling better now that he knew. "I've already contacted the FBI and spoke to someone named David Braggs. He's agreed to get in touch with the local police force in New York and go from there. The feds have more power to follow up on this so hopefully that means we'll get some help at this end as well if there is a connection."

She jerked, startled when the cell phone rang. Glancing at the number, she relaxed. "It's someone I know," she said, answering.

"Afternoon, Kat," Tim Carson's voice said on the other end. "I've got something for you if you can talk."

"I can, Tim. Mind if I put this on speaker phone so a friend of mine can hear as well?"

"No problem."

He waited while she pushed a button then continued. "I've looked over what you've given me, Kat, and here's what I've come up with. Your man is tall. I would guess about six two or three. The angle of Allison Sandoval's wound tells me that. The severity of it, especially being post-mortem, means he was angry with her. That kind of depth wasn't necessary since she was already dead."

"Do you think the murders I gave you backgrounds on are connected?"

"Without a doubt. Your parents' deaths weren't planned, especially after you told me what you've dreamed but the reality is he's gotten away with it for fifteen years. He thought he was home free then found out that wasn't the case. He's running scared, Kat. The similarities between the deaths can't be ignored. It's obvious your friend's father discovered something, whether it was those narcotic vials you mentioned or something else, and paid for it with he and his wife's life."

212

"What about Allie Sandoval? She wasn't killed the same way."

"That's because he killed her for a different reason if what you suspect is true. Blackmail can elicit violent reactions. What concerns me is her death was hands-on. That means he's gone past using a weapon that doesn't require physical contact. It also means he's growing bolder."

"Are you sure Allie Sandoval was killed by the same person?"

"It ties in, Kat. Five people killed, six if you include the old man murdered right after your parents were, in a small town like Brookdale makes me think that's the case. I've spent some time analyzing all of this and have come to the conclusion that our man could be very capable of functioning day to day. However, mentally he's walking a very fine line between sanity and psychosis. If he's responsible for those threatening phone calls, then he might very well have gone over it. Believe me, he will do anything he can to avoid detection, even kill again."

"Any physical characteristics we can look for?"

"Other than being tall and left-handed, there isn't much else I can tell you. My guess is he must have either a job he doesn't want to lose or is prominent enough to kill to prevent someone from delving into his past. He can't handle that. Desperate men don't stick around the scene of a crime or crimes unless they've got some kind of vested interest."

"Then you think the killer is someone who lives here?" Cole asked.

"Cole Collins, Tim Carson." Kat introduced them. "Cole's the sheriff here in Brookdale."

"Nice to meet you, Cole," Tim said over the phone, "and to answer your question, I think the evidence suggests that. Comfortable surroundings, he knows the geography, the routines of the people. Easier to escape detection that way. He might be scared but he's also feeling infallible right now. Don't rule out the possibility of an accomplice in all of this as well. Someone who can make those threatening phone calls, do his dirty work. If that's the case, you're talking about a very dangerous combination. Watch your step."

"One more question, Tim," Kat said. "He's called both my

cell phone and my private unlisted number even though I've changed them several times. The police in New York are certain the calls are coming from there, which means either he's traveling back and forth or he's using that accomplice you spoke of. Why would he expose himself that way?"

Tim was silent for a moment, mulling that thought. "Could be he doesn't think he is. Do you recognize the voice?"

"I thought I did, but now I'm just not sure. He disguises it."

"That's the one other thing I've come up with. The man is intelligent. Aside from him managing to avoid detection all these years, he hasn't left a single clue. No fingerprints, no careless fibers left behind, nothing. He just might have been lucky avoiding detection with the first murders but it isn't a coincidence that he hasn't left further clues. He knows what he's about. There's a good chance he's got someone else making those calls just to throw a wrench into the investigation."

Cole turned the car into her aunt's driveway and turned off the engine. "We've come up with a few more things since I last talked to Kat, Tim. Okay if I send them your way?"

"Sure. I'd be happy to help however I can. Katarina has my fax and phone numbers."

"Thanks, Tim. I really appreciate it," Kat said.

"Always glad to oblige my pretty lady lawyer," he quipped. "Talk to you soon."

She thoughtfully flipped the phone closed. "I represented Tim a few months back. He's a renowned serial profiler and I respect his opinion." She sighed. "Same problem again, more clues and still no suspect."

"No, but I've got another connection. Dale Cowls called me just before I left to pick you up. You know that hair he found on the backpack? It belonged to Tanner Gordon."

She was surprised and it showed in her expression. "That's totally unexpected." She shook her head. "Tanner wasn't the nicest person, even back in high school, although he was more Andy's age than mine." She frowned thoughtfully. "As a matter of fact, if memory serves he and Brian Landers were good friends."

"Your memory is correct. He was at Gordon's funeral. Most of the town was there as well. I figured I should put in an appearance. Brian was pretty shook up. A couple of times I had the feeling he wanted to approach me but he never did. It's a sure bet he knows more than he's saying about a whole lot of things."

"Poor Brian," Kat said sympathetically. "I remember he, Tanner and Dan hung around with the same crowd growing up. I wonder if anyone's told Dan about his death."

"I doubt it unless Brian did. Tanner didn't have any close relatives except a mother in a nursing home."

Their conversation was interrupted by Olivia's voice calling from the front porch.

"Daddy, should I come out now?"

"Yeah, you've been sitting out there like forever," Tiffany complained, standing next to her friend on the front steps.

Kat's amused glance met Cole's. "It appears we're being summoned."

"It seems so," he answered, holding her gaze.

She paused with her hand on the door handle. "What's that about?"

"What?" he asked innocently.

"That look."

"What look?"

"You're hiding something. What's going on?"

Unable to wait any longer, both girls appeared at the side of the car.

"Hi, Kat," Olivia said, her face flushed with excitement.

"What took you so long?" Tiffany complained indignantly. "Everyone is waiting."

Kat reached behind the seat to grab her purse, glancing at Cole over the girls' heads. "And who is everyone?"

"A whole bunch of people," Tiffany said importantly. "Your aunt and brother, Ellie and Sam Sulin and even Liv's Grandpa Collins," she ticked off on her fingers one by one.

Cole slid his long legs out of the car and tapped the girl's nose. "Anyone ever tell you that you have a big mouth, Tiffany Ross?"

"All the time," Deanna said, overhearing the conversation

as she walked down the porch steps. "Welcome home, Kat," she said, hugging her friend long and hard. "You have no idea how excited I am to have you back in town permanently."

It was then Kat caught sight of the line of cars parked down the road. She moved around the hood, glancing up at Cole, eyes narrowed. "What is this, a welcome home party?"

Deanna put a finger across Tiffany's lips before she could reply, a warning light in her eyes. "Not another word, young lady." She took her by the hand. "You come with me. We'll wait for you inside," she tossed over her shoulder, moving back up the steps with a reluctant Tiffany in tow.

"Remember what I told you to ask, Liv," Tiffany shouted just before her mother ushered her inside.

"I won't," Olivia shouted back, her eyes brimming with excitement.

Kat put her purse down on the hood of the car and held out her arms. "I think I need a hug from my best girl."

Olivia didn't need any further encouragement. She ran forward, wrapping her small arms around Kat's waist and burying her face against her. "I've really missed you, Kat. So has Dad."

"Well that's good to hear," Kat murmured, kissing the top of the girl's dark curls, her heart full.

Olivia turned in her arms toward her father. "Can I do it now, Daddy?"

He leaned inside the car, opening the middle console and palming a small brightly wrapped package. "You can," he said solemnly, handing it to his daughter.

"Kat, Daddy thought that I should be the one to ask you," she said shyly, holding out the box.

"Ask me what?"

"To marry us," she responded, laying the small box in Kat's hand. "Please say yes," she pleaded, "because Daddy needs you and I do too. It's not the same when you're not here. Daddy says we come as a package and we should ask you together. Does that make sense?"

Kat could feel the tears welling in her eyes as she bent down to hug the girl close to her. "It makes perfect sense, my love. I can't think of anything I'd like more than being your mother," she murmured huskily.

The girl wiggled excitedly out of her grasp. "I *knew* you'd say yes! I just knew it! Wait'll I tell Tiff!" She spun around to run back toward the house then stopped abruptly. "That means you want to be Daddy's wife too, right?"

"Why don't you let me talk to your father about that," Kat drawled, glancing at Cole.

"Okay," she said, skipping up the steps, "but don't be too long." She giggled. "I forgot. Tiff said I was supposed to make you promise to give me a brother or sister for my birthday next year. It's Christmas Eve and Tiff says it takes nine months so with a wedding and all that should be about right."

Cole groaned under his breath while Kat couldn't help laughing outright.

"We'll discuss it, okay?"

"Okay," the girl said happily, disappearing inside.

Kat turned back to the man standing behind, her tracing his lean jaw with a finger. "Very clever, Cole Collins, having your daughter make me an offer I can't refuse."

He grinned but his eyes held a different message, their expression telling her there was a wealth of emotion just below the surface. "I wanted you to be sure about this move home before I made it official, Kat. Liv's right, we are a package. A father and daughter who desperately need you in their lives. You up to the challenge?"

She didn't answer but simply drew his mouth to hers.

"I take it that's a yes," he teased, brushing his thumbs lightly against her neck, the caress sending shivers of need through her.

"Most definitely," she confirmed, taking the gift she still held in her hands and pulling the paper away. She lifted the lid of the black velvet box and gasped. "Cole, this is absolutely gorgeous!"

He removed the thick circle of rubies and diamonds and, lifting her hand, slid it on. It fit perfectly. "The stones reminded me of you. Fire and ice."

She raised a brow. "I'm not sure I like that comparison."

His smile was dark and sexy. "You would if you knew what I was thinking when I bought that ring."

"And what was that?" she asked, wrapping her arms around his neck while admiring the sparkle of the stones.

"You're cool, calm and icy on the outside, lady, but underneath you're all fire. Hot, molten fire."

Kat's felt the sting of tears. "I love you."

"Come *on*, you two!" Tiffany yelled from the opened window in the living room, just loud enough to startle them.

Kat looked up at Cole, laughing. "I guess we have kept them waiting long enough, haven't we?"

Evelyn met them at the door, misty-eyed when she saw the ring on Kat's finger. "I can't help thinking how happy your mother and father would be right now," she said, her voice thick with emotion. "How pleased they would be at your choice of husband," she finished, grabbing Cole's hand.

Tears stung Kat's eyes as she took her aunt's outstretched hands in her own. "I know they would, Aunt Evelyn."

"I'm pleased my son has such exquisite taste," Jared said warmly, wrapping an arm around Evelyn's shoulders.

The blush that stole over her aunt's cheek had Kat raising a brow. "It looks like you have the same exquisite taste, Jared."

He nodded. "That I do, young lady."

"Hey, you two," Mandy interrupted, motioning to the food laden table and the crowd of people around them. "No one else can eat without you starting things so get a move on." Her plump face was wreathed in a delighted smile as she caught Cole and then Kat close. "It's damn time the two of you decided to tie the knot. No mistaking how you feel about each other, is there, ladies and gentlemen?"

A roar of approval answered her question.

Cole caught her hand in his. "Guess we can't let them starve, now can we?"

Plates piled high with food, they settled at the table, enduring teasing with an occasional lewd comment when the children weren't around. Kat absorbed all of it, the atmosphere, the good friends, the feeling that she had just been on a long hiatus from where she really belonged. What was even more gratifying was that these people, whom she had known her entire life, had embraced Cole and his daughter with the same enthusiasm. She glanced over at Olivia, who was in the middle of a group of children her own age, holding center court. It had been slow in coming but she could see a marked change in the child, the glow about her and the confidence in her eyes.

She only wished these investigations weren't hanging over their heads. She had a feeling, a very bad feeling, things were going to get worse before they got better. She lifted a troubled gaze to Cole who was busy talking to Jerry Landers. He was in danger. She felt it, sensed it. They all were until this killer was caught. A frisson of fear trickled down her spine as she glanced around the room. It could be any one of the people standing within arm's distance of her. She didn't like suspecting people she loved and had grown up with.

"Why so gloomy?" her aunt asked, sliding into a chair across the table, her eyes searching Kat's face. "This is your engagement party, love."

"Just thinking," Kat said lightly, smiling.

Evelyn leaned forward, lowering her voice. "Something is going to happen, Kat. I've had this deep sense of foreboding the last couple of nights." She grimaced, her brown eyes dark with concern. "I didn't mean to say that. Not tonight, not now. But I'm concerned. I have my own set of instincts and they're telling me you and Cole are at the very center of what's about to happen."

Kat nodded. "You're not telling me anything I don't already know, Aunt Evelyn."

"That doesn't make me worry less."

"Would it help if I told you I have this very strong feeling that all will end as it's supposed to?"

Evelyn eyed her for a long moment. "Depends on what that means."

"It means you need to stop worrying and enjoy your niece's homecoming and engagement."

"I agree with that," Jared said, handing Evelyn a drink. "These young people know how to take care of themselves." He caught Kat's glance, his expression telling her he wasn't taking what her aunt had said lightly however.

Tiffany skipped up to them, balancing a piece of fried chicken, a biscuit and a can of soda in her hands. "I told you half the town was here," she spouted importantly. "Wait 'til you see what Liv and I have planned for your wedding. It'll be really awesome."

"Should I ask?" Kat flicked a glance at Cole, catching the soda neatly before it crashed to the floor and handing it back to the girl.

"Not if you don't want to have nightmares," Cole whispered loudly.

"That's not funny," Tiffany said haughtily. "At least Liv talked me out of the live doves I wanted to have in the church. I saw a show one time that had them flying all over the place. Everyone thought it was cool until one of them pooped on the bride."

Kat had a hard time containing her laughter. "Doesn't sound very romantic, does it?"

"Nah, but it sure was funny."

"You're something else you know that, Tiffany Ross?"

"That's what my mother keeps saying." She put her food down and flung her arms around Kat. "I'm really glad you're staying home, Kat, cuz then Mom can concentrate on someone else besides me all the time." She grabbed her food again and took a bite of the chicken, munching enthusiastically. "I wouldn't even mind babysitting next year. After all, Liv and I will be nine and perfectly able to take care of a baby."

"Go!" Kat ordered, unable to stop the laughter from escaping this time.

Much later, Kat tucked her feet under her in the leather chair by her aunt's fireplace. She took an appreciative sip of her coffee, glancing around the comfortable room. The family room was still full of people and the crowd spilled over into her aunt's big country kitchen, the front room as well as the deck out back. Tiffany had been right, almost half the town was there, including Cole's lawyer, Barry Sullivan, and his wife Gina. She and Gina had hit it off immediately while Barry had enjoyed spending some time filling her in on his and Cole's escapades in college despite Cole's threats of reprisal.

She couldn't have asked for a better homecoming, she

thought. If she hadn't been sure of her feelings regarding the move before, she was now. Her gaze slid to Cole who was talking to Andy and Sam across the room, his head bent to hear something her brother was saying above the din.

She noted again the way he listened, the way he made people feel as if he really cared about them, about their opinions. She had dated over the years, even thought she had fallen in love a few times. Nothing compared to what she felt now. She had always known that it would take a certain kind of man to push the attraction to serious. The kind of man who would challenge her, keep up with her intellectually as well as emotionally. She had found that man.

As if sensing her scrutiny, he glanced up, catching her gaze. He excused himself from the group he was with.

"Happy?" he asked, straddling the chair next to her as he searched her face.

She nodded, hiding a delicate yawn with the back of her hand. "It's good to be home."

"Sorry to interrupt," Deanna said as she and Mike joined them. "As much as I hate to leave, we have to." She glanced at her watch. "Doug has a football game tonight and he'd be crushed if we weren't there."

Mike nodded. "Only a sophomore and he's starting quarterback for the varsity team," he said proudly. "I'm just a little prejudiced but he's damned good for his age."

"That's great," Kat said. "I'd love to see him play."

"Now that you're home permanently, my friend, we'll make an evening of it," Deanna promised.

"Do I have to go to that dumb game?" Tiffany groaned as she walked up next to her mother, finishing off the last bite of cake on her plate.

"Yes, you do," her mother said firmly. "Remember he went to your school play and piano recital."

"Yeah and complained the whole time."

"Would you feel better if Olivia came too?" Mike asked, winking at Cole.

"Yeah, a lot better!"

"Okay with you, Cole?" Mike asked.

"Please, Daddy," Liv begged her father, putting an arm around her friend. She looked up at Mike. "Could we get some hot chocolate?"

"You bet," Mike answered, grinning. "Wouldn't be a football game without gorging on hot chocolate and pretzels."

"If you're sure you don't mind her tagging along," Cole said, ruffling his daughter's hair affectionately, "it's fine with me."

Deanna gave a long-suffering sigh. "Please, Cole. With Liv there, at least we'll get to enjoy the game."

Cole eyed his daughter's jeans and sweatshirt. "You're going to need a coat. It's cool this time of night."

"Don't worry. Tiffany has an extra one she can wear." Deanna glanced at her watch. "Mike, we better move or we're going to miss the kick off."

"Bye, Daddy," Olivia said, reaching up on tiptoe to kiss her father. "Bye, Kat," she repeated, hugging her. "Maybe I can call you Mom when you and Dad get married," she whispered shyly.

"I think that would be wonderful," Kat managed to say past the lump in her throat.

"She means it, Kat," Cole murmured softly as his daughter waved goodbye and skipped after Tiffany.

"I know she does," Kat said, looking up at him. "That's why I'm so touched. She could have resented me big time."

"She could have but she doesn't," he said quietly, running a finger along the curve of her jaw. "She knows the real thing, just like her father."

Before she could reply, several people came up to say goodbye. Soon the crowd thinned significantly. As usual, Mandy had everyone cleaning before they left, and by the time the last person waved goodbye, the house was back to its usual tidiness.

"How can I thank you?" Kat said, putting her arms around Mandy's plump shoulders. "What would this town do without Mandy Stanislaus?"

"Starve," she said, eyes dancing. "Now you take some of that food home, Cole. I've got it in individual containers and labeled. It's all ready for freezing."

"Yes ma'am," he drawled, bending down to kiss her cheek.

She shook a finger at him. "Don't be sassing me, young man."

Cole threw his hands up. "Not me!"

Evelyn wrapped an arm around Kat's shoulders as they walked to the car. "Are you sure you won't stay here, love? You know you're always welcome."

Kat shook her head. "I've always known that but I need some time to get myself organized, settled. The cabin is the perfect place for that."

"It's also isolated."

"Not really and I had an extra deadbolt installed on the front and back doors last time I was here. Besides, I have my cell for now. On Monday I'll hook up the house phone as well. I'll be fine, really."

"Don't worry, Evelyn," Cole said, opening the car door for Kat. "I'll check in on her."

Evelyn smiled. "I know you will. Just do me a favor and set the date for the wedding soon. I can't wait to start planning."

"Tiffany and Olivia already are," Kat said wryly. "Wait until you hear what they have in mind."

Evelyn rolled her eyes. "I can just imagine." She leaned against the open window. "You're taking some big steps all at once, Kat," she murmured as Cole walked around the hood of the car. "Marriage plans, a move back home, and a ready-made family."

"If you're asking if I've thought this through, then the answer is yes." Kat's gaze was steady as she glanced up at her aunt.

"Then that's all I need to hear." She leaned forward to press a kiss to her forehead. "Night, love."

"Goodnight, Aunt Evelyn."

Cole slid in the driver's side just as Andy appeared next to the car, offering a hand to Cole. "Always wanted a brother. Guess I'll have to settle for a brother-in-law." He leaned down to peer at Kat. "Your car arrived this morning. It's already at the cabin."

"Thanks, Andy. I appreciate it."

"No problem. Talk to both of you tomorrow."

It was only after Cole backed out of the driveway and was on the main road that he glanced over at her. "Tired?"

"Just relaxed."

"Feel like stopping at the house? I'd like to check on Ringer. He's been caged for a long time."

"That's fine. I'd love to see how much he's grown."

He arched a brow. "Considering he's five months old now and a Great Dane, suffice it to say he's significantly larger than when you saw him last."

He was, she thought, when Cole let him loose and he came bounding out, his long legs going in every direction as he slid across the tile floor. Laughing, she knelt down to stop his progress and was awarded by a sloppy kiss.

"Hi, there, boy," she crooned. "My, you've grown, haven't you?"

The puppy immediately flopped over on his side, adoration in his velvet eyes when she began to rub his stomach.

"Keep that up and he won't let you alone the rest of the night," Cole warned. "I speak from experience."

After he let the dog out and fed him, they headed to the cabin. Just as Cole made the last turn before the driveway, Kat instantly became aware of that aura that always preceded one of her visions. Reluctantly, she closed her eyes, allowing it access.

The moon was bright. The figure bent over a prone body, shadowed by the tall trees on either side of the path they were standing on. The cabin, her cabin, was visible in the distance, smoke curling from the chimney.

"What the hell were you thinking? Someone is going to miss the man sooner or later."

"How was I supposed to know the old coot was going to take a midnight stroll?"

"You killed him for Christ's sake! They find him, they're going to know it wasn't an accident."

"Then we make it look like one. Come on, help me carry him."

"Where?"

"Back to his place. I'll think of something."

"You better, because I ain't going to jail for something I didn't do."

There was silence, a menacing silence.

She saw the taller man rise to his feet and grab the other one by the neck. "You're going to do what I tell you. Got it?"

"You can't boss me around." The voice was belligerent.

"Wanna bet?"

"Okay, okay." The voice was just a shade breathless, fearful.

"Don't forget, I go down, so do you. You and that hot little girlfriend of yours. So just keep your mouth shut. Understand?"

"Yeah, I understand."

The scene faded as quickly as it had come. Kat opened her eyes slowly, sliding back to the present.

"Tanner Gordon was with the person who killed Clay Saunders."

Cole's gaze shot to hers as he braked in front of the cabin. "Another vision?"

She nodded. "I recognized the path where we found the backpack. You were right. Mr. Saunders was killed there and then carried where he was found."

"You didn't see who the killer was?"

She shook her head regretfully. "I saw Tanner's face in the moonlight but the other person was hidden by the shadows." She frowned. "However, his voice is the same one I keep hearing in my dreams. It's so familiar and yet I can't place why that is." Her gaze slid back to his. "One thing I do know. Tanner was afraid of whoever it was, really afraid."

"Because he had something on him?"

"That's the impression I got. There was a mention of a hot girlfriend." Her gaze found his. "I have a feeling they were talking about Allie."

His jaw tightened. "I know they were. I've done some investigating into Gordon's past since he was killed. He and Allie were an item the entire summer she was here." He rubbed

225

a hand across his jaw thoughtfully. "If your instincts are right, that means Allie, Tanner and whoever this person is were involved in your parents' murders as well. Same weekend, late at night, the backpack, it all makes sense."

"Could Tanner have been the father of Allie's baby?"

Cole shook his head. "Ruled him out yesterday. Dale was able to get enough DNA to confirm Gordon wasn't the father. Besides, no one in the town saw the two of them together after that summer. My guess is they went their separate ways or they didn't want to be linked with each other for fear of being discovered."

"Do you think Allie was actually involved with killing my parents?"

He shook his head. "I really don't, Kat. She was a lot of things but I can't see her murdering someone. More than likely she was driving the getaway car, if you want to call it that. She probably had no idea what had happened. She could have been drunk or high or both at the time. Barry did some investigation into her background when she was trying to obtain custody again and discovered she had a drug and alcohol problem even back in high school. Rumor has it Tanner dabbled in drugs that summer as well."

She opened the car door. "We're getting close, Cole. Sooner or later, either you'll find the evidence that links us to the right person or I'm going to recognize that voice."

He reached behind and swung the suitcases out of the back, giving her a wry look. "Kind of hard to get excited about us when there is so much hanging over our heads, isn't it?"

"Oh, I don't know," she murmured, dropping her purse on the ground and wrapping her arms around his neck. "I imagine I can get rather excited if the right situation arose."

His eyes grew dark as he bent his head. "A situation like this, maybe?" he asked, dropping the cases and gathering her in his arms.

"Could be," she teased, rubbing suggestively against him.

He groaned. "It's been a long two months, Kat. Keep it up and we won't even make it inside the door."

"Then I guess you better hurry," she murmured, licking her lips provocatively.

The suitcases forgotten, he hauled her up into his arms, struggling to open the door with one hand while she rained kisses down the side of his jaw and neck, her hands busy unbuttoning his jacket. He used his back to shut the door, making it as far as the couch. Lowering her onto its soft cushions, he stilled her hands with one of his.

"My turn," he said hoarsely.

His lips found the scented softness of her neck, his tongue sliding across the hollow where her pulse was roaring. She arched as his tormenting mouth lowered, searching and finding the bare skin of her breasts. He shoved her shirt then the lacy bra aside, capturing one turgid nipple deep in his mouth. She whimpered her need as she freed her hands. Frantically, she splayed them across his back, her nails digging deep as she threw her head back, allowing him free access.

He ran his tongue across the soft flesh, finding the other breast, feeling her trembling beneath him. When she reached down and found him, it was his turn to groan with enjoyment. Somehow, instead of the softness of the couch, they were on the floor, clothes scattered around them. Her erect nipples taunted him, almost causing him to lose what little control he had left.

He poised above her for one brief moment, his gaze locking with hers. "I love you, Kat," he growled, taking in her swollen lips and flushed cheeks and the deep passionate blue of her eyes as she looked up at him.

"Then show me," she whispered.

He responded by burying himself deep within her. Her breath caught in a gasp and then she was meeting him with a thrust of her own.

Heat threatened to turn her limbs to liquid, her eyes growing opaque as she moved with him, against him, her long slender body fitting his perfectly.

Grabbing a fistful of hair, she guided his lips to hers, needing to taste the heat, the maleness of his mouth. It was all there, the love, the lust, the strength.

He explored her mouth, nibbled on her full lips, his thumbs brushing her already sensitive nipples. She could feel herself reaching, climbing and grabbed him, needing to pull him with her.

"Sweet Lord, now, Cole!" she gasped, her nails raking his back as he dove deeper, harder. "Right now!"

When it came, the climax was more powerful than either of them had ever experienced. It left Kat feeling limp and deliciously satisfied.

"What's that saying?" he murmured, his breath warm and sweet against her cheek. "There's no place like home?"

"That doesn't even begin to describe the last few minutes," she said, her voice still husky with passion.

He growled a laugh and then glanced around. "Do you think just once we might make it into the bedroom?"

She wound her arms around his neck, shrugging. "Maybe when we've been married for twenty years or so. By then arthritis might make this floor just a little cold."

His gaze slid back to hers. "Want to make a bet?"

She laughed, pressing her lips to his broad chest. "Nope. Not me."

Cole's cell phone rang, startling both of them. He reached over and pulled it out of his jacket, answering.

"Sorry to bother you, Cole," Betty said on the other end. "But I just received a phone call from Brian Landers. He wants to meet you at the office in about half an hour. It sounded like it was urgent so I thought I better call you."

Cole glanced at his watch. "That'll work for me, Betty. Let him know I'll be there. Thanks."

He disconnected the call thoughtfully.

"Emergency?"

He shook his head. "Brian Landers wants to meet with me in a few. I've a hunch he wants to come clean." He bent his head, brushing her lips and then groaned. "Better not do that again or I won't be going anywhere."

She smiled, stretching seductively. "Can't say that would upset me."

"You're a cruel woman," he complained as he reluctantly stood and tugged on his jeans.

She rose, tossing him the shirt still hanging half off the

couch. She reached for her own clothing. "I'll go with you."

He shook his head. "Won't work, Kat. I'm not exactly one of his favorite people. The two of us walk in there together and he might feel threatened. I'll be back as soon as I can."

She frowned and then nodded. "Okay, I'll buy that." She stopped him from buttoning his shirt, trailing a nail across his hard abdomen. "Don't worry, I'll be waiting for you when you're done," she said, her voice low and sexy.

"Then Landers better talk fast," he said darkly.

Laughing, she made her way to the bedroom while he finished dressing. She slipped on a warm terry robe, walking back into the main room just as he was shrugging into his jacket. Her expression was no longer seductive but serious as she put a hand on his arm.

"Be careful, will you? I'm getting some bad vibes."

He looked down at her. "About Brian Landers?"

"I don't know. Aunt Evelyn told me she felt the same way. Maybe it wouldn't hurt to call Jerry to meet the two of you just in case."

He shook his head. "I've got a feeling Brian would clam up immediately if his father was anywhere around."

"Then call me as soon as you can. I just want to make sure you're safe."

He pulled her to him, inhaling the fragrance of her hair. "I promise."

After carrying her suitcases in, he kissed her again and drove away.

She watched him go, a feeling of trepidation she couldn't shake flowing through her. Impatiently, she turned toward the bedroom and took a long, hot shower, letting the needles of water ease the tension from her. Afterward, she donned one of her favorite sweat suits and touched a match to the waiting wood, gazing pensively into the flames.

Cole was right. She should be ecstatically happy right now. She was marrying a man she adored, becoming the mother to a child she'd already bonded with. In addition, she was moving back to a town she had come to realize she always intended to return to. Yet there was a murderer out there, lurking just beyond the shadows both literally and in her mind. A person that could destroy everything.

She spun around, her heart in her throat when she heard the creak of the front porch steps. Damn! Someone was out there and she'd foolishly forgotten to lock the door. *Calm down, Kat,* she told herself. *You're letting your imagination get the better of you.*

Still, until she knew who it was, she had no intention of letting anyone in. Silently she eased toward the door but it was too late. Just as she reached for the lock, it swung open. A scream rose and then disappeared as she recognized the man standing in front of her.

Relaxing, she shook her head, arching a brow. "You scared me half to death! What are you doing here?"

He didn't answer but instead turned, closing the door. Then very deliberately he shoved the deadbolt home. *Shoved it home with his left hand!*

Even before he turned, she was backing away, her senses on high alert. Something was wrong, she thought. She'd never seen him like this, seen those eyes bore into her, cold and flat.

"I'm sorry. Really sorry," he said, moving toward her.

That voice! She closed her eyes and at once the scene was in front of her. Her father standing over her mother's crumpled body, staring in total shock at the boy holding the gun aimed directly at him. Staring at...

I'm sorry. Really sorry...

Her eyes widened in horror, disbelief. "Oh, my God! It was you!"

Chapter Fourteen

The man sitting across the desk from him was nervous, Cole thought, but the animosity was gone. Betty had tactfully waved goodnight as she closed the door, leaving them alone. Cole leaned back in his chair and waited.

"Listen, Cole," Brian began, clearing his throat, "it's no secret I wasn't happy about you taking the job I thought belonged to my father." He shook his head ruefully. "Hell, I think I blamed you for my parents' marriage breaking up, Dad not being sheriff and God knows what else." His gaze found Cole's, his eyes very much like his father's. "I was wrong. I'm not proud about the way I've behaved but I'm man enough to admit it."

Cole nodded. "Maybe I would have felt the same way if the situation had been reversed. But I have a feeling that's not why you're here."

"No it isn't." He was silent for a moment, shifting in his chair, obviously searching for the right words. "I know for a fact Tanner was chasing you the day he was killed." Grief flashed in his eyes. "I tried to warn him what he was doing went way beyond the harmless pranks we'd pulled growing up. He didn't listen. He liked speed, liked his hot car and when he was asked to use both, he couldn't resist."

"Who did the asking?"

"I don't know the man's name but I do know whoever it was had called him before. Asked him to do stuff aimed at running you out of town." His face flushed lightly but he kept his gaze on Cole's. "Because I wasn't all that thrilled with your being here, I didn't discourage him. Maybe if I had he wouldn't be lying in that damn cemetery."

"Like defacing the squad car?" Cole asked.

Brian nodded. "That and spreading rumors around town about you. Leaving notes in the Sandoval's mailbox saying you weren't a fit father for your little girl."

"Did Tanner ever tell you why this person had it in for me?"

"No, but whoever it was apparently knew his weaknesses. Tanner liked to show off, see how much he could get away with. Always did. He had rich tastes and this jerk paid him well. That's how he got enough money to buy that sweet ride."

"Any idea who you think this might be?"

Brian kept his gaze on Cole's. "I figure it has to be someone who knows the area. Someone who lived here long enough to go after a person who would do what he asked without question. Whoever it was had to have kept in contact with Tanner after high school."

"Any names come to mind?" Cole asked casually.

"I'm working on it. I'll get back to you."

Cole rose and put out his hand. "It took guts to do what you just did, Brian. I appreciate that."

After a brief hesitation, Brian extended his own. "My father likes you, Collins, respects you. That's probably why I resented you so much. I've always felt like I failed him, not following in his footsteps." He moved toward the door. "That's not why I decided to come here, however. I came because I appreciate the way you treat him. Like an equal."

"That's because he is," Cole said simply.

"I think you mean that. He believes..." His voice trailed off as he caught sight of the bagged knife sitting on the table near the door. He leaned closer, picking it up and examining the plastic-covered bottom. He glanced over at Cole. "Why do you have Dan Rogers's knife?"

Cole raised a brow. "I wasn't aware it was his knife. The initials aren't very clear."

"I recognize the style. We all bought one our senior year. Since they were the same, each of us carved our initials in the bottom. I think I still have mine somewhere at home."

"Who else had knives like that?"

"Me, Tanner, Dan, Andy, and Sam Sulin. Some guy was selling them at a local knife and gun show. Reason I know it's Dan's is because Andy carved a RA in his so they wouldn't get them confused." He pointed to the faint R carved into the bottom of the handle. "We all scratched the first initial of our last name on the base here." He pointed to the side. "Andy scratched an A right here so this has got to be Dan's. He shrugged. "We thought we were tough stuff," he reminisced. "Dumb teenagers I guess."

The knife is the key. Remember the knife.

The words, their warning, flashed through Cole's memory. "Any of those men left-handed?"

Brian's expression tightened. "You know I am."

"Besides you," Cole said.

Brian scanned his face for a moment. Apparently satisfied that Cole wasn't accusing him, he answered. "Sam and Dan are. The baseball coach was in heaven in high school with two of the three of us pitchers. Sam was even approached by a couple of minor leagues, he was that good." He raised his head suddenly. "Come on! You don't think one of them...?"

His cell phone rang and Cole glanced at his watch. It was seven-thirty. Not late enough for the high school football game to have ended. He eyed the number. Long distance and not one he recognized.

"Can you wait just a minute while I answer this, Brian?"

The other man nodded, still holding the knife in his hands, frowning.

"Hello?"

"Cole Collins?"

"Yes?"

"Good, I was hoping I could reach you. Lucky Kat gave me a card with your number on it before she left. This is Jack Steinman. We met when you came north for the weekend."

"I remember. How are you, Jack?"

"I'm fine, busy as usual. Is Kat with you by any chance?"

"No, she's at the cabin. Did you try her cell phone?"

"Actually I did and that's why I'm calling." There was a brief pause. "To be frank, I'm worried about her."

"Why?"

"This might sound strange but something's been nagging me for the past couple of weeks and I'd like to run it by you. Keep this between you and me because Kat'll strangle me if I'm wrong."

"Go on."

"My fiancée and I are thinking of a cruise for our honeymoon. Kat suggested I ask Dan Rogers who he would recommend since he was on one a while back. That's the part that bothers me."

"What?"

"The cruise he told me he went on was at dock for repairs the week he was gone."

"Maybe he simply changed his plans and booked another line and forgot to mention it."

"I thought of that, but since Dan was unavailable that day and the wedding is only about a month away, Kat gave me his parents' number to expedite things. They were supposed to have taken the cruise with him."

"Supposed to have?"

"They didn't have a clue as to what I was talking about when I phoned. They told me they had purchased a vacation home in the Florida Keys about a month before Dan was supposed to go on that cruise and they'd been there since then."

Cole was getting a bad feeling, a very bad feeling, but he decided to continue to play devil's advocate. "He's rich and single. Maybe he wanted to take a vacation with a significant other and just didn't want anyone to know."

"Okay, I'm going out on a limb here, Cole, and I know it. Hell, maybe I'm even jeopardizing my future but I've got to tell you there's something about Dan Rogers that rubs me the wrong way. At first I thought it was simply that I was the junior partner and he just didn't have a lot of patience with someone new. I don't believe that anymore."

"Why is that?"

"Because I've seen him do things I know Kat would never approve of. For instance, the last case he took simply because the woman had bucks. Knew she was guilty as hell but that didn't stop him having an affair with her anyway. Don't ask how I know, I just do. Another time, he deliberately falsified evidence. I knew it but I had no way of proving it. He won both cases so his reputation remained intact. However, he's pushing the envelope. Sooner or later, he keeps this unethical behavior up and someone is going to notice."

"I wasn't overly impressed with the man myself, Jack. What is it you're trying to suggest?"

"Something that probably is way off-base. However, I'll let you make that determination." Again there was another pause. "Kat and I have had several conversations about the murders in her hometown. Her parents, the Sulin couple, your ex-wife. She even told me about the old man that you suspect didn't die from natural causes. So, on a hunch, I did some checking."

"On what?"

"On where Dan was when those people were killed. I know this sounds crazy but he was away on vacation when that couple were murdered. Away as in Brookdale. And when I talked with his secretary, she told me that she had arranged for an early flight for him the morning your ex-wife was killed, this time to Birmingham."

"Are you saying you think Dan Rogers is guilty of murdering those people?" Cole asked incredulously.

"I'm saying there's another side to that man. I've been with the firm for over a year now. Since Kat has eased back, I've been working closely with him on a number of cases. He isn't a nice person." He paused. "This has been on my mind for a long time so forgive me if I'm going off here. Dan has a thing for her that he's managed to disguise rather well. However, I've seen the look in his eyes when she mentions you. He resents her leaving and I think he blames you."

"That doesn't make him a killer, Jack."

"No, but the man likes where he's at right now. Trust me when I tell you he's there because Kat put him there. He isn't half the lawyer she is and that isn't envy talking, that's simply the truth."

"Frankly that isn't an issue now. With Kat moving home and he being in New York, unfortunately it looks like his

235

behavior is something you're going to have to deal with one way or another."

"You don't understand, Cole. That's why I phoned Kat tonight. When I was talking to Jenny, Dan's secretary, she let it slip that she had to stay late to catch up on some work Dan had left for her because he was going out of town again."

"Are you saying he's headed back to Brookdale?"

"That's what his secretary told me. If he is, Cole, I'd feel better knowing Kat knew that. Even if I'm totally wrong about what I suspect, I don't like the idea of her being alone with him. She saw just a glimpse of what I'm talking about last night at dinner with all the members of the firm there and I could tell it upset her."

Cole could feel the muscles in his neck and back tense when he thought of Kat alone at that cabin. He'd only met Jack Steinman once but it had been apparent almost immediately that the man was steady and not the type of person to jump to conclusions. It was obvious he had thought this through long and hard.

"I appreciate you calling me, Jack. I promise you the first thing I'm going to do is call Kat. If she doesn't answer, I'll check on her myself. As far as your suspicions, you've given me another suspect I hadn't even considered. I hope to God you're wrong but that doesn't mean I won't follow up on what you've told me."

"I know you will. Thanks, Cole. Call me when you get a chance and let me know everything is okay, will you?"

"Count on it."

Cole's glance slid to Brian after he disconnected the call. "Sorry about that, Brian. I hate to ask, but you mind sticking around for just a few minutes longer while I give Kat a call?"

"No," he answered, still holding the knife in his hand. "I overheard part of that conversation, Cole. I have a feeling whoever that caller was might be on to something."

Cole was busy punching in Kat's cell number, his eyes holding the other man's gaze. "Hold that thought, Brian, for just a minute." He was immensely relieved when she answered.

"Hello?"

"Everything okay, Kat?"

"Why do you ask, Cole?"

"Just worried about you there alone, that's all."

"Sometimes it pays to worry, doesn't it? Listen, I have to go. I'm in the middle of things I have to deal with before I can really call Brookdale home again. New York still has a hold on me. I think it will be that way for longer than I ever imagined. Night, Cole. I love you."

Before he could respond, all he heard was a dial tone. He hung up the phone slowly. It wasn't like Kat to be so abrupt, he thought, concerned. After he finished talking to Brian, he would ask Deanna if she wouldn't mind keeping Liv just a little longer so he could swing by the cabin and see for himself that everything was okay.

Brian interrupted his thoughts, putting the knife in front of him and resuming his seat, still frowning. "I just thought of something while you were talking, especially after you mentioned Dan Rogers. The night the Ramons were killed, me, Andy, Dan, Sam and Allie did some cruising in Andy's old Buick. I remember because Dad was ticked that I was hanging around Allie." He grimaced. "Sorry. I keep forgetting she was your wife."

"That was long before I met her, Brian."

He nodded. "Yeah, I know but it still doesn't seem real that she's dead." He took a deep breath. "Anyway, Dad grilled me pretty hard the next day. I think he was worried I had something to do with those murders. Because of that, I distinctly remember we stopped for pizza earlier in the evening. Andy flipped Dan his keys while we waited to get some beer because Allie kept bugging us about it." He frowned again, rubbing his forehead absently. "I also remember her asking Andy if he had a way to get his hands on some drugs to get high."

"Andy gave her his father's keys?"

Brian shook his head. "No way. He was always straight but I do remember Sam teasing him, saying all he had to do was use those keys he kept in his car. The ones to his father's office he kept in the console between the seats."

"So you're saying Dan might have taken those keys when he made his run for beer?"

Brian shrugged. "He could have."

Cole was putting the pieces together and didn't like the way they were fitting. "Did you happen to see Allie driving her Mustang later that night?"

"I didn't see her but I wouldn't be surprised if she did. She was pretty well lit by the time we dropped her off. She was seriously pissed that we wouldn't party with her anymore." He looked slightly uncomfortable. "She had a problem way back then with booze. I thought it was cool at the time but even I knew she was over the edge with the drugs." He paled slightly as he shot Cole a look. "I forgot. Dan didn't go home with us although he was feeling no pain as well. He stayed with Allie. If he had those keys..."

Cole pointed to the knife. "I found that in back of the Sulin house. Did Dan carry that knife with him?"

"He did back then."

"One more question, Brian. Did Dan visit the Sulin house often?"

"Sure, we all did."

Cole rose and shook Brian's hand warmly. "Thanks, Brian. What you've told me might very well go a long way to solving all three of these cases."

Brian opened the door and then looked back. "You know, when I think about it, Dan was never really one of us. It was pretty clear he just hung around with Andy so he could see Kat. He had a thing for her way back in high school."

At that exact moment, it hit him like a ton of bricks, fear almost knocking the breath out of him.

...it pays to worry...things I have to deal with...New York has a hold on me...

He reached in his desk and grabbed his gun and holster, strapping it on as he strode to the door, startling Brian.

"He's at the cabin, Brian. I was stupid not to have known it. Kat was scared. I could hear it in her voice."

He swung the door open, striding through and slamming it forcefully. Brian was right behind him. Cole glanced at him, his jaw working furiously., "If he's done anything to her, I'll kill him."

Brian was already reaching for his cell phone. Ignoring Cole's scowl, he slid into the passenger side of the 'Vette.

"I'm going with you," he said firmly. He finished dialing the phone. "Dad, Cole needs to talk to you."

He handed the phone to Cole.

"Jerry, our killer is Dan Rogers. Meet me at Kat's cabin and for God's sake don't put your siren on. Park about half a mile back and I'll call you if I need backup. Yeah, I'm sure. Damn sure."

He put the car in gear and tore out of the parking lot, tires squealing. Damn it all to hell! She wouldn't even begin to suspect her partner. She'd welcome the bastard with open arms and might end up dead as a result.

His knuckles clenched white on the wheel, fear like he had never known clutching at him with icy fingers. And he did the only thing he could as he tore down the road urging the car faster and faster.

He prayed.

Chapter Fifteen

Her hands trembled slightly as she disconnected the call and turned back toward the man standing just behind her. He wasn't aiming the gun he held casually in his hand and that made its presence even more frightening.

"Very well done, Kat," he said calmly.

The trembling ceased as fury rushed through her. "All that time working side by side. All those late nights, those pizzas we grabbed on the run, you sat across from me knowing you'd destroyed my life." Her fists clenched at her side, nails biting into her palms. "I trusted you, Dan. Even felt better knowing you were with me in those first years. Damn you!"

He jerked as if she'd slapped him, his eyes losing their coldness as he moved closer to her. She put her hands up, backing away.

"Don't touch me!"

"You don't understand how it was, Kat," he pleaded. "That night I was drunk. Allie and I both were."

Her eyes widened. "Allie was part of this?"

He nodded. "She drove. I stole those keys from your brother's car. All we wanted to do was juice up. We headed around back because I figured the office was closed." He shook his head. "I didn't even know Allie had thrown her uncle's loaded gun in the backpack until your mother startled me. I swear to God! I had this stupid idea to throw the vials at her and run. That's when I found the gun. I was so damn scared and so drunk that I pulled that trigger without even realizing I'd done it. When your father came in, I panicked again."

Tears were streaming down her cheeks without her even realizing it. "Do you have any idea what you did to Andy and me that night?" She strode forward, surprising him. Raising her hand, she slapped his cheek hard. So hard he jerked backward.

Instantly the cold, flat look in those eyes returned as he grabbed her arm and twisted it until she cried out in pain. "Listen, you're the one that wanted me to join the practice. If it weren't for me, you'd never have made it as far as you did. I can't change what happened to your parents but I'm sure as hell not going to jail for it."

Don't be stupid, she told herself. *He's obviously unbalanced. You know what he likes, feed into it. Buy some time.*

"Let go of my arm," she said calmly, rubbing her aching shoulder when he finally did what she asked.

He moved to the bar and poured himself a shot of whiskey. Lifting it to his lips, he swallowed it in one gulp, still watching her closely.

"You're right, Dan. You were invaluable to me in those early days. I'd forgotten. Besides, it's been so long since Mom and Dad died that the police would never be able to prove you had anything to do with their deaths now."

He snorted derisively, slamming the shot glass on the bar. "So I thought until out of the blue I got a call from Paul Sulin. The son of a bitch calmly informed me that he'd already spoken to Allie and she as much as admitted the two of us were together in that car of hers the night your parents were killed. Said the vials he had were proof of that. Practically accused me of murder over the phone. Fifteen damn years later!"

The shaking started inside of her again as she began to put the pieces together. "You were on vacation that week, weren't you? The week the Sulins were killed?"

His expression was ugly. "I couldn't allow him to stir up what I thought was long forgotten, now could I?" His lips curved in a sneer. "It was so incredibly easy. The back door lock was a joke. Even remembered that squeaky step." He raised the gun. "Bang, bang and it was done. No muss, no fuss."

Kat felt the nausea rolling in her stomach at the satisfied look on his face. God! How could she have been so gullible, so very stupid? She'd worked closely with this man for years.

Thought she knew him. Granted, there had been things that had bothered her. Small things like his need for taking credit for cases he had little input in or the way he would look at her on certain occasions. Yet she had never, in her wildest imagination, thought him capable of any crime, let alone murder.

Her cell phone rang again and she jumped, her heart beating madly. She leaned forward to grab it but he beat her, palming it himself. He glanced at the name that came up and his expression darkened. "Your lover is calling," he snarled. In one hard, swift motion, he flung the cell phone against the wall, watching as it fell in pieces to the floor. He spun back, his jaw clenched, eyes hard.

"I wanted you, Kat. I've always loved you from as early as when you were fifteen. Do you think I liked working so damned hard every night? That I really liked representing those penniless low lifes you grabbed off the street those first few years? I did it for you. So we could be together. It was all going so nicely, just as I planned, until Collins arrived."

She moved slowly behind the couch, putting as much distance as she dared between them. There was no doubt in her mind Dan Rogers was a sociopath. The signs were all there, the swift change of personality, the lack of remorse, the intelligence. She was in grave danger and suddenly she simply didn't care. He had used her, killed her family, threatened her... Realization hit her just that quickly.

"It was your voice on the phone! You were the one making those threatening calls, you bastard!"

He smiled. He had the nerve to smile, she thought, incensed.

"Not initially as it happens," he said conversationally. "I was able to get our friend Adam Frank to make those first calls. It's amazing what a criminal will do if you promise him the right things and I had the power to do that." The smile grew wider, uglier. "He doesn't like you very much, you know."

She had to grab the back of the couch to stop from striking that handsome face again. "Do you know how sick you are, Dan?"

He poured himself another shot of whiskey, his lack of expression chilling her. "Not sick, Kat, just very smart and very determined. Found someone in my lovely hometown who was willing to do a whole lot for cash as well. Of course that meant traveling here a few more times than I would have liked including that week I was supposed to be on vacation." He smiled grimly. "Trust you to notice I didn't have a tan." He tossed the drink back. "You always were too smart for your own good."

When his gaze roamed back to her she could feel the familiar aura, knowing she had linked with his thoughts, his memories. She tried desperately to pull herself away but the images began to form in front of her despite her attempts to stop them.

The sunlight was bright, blinding, as the woman waited in front of the old barn. She checked her watch and paced, blonde hair flying in the wind. She strode up to the car as it bumped its way toward her, pulling the door open angrily as Dan stepped out.

"Where the hell have you been? I've been waiting in this God forsaken place for half an hour."

"I have other things to do besides meet with you every two minutes, Allie. I don't appreciate having to catch a plane and drive for an hour for another one of your ridiculous demands. I'm warning you I'm getting damn tired of being at your beck and call."

The smile was dark and triumphant. "Well, you better get used to it, my friend, because we've got a problem." She pulled out a cigarette, lighting it and inhaling deeply. "Ever hear the saying those who play must pay?"

Fury lit his eyes. "What's that supposed to mean?"

"It means I'm pregnant, Dan, with your child. Imagine that."

"That's ridiculous! You're on the pill."

"Was on the pill." She took another drag of her cigarette, blowing the smoke in his face. "Funny thing is little old me must have forgotten to take it a few times."

The look on his face had her continuing hurriedly. "Dan, calm down. I can get rid of it easily enough. I'm sure we can come to some kind of financial arrangement," she finished slyly, stepping forward to wrap her arms around his neck. "After all,

243

you wouldn't want this backwater town to know you're screwing the sheriff's ex-wife now would you? Wouldn't do that reputation of yours much good." She shrugged delicately. "Now me, I couldn't give a shit. I'm not exactly popular here anyway." She reached up to kiss his lips, ignoring the fact that he held himself stiffly, eyes cold. "How about it? Say about a hundred thousand or so to get rid of junior? Sound reasonable?"

It took a few moments for her to recognize his intention when he grabbed her by the shoulders his hands sliding up to encircle her neck.

"What are you doing?" she asked in alarm, beginning to struggle. "Dan, wait. You're hurting me. Stop! I can't breathe." Fighting desperately, she grabbed his hands in a vain attempt to release his fingers.

"That's the general idea, my dear," he said smoothly, pressing harder.

Within minutes she grew limp in his arms. He let her fall to the ground, staring down contemptuously at her lifeless body.

"So much for that financial arrangement, you bitch..."

Her eyes snapped open. She was still standing in back of the couch but Dan was no longer in front of it but instead stood next to her.

"What was that all about?" he asked, putting a hand under her chin and jerking her face upward. "If you're trying to pull that ESP crap, don't bother. I'm not buying it."

She reached up and grabbed his hand, flinging it away, unable to hide her distaste. "I told you don't touch me."

He grabbed her hair and yanked it hard, pulling her against him. "I'll damn well touch you any time I want. Might as well get my fill of what I've wanted to do for so very long."

She stilled. "What is that supposed to mean?"

"It means just what you think it means, my love."

"So the big rich lawyer isn't above rape?" she taunted, trying desperately to keep the fear from showing in her voice.

He merely smiled. "No one will think it was that, my dear." He yanked her head back again, covering her mouth with his while she twisted and turned futilely.

She could smell his expensive cologne and feel the scrape of the diamond on his finger against her skin. His grip was cruel and effortless as he ground his lips against hers. At her lack of response, he lifted his head, angry. "Especially since you and that lover of yours have made this your personal hideaway. DNA is so handy unless you don't have someone to compare it with."

She looked up at him contemptuously. "You can't be assuming I would let you sexually assault me and not say something?"

"I assume nothing. You don't think I can let you live now, do you? Expose me to the good people of Brookdale and that big, bad cop of yours?" He slid his hand from her waist upward, finding the bare skin of her abdomen. She couldn't prevent a shiver of loathing, trying again to escape the firm hold he had on her. "Come on, Kat, you're smarter than that."

Despite her terror her mind was racing. "Do you get your jollies out of manhandling women, Dan? Like when you strangled Allie in that field? So much for being a loving father to the child she was carrying. I guess kids didn't play a part in your future, did they?"

His eyes widened in shock, his grip loosening as he stared at her. She was ready. In one quick, desperate motion she grabbed his arm. Using her weight, she flipped him onto the floor, stomping her foot hard on the hand that still held the gun. He roared with pain as it skittered across the wood, the sound loud in the room.

She leaned sideways to grab it and found herself flat on her back, Dan's hands around her throat.

"You bitch!" he screamed. "I'll kill you right now!"

Spots were floating in front of her eyes as he pressed harder. Fighting the darkness that threatened to consume her, she summoned every bit of strength she had left. Fisting her fingers, she aimed under his chin, almost feeling his teeth rattle as she connected.

He fell, grabbing his jaw as he bellowed in pain. She scrambled around his prone body, crawling toward the gun.

Her fingers settled around it just as his hand did the same. They fought, groaning and panting across the floor, Kat using all her karate skills while Dan used his brute strength. Finally he wrenched the weapon from her and stood, bloody and gasping for air, his hand shaking as he aimed the gun. He backed away as she struggled to her feet, stopping only when the edge of the stone fireplace came in contact with his legs.

"I'd forgotten about the karate. You're rather good," he panted, spitting blood as he wiped the back of his mouth with his shirt. He cocked the trigger. "Just not good enough." He raised the gun, his smile cold. "We could have had something together, Kat, made millions more. The provisions you made for the firm in the event of your death make me sole owner, imagine that." He bowed his head mockingly. "I thank you."

"You'll never make it back to New York, Dan," she said, rubbing her sore neck, her voice thick. "Cole will put it together and if something happens to me, he'll go after you with a vengeance."

"He won't have the opportunity," he said smugly. "After you, he's next on my list. It won't be hard to set that up. Dark night, call coming in about seeing a strange car parked by your cabin. He'll make a beeline here and...the rest is history."

"There has to be some part of you still in there that doesn't want to do this, Dan," she pleaded, moving toward him. "You need help. Just stop now and give yourself up. I'll represent you. See that you get all the psychiatric care that you require."

His eyes flashed fire. "I'm not crazy, Kat, far from it. I won't need an attorney because I've covered all the bases just like you've always insisted during our years together." He grinned unpleasantly. "Being methodical is boring but it has its uses."

She eyed him with a calm she was far from feeling. "Think about it, Dan. Your fingerprints are everywhere. People are going to wonder why that is. You had to have rented a car. Someone is going to investigate that. It would only be a matter of time before they put the pieces together." She moved closer, keeping her gaze locked with his.

"Not going to happen," he said calmly. "I was just visiting an old friend. She was alive when I left. We even had consensual sex." His eyes narrowed. "Can't you hear the gossip, Kat? Maybe the cop got mad when he found out. Maybe he murdered her. After all, some people think he killed his ex-wife."

...tell him you know about the knife he left there...the one he was searching for with the letter R on the handle ...the one Cole found behind the Sulin house with his fingerprints on it...tell him now, Kat!...

The words were crystal clear and she repeated them verbatim without thinking, knowing she was being guided by forces she couldn't see.

For just a moment, she saw the confusion, the shock, in his eyes. This time she aimed lower and harder, kicking with all her might. He doubled over and when he came up, she was ready, lashing out at his chin. His head snapped back, the gun discharging harmlessly into the ceiling as he fell. With a loud crack, his head connected with the corner of the fireplace. For one brief moment his eyes cleared as he looked up at her. Then they dulled and grew lifeless. His head lolled to the side as his body slumped forward.

For a split second she froze and then reaction set in as she sank to the floor, shivering uncontrollably. "Oh, my God, Dan, no!" she cried, tears clouding her vision.

She didn't move when the door crashed open. Everything was suddenly moving in very slow motion. It was only when she heard Cole's frantic voice that she was able to pull herself together.

"Kat, where are you? Damn it, answer me!" he shouted, barreling into the room.

"I'm here, Cole," she whispered hoarsely.

He rounded the couch and had her in his arms, frantically running his hands up and down her back, her neck, her face. Finally satisfied, he buried his face in her hair.

"Thank God!"

The tremors Kat felt as she leaned against him matched her own.

"Just hold me," she pleaded, tears still streaming down her face.

"Did he hurt you, Kat?" he demanded violently, pushing her back slightly so he could see her face.

She shook her head mutely.

Cole's gaze slid to the still body by the fireplace. Brian

247

caught the look above Kat's bent head and walked around them, leaning down to place a hand on Dan's neck, feeling for a pulse. After a moment he shook his head, his expression grim.

"He was so sick, Cole," she said brokenly, "I should have seen the signs."

Cole's hands continued to soothe. "He hid it well, Kat," he said tersely.

She lifted a tear-stained face. "I'll have to call his parents. Let them know. It'll devastate them."

Cole's mouth was set in a grim line. "Forgive me if I'm not feeling as magnanimous at the moment."

She shuddered against him. "They're good people, Cole. He was their only child."

Jerry strode in at that moment, his anxious gaze going from Kat to Cole to his son. "Everyone all right in here?"

"All except for Dan," Brian said harshly, motioning toward the still figure of the man. "Damn! I'd never have made the connection. Guy had it all, fancy clothes, fancy car, big New York City address."

"Guess it depends on what having it all means to you," Jerry said quietly.

"Yeah, I guess it does at that," Brian agreed solemnly.

Jerry flipped his cell phone open and called Dale Cowls, arranging for the coroner's wagon to pick up the body. He put a hand on Kat's shoulder. "I'm sorry about this, Kat. Real sorry."

She squeezed his hand briefly. "Thanks, Jerry."

He looked back at the body. "Kind of strange coincidence isn't it. Cracked his head at almost the exact spot we found old man Saunders."

Kat closed her eyes, an image of Clay Saunders flashing in front of her. It had been his voice speaking those words. She was as sure of that as she could be. Thanking him silently, she slowly rose with Cole's help, every bone in her body protesting.

He turned her away from Dan's body and led her toward the kitchen, stopping only long enough to splash a shot of whiskey in a glass.

"Drink it," he insisted.

She slowly raised the glass to her lips and then swallowed.

Coughing, she handed it back to him.

"Better?"

She nodded, taking a deep breath, feeling slightly better. "I missed the signs, Cole. I saw him every day and I still missed what I've been trained to see."

He shook his head. "He was very, very clever, Kat. He knew what buttons to push, how to get what he wanted. He had the money, the power and familiarity on his side." He slid an arm around her. "No one wants to believe someone who is close to us is capable of doing unimaginable evil. You know that."

"But killing people he grew up with?" she said numbly. "The Sulins were practically family, Cole. Dan ate at their dinner table, spent hours in that house." Her eyes filled with tears. "How could he have been that cruel, that inhuman?"

He glanced at the body. "Guess we'll never know the answer to that one."

They both turned when the front door opened and Dale Cowls walked in, followed by several of his assistants. He assessed the scene quickly, walking over to the body, his gaze locking with Cole's.

"You got to be kidding me. Dan Rogers?"

Cole nodded grimly.

"Well I'll be a son of a..." he began and then stopped, catching sight of Kat's expression. "Hell, I'm sorry, Kat. This can't be easy for you." He caught Cole's eye. "Was he the one who killed all of them?"

"Looks like it."

He whistled softly, shaking his head. "Never would have guessed it." He knelt in front of Dan's prone body, his skilled eye taking in the head wound and the positioning. "Want me to cordon off the area?"

Cole shook his head. "No need. Do me a favor and keep this quiet for a little while. At least until we can inform Rogers's parents, okay?"

"You got it."

Kat stood silently by Cole's side as Dale directed one of his assistants to bring in a gurney. Unable to bear seeing the still figure of her partner zipped into a body bag, she put an arm through Cole's. "I can't watch this."

He nodded, tucking her against him as he guided her outside. She took a deep breath as the coroner's wagon backed up to the porch, tears again misting her vision.

Cole brushed it away with his thumb. "You okay?"

She nodded. "For now. I don't think it's all sunk in just yet." She looked up at him. "He would have killed me, Cole. You as well."

They watched as the shrouded body was loaded into the wagon. Cole gently pushed her inside the car, his expression grim. "He could have but he didn't. God knows if that's because we were just damned lucky or there were outside forces at work. Either way it's over."

She grabbed his hand, her gaze finding his. "It won't be that easy, Cole. People were hurt, are going to be hurt. They'll be inquiries, an investigation, and gossip. We'll have to deal with that."

He tipped her chin up, his gaze scanning her pale face. "I know that." He lifted her hand and brushed her knuckles with his lips. "We have each other and our friends and family. We'll manage."

She smiled slightly, nodding but, as he rounded the front of the car, a single tear was poised on the tip of her lashes. It shimmered there for a long moment before sliding silently down her cheek.

Epilogue

"Is she finally asleep?" Cole asked as Kat curled next to him on the couch. The lights from the Christmas tree twinkled on the brass, turning it to burnished gold.

She nodded, resting her head against his shoulder. "I remember feeling just like she feels right now. Not sure if she wants to believe anymore but afraid not to. There's nothing like the excitement or that sense of anticipation a child feels on Christmas Eve."

"Not to mention she has been sinfully indulged with a birthday party to end all birthday parties today," he said dryly.

Kat smiled, brushing a kiss along his jaw. "She deserved something with balloons, rowdy kids and loads of gifts. She hasn't had much of a chance to do that kind of thing thus far."

He sighed, tucking her closer. "I know and I still feel guilty about that."

"Don't. She's a normal, newly turned nine-year-old now, complete with mood swings and attitude. I think it's great. Besides, the height of the party was actually the hours before when Sonya Sandoval flitted around in jeans and a t-shirt helping to hang decorations. I think she had more fun than Liv. I don't think I've ever seen the woman laugh before."

He smiled, stroking her hair. "Trust you to include her in the preparations." His eyes darkened. "They need Liv in their life as much as she needs them in hers."

"I know that," she said quietly. "And I think she knows that as well. They can't bring back their daughter but at least they have a part of her in Olivia."

"Liv loves you, Kat."

"And I love her with all my heart. She's been through a lot these past few months with her mother dying, our getting married, slowly accepting the Sandovals again. I think she's been surprisingly resilient."

He smiled in the darkness. "Remember, getting married quickly was your idea. I was willing to wait until things settled a little."

She gazed pensively into the flames. "I know that but after what happened with Dan, a big wedding somehow didn't seem so important anymore. Being husband and wife and the mother of that little girl up there did."

He tilted her chin upward, scanning her face. "Still having trouble dealing with the memories?"

She shrugged. "I have my moments. He wasn't all bad, Cole."

"Don't even go there, Kat. He almost killed you, would have if you hadn't been able to defend yourself."

"I know that but he was sick, Cole. At his funeral his mother told me that she had taken him several times to a psychiatrist when he was a child for aggression at school and severe temper tantrums. By the time he was in high school, he'd learned to hide those traits. I called Tim Carson a few days after Dan died, hoping he might give me some answers."

"Did he?"

"He said that Dan's behavior was classic sociopath. His focus on me, his intelligence, his manipulation of people for his own ends without remorse." She shuddered. "He kissed me after dinner the night before I moved back home. I remember thinking how strange it was that I felt so little except guilty that I couldn't feel the same things he felt for me. You'd think with all that talk of my inherent talent, I would have sensed something, seen something, but I didn't."

"He was too close to you, Kat. Even if you had sensed something I doubt you would have believed it." He paused. "I don't know if you want to hear this but I think you should know. Dale Cowls was able to match Dan's DNA to that fetus. He was the father."

She closed her eyes, not wanting him to see her expression, see that she had already known. She still had flashes of that vision. Of the way Dan had killed the woman who was carrying his child without a flicker of emotion. It haunted her, that laugh, the expression on his face. Cole didn't need to know those things.

"I know this hurts, Kat. I only wish I could have spared you some of the pain."

She shook her head. "I'm a big girl, Cole. I've seen more heinous crimes."

He tucked a silken curl behind her ear. "Maybe, but not with someone so close to you."

"You know what hurts the most? Jack told me Dan had arranged for Adam Frank's early release and was the one that provided him with the cell phone he used to call me in the beginning."

"That bastard," Cole muttered, his jaw tightening.

She was silent for a long moment, reliving the sorrow and pain for just a little longer, grieving for what could have been and then purposely pushed it away. It was the time and season to forgive and forget and besides there were other things to talk about, more exciting things.

She rose, placing another log on the fire. "I think it's safe to get the gifts now." She went to the closet under the stairs and unlocked the door, pulling out several large bags full of gaily wrapped packages.

"You keep this up that child is going to end up spoiled," he warned good-naturedly as he helped her put the presents under the tree.

"Don't worry, some of these are for you," she tossed back, lips curving.

Bending down, she put the last gift under the tree and when she straightened, she found herself wrapped in her husband's arms.

"Merry Christmas, wife," he said, his gaze dark with purpose as he bent his head.

She still grew weak at the knees when he kissed her like this. "I don't see any mistletoe," she teasingly whispered against his lips.

"I don't need incentive to kiss my wife," he murmured,

sucking gently on her lower lip.

"Speaking of that," she said casually, leaning back to look up at him. "I'm especially excited about being able to give Liv what she really wanted the most."

He kissed the tip of her nose. "And what, among the million things she asked for, was that?"

Her eyes danced in the firelight as she looked up at him. "Oh, nothing special. Just a little brother or sister."

She watched his expression go from confusion to realization.

"You're pregnant?"

She nodded. "About six weeks or so according to Ellie."

This time the kiss was longer and sweeter. "Are you happy about this?"

"Ecstatic."

"Then that makes two of us." He edged her back toward the couch, settling down with her in the crook of his arm. "Does Doctor Sulin have any objection to her pregnant patient making love with her new husband?"

She stretched out languidly on the couch, loosening the belt of her robe. "She told me I'm completely healthy."

"And completely beautiful," he said softly, easing down beside her, his hands caressing her delicate jaw, the line of her neck, her breasts. She arched, his touch instantly arousing her as it always did. Yet he stopped when his palm found her still flat abdomen, his big hand spanning its width.

"A baby," he said wonderingly.

Her heart melted at the expression on his face. She was so very lucky. Both of them were.

And, as the snow fell gently outside and the fire flickered, she made love to her very handsome and very wonderful husband. Afterward, deliciously warm and satisfied, she looked up and began to laugh.

"And what's so funny?" he asked, pretending to be affronted.

She pointed toward the ceiling. "I don't know who did it or how they did it but look."

He turned, his eyes following where she was pointing.

A sprig of mistletoe hung from the very peak of the ceiling some fifteen feet up.

"Did you put that there?" she asked.

"No."

She frowned. "Then I wonder who did?"

"A very, very smart person in my opinion," he murmured sleepily, his head resting on her breasts.

She smiled softly, yawning. "I couldn't agree more."

And, just for a second, through the frosted glass of the tall window in front of her, she thought she caught a glimpse of a falling star. Smiling, her eyes fluttered closed and she fell asleep in the arms of the man she loved.

About the Author

To learn more about Anita Whiting please visit
http://anitawhiting.tripod.com. Send an email to Anita Whiting
at timwhite@windstream.net or join her Yahoo! group to join in
the fun with other readers as well as Anita Whiting
http://groups.yahoo.com/group/ Samhain Authors.

Can a psychic investigator disprove an accidental death before she and her lover are next to die?

A Killer's Agenda
© 2007 Anita M. Whiting

Brad Norton doesn't believe his aunt's death is the accidental shooting the police claim it to be. His instincts tell him there's a more sinister explanation. In order to get to the bottom of it, he's going to need professional help.

Pairing up with Alex Leahy, a clairvoyant private investigator, wasn't exactly in his plans. He didn't expect the fiery redhead to take over the case and get under his skin so quickly, but things happen fast when Alex is around.

Still, they can't plan a future together with a killer on the loose. When their investigation intensifies they bring him out of hiding. The danger grows to an entirely new level, however, when attempts are made on their lives.

With six deaths already confirmed, it's a race to stop their man before Alex and Brad are next on the list.

Available now in ebook and print from Samhain Publishing.

Enjoy the following excerpt from A Killer's Agenda...

The day dawned gloomy and dark with torrential rain that sometimes plagued the area. No open windows this morning, Brad thought. The windshield wipers were barely keeping up with the blast of water. Why he had agreed to help a woman he barely knew move was beyond him. No, he knew why. She intrigued him. Maybe it was this clairvoyance she professed to or maybe it was the fact that she had an answer to his every question. Either way, he wasn't at all sure he liked it. Not one bit.

He welcomed the chill of the rain as he walked swiftly up the porch steps. It served to clear his brain if nothing else. Before he could knock, the door opened and Alicia rushed out, a cap pulled low over her dark curls and a back pack slung over her shoulder.

"I'll be home about one or two," she tossed back as she barreled directly into Brad. He caught her before she lost her balance. Startled, she looked up and then grinned, reminding him of her sister. "Sorry about that, Mr. Norton. Alex said you were coming this morning." She took a few steps backward, closing the door against the rain. "Nice body," she remarked, gazing at the damp black tee shirt that molded his chest and shoulders.

He raised a brow in surprise, his lips twitching. In her own way, Alicia threw him off balance just as easily as her sister did.

"Don't move," she commanded, closing her eyes for a brief second. She stood perfectly still for a few moments and then flung her arms out dramatically, her expression suddenly intense. "I see the scene. Pouring rain. She doesn't know he's returned from the war. She rushes out the door, late for work and he's standing there. She doesn't see him and before she knows it, she's in his arms. Tears mingle with the rain as their lips lock and he pulls her close. Scene fades with fog swirling around both of them." She sighed, leaning against the doorjamb, her dreamy blue eyes opening and finding his. "We'd be a natural. Care to wait for five or six years and then take Hollywood by storm?"

Suppressing laughter, he shook his head. "I don't think so," he said dryly. "Although thanks for the compliment."

"Darn! I guess it's just as well. By then I'd be in my prime and you'd be getting old."

Brad's gaze snapped to hers. When she grinned impishly, he couldn't help laughing.

"I figured that would get a reaction," she said mischievously. "Go on in. Alex is somewhere in there, cleaning like mad." She skipped down the stairs. "By the way, I meant it about the nice bod. See you later."

He watched her drive away, amused, and then turned and rang the doorbell. It was flung open almost immediately. Alan stood there, dressed in sweats, a sandwich in one hand and a large glass of milk in the other.

"Hey, man, come on in. Thanks for helping Alex this morning," he said, swallowing a mouthful of food. "We don't normally practice on Sunday but it's a really big game next weekend. I can't miss it or the coach'll have my head. Alex told me to tell you coffee's on in the kitchen if you want some. Gotta go."

He reached behind Brad and grabbed a helmet sitting on the foyer table, then grimaced at the rain. "Lousy morning to practice in." He glanced back at Brad. "Yeah, yeah, I know. I'm young. I can take it." He began to whistle as he slammed the door behind him.

Brad found himself grinning as he saw him pull a hood over his head and jump into a car that pulled to the curb minutes later.

For some reason, he found himself wondering how his father would have reacted to the last ten minutes. *Yeah, right.* No child of Andrew Norton's would have been as spontaneous, as sure of themselves. It was then it struck him like a lightning bolt. Hell! He was becoming his father without even realizing it. He liked order, predictability. *That* was the reason Alex Leahy mesmerized him. She was impetuous, mysterious, and contradictory. Everything he wasn't and yet he was drawn to her like a moth to a flame. Like a forbidden fruit that he desperately wanted to savor.

The sound of the vacuum cleaner interrupted his thoughts. Instead of climbing the stairs, however, he wandered into the kitchen, helping himself to the coffee Alan had mentioned. He liked this room, liked the way it made him feel with its warm oak cabinets and table. A pang of memory shot through him. Besides Maggie's cozy domain, the kitchen had often been his favorite place at his aunt's as well. She had given him her unbiased and complete love when he had so desperately needed it. There had been long talks around the kitchen table, dinner conversation that skillfully guided a lost teenager out of his shell. The sting of unexpected tears surprised him. Guess it would be a long time before the pain disappeared entirely. His memory of her deserved as much.

He took a deep, steady breath, inhaling the fragrance of the coffee. As he took another sip, the noise upstairs stopped. No point in reliving the past. His job now was to find this creep and make him pay.

Moments later, Alex appeared, her curls tamed in a casual pony tail. She wore scruffy jeans and a Panthers tee shirt that was about two sizes too big for her. The pull was there again the minute he set eyes on her. Not one of the women he had dated would have been caught dead in the outfit she was wearing, at least not in front of him. Her lack of artifice was immensely appealing, not to mention the fact that those scruffy jeans hugged her curves admirably.

"Morning, Brad. Thanks again for coming over." She sighed, lips curving as she helped herself to a cup of coffee. "I'm almost done. My idea of a clean room and my siblings' differ markedly, but I promise I won't keep you long." She tucked one leg underneath her as she curled into a kitchen chair, taking a sip of coffee with obvious enjoyment. "I gather Alan and Alicia have already welcomed you? I heard your car drive in before my sister left."

"Welcomed is a mild way of putting it," he responded wryly.

She laughed. "I know exactly what you mean. Alicia doesn't just live life, she embraces it. Things are never dull when she's around."

He leaned back in his chair, wrapping his big hands around the mug of coffee. "Do any of you ever stop for a breather?"

"Sure. If we have to. This is minor. Just imagine my mother and father and my twin brothers here as well."

"I'd rather not."

"Chicken," she teased, setting her cup down. "Have you contacted the attorney in Charlotte?"

"Last night. He's agreed to meet with us Monday afternoon if that works for you."

"It does only because I purposely kept my schedule light due to my parents being away. As a matter of fact, I've got a few weeks relatively free."

"Good. Then we'll leave tomorrow about eight. It'll take half a day to drive there without rushing."

"Sounds fine." She warmed both their cups with fresh coffee. "If you don't mind a suggestion, instead of wasting time going back and forth, why don't we continue north after tomorrow? We'll compile notes as we go."

He arched a brow. "You okay with that?"

She gave him an impatient look. "I wouldn't have suggested it if I wasn't."

"Okay. Are your parents okay with you traveling with a strange man for over a week then?"

"You're not serious?"

"Perfectly."

Her eyes narrowed. "You going to ravish me?"

"The thought has crossed my mind once or twice."

"Odd. You're not alone in that then."

He laughed. "Are you always so frank?"

"I try to be." She leaned forward. "Brad, I'm getting the distinct feeling that this whole thing is going to get a lot more complicated than either of us first thought."

"Emotionally or investigative wise?"

"Both."

"You backing down?"

"Absolutely not. I'm just warning you."

"Lady, you're way too late for that." He captured one of her hands, pulling her up as he stood. "Way too late."

Just before he leaned down to capture her lips, he told himself he was acting totally out of character. It wasn't in his nature to move so quickly or act so spontaneously. Yet she stood there, lips slightly parted, her green eyes deep and dark and he had to kiss her. Wasn't sure he should but that made no difference.

Sensations rocketed through him as his lips crushed hers. When he trailed them along her neck, she melted against him, winding her fingers in his thick hair.

He was the one who finally pulled away enough to look down at her, shaking his head ruefully. "I'm beginning to think the only way to get you out of my system is to sleep with you."

She arched a delicate brow. "Sleep or have sex?"

"Both."

"One doesn't have to include the other."

He ran a finger along her lower lip. "With us it would."

"Don't be too sure."

"About the sex?"

"About sleeping."

GREAT
CHEAP
FUN

Discover eBooks!

THE FASTEST WAY TO GET THE HOTTEST NAMES

Get your favorite authors on your favorite reader, long before they're out in print! Ebooks from Samhain go wherever you go, and work with whatever you carry—Palm, PDF, Mobi, and more.

Printed in the United States
129379LV00001B/70/P